HOW TO GET OVER YOUR EX IN Ninety DAYS

JENNIFER PEEL

To Mrs. Davis and Mr. Craft,

Thank you for bringing the world of theater to my children.
The world needs more teachers like you.

Prologue

♥

Jackson Montgomery is replacing Steve Jones as Vice Principal of River-ton High School. There it was in black in white. I was so proud of my guy. Although he could have given me a heads up. A girlfriend shouldn't have to read about her boyfriend's promotion in the *Riverton Record*, but I understood why he had to keep it confidential. I had already forgiven him by phone and I was looking forward to him making it up to me when he came over for dinner later.

He said he needed to talk to me about something important. I made a mental note to pick out my wedding dress. I mean, we had already named the four children we were going to have. Bear, Nick, Bryant, and Liliana. Jackson was a huge Alabama fan and had played football in high school, so I gave in and let him pick out the boys' names. I was also pretty accommodating with the girl name too. Liliana was his grandma's name and we both adored her as much as she adored me.

I smiled when I thought of how happy Miss Liliana was going to be when she found out that Jackson had finally proposed. She had been after him to do it for months. I don't think I had been dating Jackson two months when she told him I was the one for him. He never denied it. He would always look at me with those soft brown eyes of his, with the long-curled lashes that always seemed to have a hint of mischief in them and say, "When the time is right."

I wasn't pushing him for a proposal. We had only known each other for a year and had only been dating since October. Best nine months of my life. But I wanted nothing more than to be Mrs. Jackson Montgomery. If ever two people were meant to be together, it was us.

We'd met at a teacher in-service workshop where we role played how to deal with different disturbances in the classroom. We'd had an instant attraction. As a drama teacher, I loved role playing, and as a ham and former golden boy who had attended the high school where we taught, Jackson was all for giving it his best. He was cast as the lovesick teen boy that had a crush on his young teacher—that would be me. He wrote "hot for teacher" on his pad of paper and flashed it at me. I then had to break his heart with gentle firmness. Sometimes, for fun during the course of last year, he would walk by my classroom and flash me that note.

I couldn't wait to get back to my job.

I wondered how different work would be now since he wasn't teaching World and American History and coaching. I knew giving up his assistant football coaching position was going to be hard for him, but being in administration had always been his goal, or at least his father's. At thirty-one he was on the younger side for the position, but no one was more qualified than him. Not only was he brilliant, but he loved the kids and they loved him, too.

His new position probably meant we couldn't make-out in the prop room anymore. That was going to be a bummer.

I jumped up off the couch and checked the lemon rosemary garlic chicken and potatoes I had baking in the oven. It sure smelled good. I also peeked in the fridge at the chocolate covered strawberries I was going to let him feed me later.

I held my stomach and hoped I would always feel that anticipation deep in the pit of my soul when I was about to see him.

I dashed to the bathroom in my small studio apartment and did a quick check in the mirror. My light brown hair was braided romantically to the side and I had primed my lips with moisturizer. My green eyes were bright and told the story of how much I loved Jackson. I added a quick layer of mascara to my long dark lashes and a tint of color on my cheeks. One of the things I loved about Jackson was that he loved casual. I looked down at my white t-shirt and cut-off jeans. It was the perfect outfit for him. Besides, when school started the next week, I would be missing my comfortable clothes and lazy summer days.

I was adding an extra layer of lip gloss when there was a knock on my door. I smiled. He was early. I didn't waste any time. I rushed to the door and opened it with fervor. I didn't squander a breath before jumping in his arms and wrapping my legs around him and kissing him like I hadn't seen him in days. In reality, it had been less than twenty-four hours.

I heard him laugh right before our lips met for their usual long, slow dance. He held me to him nicely and walked us in and shut the door behind us with his foot. He was talented like that—or at least well practiced. He could even unlock a door while holding me and kissing me like...well...like he meant it.

I ran my fingers up through his perfectly styled chestnut hair as he kissed me deeper. I could taste the cinnamon gum he had just chewed.

I loved when he pulled me tighter against him, like he wanted to evaporate any space that came between us.

We had about made it to the couch when he released my lips abruptly. He groaned and squeezed me tighter. "You're making this hard on me."

I smiled and looked into his eyes—they weren't their playful selves. "What do you mean?"

He kissed me softly once and leaned his forehead against mine. "We need to talk." The way he said it was unlike him. Unlike any way he had ever spoken to me before.

I released my legs from around him and basically slid down his tall frame.

He took my hand and led me to my sofa. We both sat down at the same time and faced each other.

"Congratulations," I whispered. "I'm so proud of you."

He ran his hand down my braid, but he didn't smile like I thought he would.

"What's going on?" I pulled on his tie to bring him in for another kiss. He barely brushed my mouth.

Okay. I knew something was up. We took our kissing seriously. Like gold medal, first place every time. "Jackson?"

He took up my hand and rubbed his thumb across it. Back and forth and back and forth. He emptied his lungs in a tense breath. "Dr. Walters is planning to retire in two years." Dr. Walters was the beloved principal of Riverton High School. "The superintendent has already mentioned to me that I could be in the running, but they want someone with a doctorate."

"You're totally up for the challenge. All you have is twelve hours left, and your dissertation." He was already working on his Doctorate in Education Administration.

"You say it like it's not a big deal."

"Jackson, I say it like I believe you can do it. I know how difficult it will be." I had barely finished my master's the year before and that was tough enough.

"Then I hope you'll understand when I say that I need to quit messing around."

"Sure...I get that." Though I couldn't think of how he had been messing around.

"If I want to reach the top levels of education administration in the state, I need to focus."

"Tell me what I can do to help. I'll help you study, make you dinner every night, you name it."

He gave me a smallish sort of grin. "You'll always be the best girlfriend I've ever had."

I paused, not sure I heard him right. "What do you mean, had? Are you finally ready to change my title?" That's what he meant, right?

"Presley...maybe if we had met later..."

I pulled my hand away from his. I did not like where this was going. For a moment I couldn't breathe. "What are you saying?"

"I have goals. My father has goals for me. Now is the time for me to realize those. And dating you has become a distraction."

I think I shook my head a dozen times trying to figure out how to make that sound not as bad as it was, but there was no getting over how terrible of a thing that was to say to me. "I'm a distraction? I thought you loved me."

"I do love you, but—"

"No, Jackson. There are no buts when you love someone. Do you love me or not? Because I know that I love you."

He reached out to touch my cheek, but I scooted back.

"Presley, with my new position comes new responsibilities, and the district frowns on administrators dating teachers."

"There isn't a rule against it."

"It's an unwritten rule."

"So that's all you have to say to me?" I felt the tears forming and I was doing my best to not let them present themselves.

"Presley, I'm sorry. Maybe we can revisit us later on down the road."

"You can't put me on layaway, Jackson. You either love me like you mean it, or let me go."

He paused for several long seconds. He shouldn't have had to think about it. That was my answer.

I stood up and turned from him. The tears found their way out. I hugged myself and tried to breathe.

"Presley." He barely spoke above a whisper. "I don't want it to be uncomfortable between us when school starts up. We can still be friends, right?"

I couldn't look at him. He sounded like he was a high school student. "No, Jackson. I can't be friends with you."

I could hear him stand up. "I'm sorry to hear that. And I'm sorry to hurt you. I know you won't believe it, but this hurts me, too. I didn't come to this decision lightly."

"You're right," I choked out. "I don't believe you."

He barely skimmed my cheek with his lips from behind before he walked out my door.

I stood there completely stunned. How did that happen? I felt used, and like I had entered an alternate reality. I snapped out of it, momentarily, when the kitchen timer went off, letting me know his celebratory dinner was done. That's when I lost it.

I turned off the oven in between racking sobs, grabbed my purse and keys, and headed straight for Capri's house. I called Jackson every name in the book—and I'm not talking about the Good Book—in my head on the way over to my best friend and fellow teacher's house. I was blaming her, too. If it hadn't been for her, I would have never moved here. I could have stayed in Colorado and taught school in Littleton, where my parents lived. But no, I wanted adventure. Well if you call living in Riverton, Alabama, an adventure. It had kind of felt like it, but that was all over now.

How could he just walk away from us? The night before he'd acted like he didn't want to leave, and he must have told me he loved me a dozen times. In light of what just happened, that made more sense. I'm sure his dad—or like everyone down here called the male parental figure, daddy—had something to do with it. They had been spending a lot of time together the past few weeks and Jackson seemed anxious. His dad was always on Jackson about making something out of his life. And I knew Jackson's dad didn't like me. I was too middle class for him. I didn't come with a pedigree. My parents, Bobby and Jan Benson, were blue collar all the way and the best people I knew. My dad was an auto mechanic and my mom was a homemaker. They raised five healthy, mostly well-adjusted girls. I was lucky enough to be the baby of the family.

His dad lived up on his high horse all alone, where all the other wealthy people in Riverton lived—in the Coves that sat above the city. The people who lived here called it their mountain. I laughed when Capri told me that. Colorado had mountains; Alabama had hills—baby hills.

Daniel Montgomery II was a piece of work. He was the CEO for some huge high tech firm in the area. A thousand aerospace companies surrounded us, with NASA and Marshall Flight Center nearby. His dad ran one that had developed some type of material that was used in space flights to prevent lighting damage. I didn't really understand it. All I knew was he had made a fortune and a name for himself. He expected his sons to do the same. Daniel Montgomery III, Jackson's older brother, was already well on his way. He was a newly elected judge in the Alabama appellate courts.

Mr. Montgomery, like I was expected to call him, was disappointed his son chose to be an educator. He felt like it was beneath him. I felt like being a teacher was a higher calling. He relented and let Jackson pursue his dream, but only with the promise that he would reach the highest level.

How Miss Liliana had raised such a son, I would never know. I knew she loved Mr. Montgomery, but I could tell that for all of his success she was disappointed that her son hadn't turned out to be a better human being.

I guess it didn't matter now. I would have nothing to do with any of their lives. Except that Jackson was going to be my boss now. I knew in his new role he would be evaluating me and I would have to get his approval for afterschool rehearsals and even the plays I would choose. This wasn't happening. If only I hadn't signed my contract for the year.

The tears and the speed of my VW Beetle increased as I zoomed to Capri and David's place. I had thought I would be joining the newlyweds in wedded bliss soon. I had even told Capri I thought Jackson was going to be popping the question tonight. I wanted to crawl into a hole and die.

I pulled in front of the cute, one-story brick home in an older, well-kept part of Riverton. Capri was so thrilled when they purchased the little fixer upper and moved in last month. Jackson and I had helped them. Everything in this stupid town reminded me of him.

I ran to their front door and pounded on it.

Capri took her time opening it. There she stood in her smock, covered in paint. I'm sure she was working on her next masterpiece. Could she look any cuter splattered in paint with her short blonde, bobbed hair and bright blue eyes? She'd looked the same since we'd met in our freshman year of college eight years ago. At eighteen, we thought we were on top of the world. Now I felt like I was in the pit of despair.

She tilted her head. "Honey, what's wrong?"

I fell into her arms, not worrying that I was staining my white cotton tee. We stood there embracing while the only thing that came out of me were sobs and more sobs. I noticed David come around the corner, look at the scene, and hightail it out of there. When the sobbing was under control, Capri led me to her colorful kitchen table that she had hand painted with gorgeous sunflowers.

We sat down and she handed me a box of tissues. I was probably going to need the whole thing and then some. I had never felt pain like this. I physically ached from it.

She took up my free, non-tissue holding hand. "So tell me what's wrong? I've never seen you like this." And we had been roommates long enough to go through some breakups, but I had never been in love like this before. I thought he was the one.

"Jackson," I shuddered. "He broke up with me. He told me I was a distraction and he was wasting his time messing around with me."

Her eyes widened. "He did not."

I nodded my head.

"I can't believe it."

"I can't believe it either, but it's true. We're over and I didn't even get a say in it."

"He's a man slut."

I had to laugh some. We hadn't used that phrase since junior year. I guess it was better than the "ovaries before brovaries" saying we used.

All joking aside. "Capri, what am I going to do? I love him. I pictured myself married to him and having his children."

Her face lit up in one of those aha moments she always got. She jumped up and went to the tiny built-in desk in her kitchen and retrieved her laptop. She brought it back and pulled up an article she had bookmarked. "I knew this would come in handy someday." She turned the screen toward me.

The headline read, 'How to Get Over Your Ex in 90 Days the Healthy Way'.

"Why did you bookmark this? You've only been married for two months."

"I told you, I had this feeling. Now aren't you glad I did?"

I shrugged. I usually never put much stock into her online reading habits. She was always reading about weird polls and articles about sex and love. I mostly used to laugh at them because most were absurd, like ten things to make your man insanely jealous. I mean, who comes up with that crap?

Through my tear-filled eyes, I started to read the article. *"You probably feel like you've been hit by a truck."* I nodded my head. That's exactly how I felt. The next part, though, was bad news for me. It suggested I break off all contact for ninety days. How was I going to do that when we worked together? It said our bodies craved that person on a chemical level and seeing them would only fuel that desire. "How can I stay away from him?" I turned to Capri for guidance.

"We'll figure something out. I'll try and run interference at school."

I didn't know how well that would work. The drama department and theater were on the same floor as the art department, but they were on opposite ends of the school.

"What if I petitioned to get out of my contract?"

Her face dropped. "Presley, you can't leave now. You're doing such great things with the drama department. I thought you wanted to enter the kids into the one act play competition this year?"

"I did. I do. But how can I work with Jackson?"

"They could take away your teaching credentials for a year for breaking your contract," she reminded me.

I sighed. "I do like eating and paying my bills."

"Don't let him take this away from you. The kids love you and you love them."

I rubbed my face with my hands. "Okay, what else does this article say?"

"Stay off social media, especially Facebook."

"Good idea." I didn't need to see him living it up while I was dying inside. "I can do that. What else?"

"Keep a daily journal marking your progress and venting out your frustrations."

I nodded my head. I already kept a journal.

"Try and remember the things you liked to do when you were single and revisit those activities."

In theory that sounded good, but everything I liked to do as a single girl was made better when Jackson was involved.

"Be careful about rebounds. Think carefully about starting any new romantic attachments."

I couldn't even think about being with anyone else at the moment.

"And wine, lots of wine."

I took the laptop back from her. "Does it really say that?"

"No," she laughed. "But it couldn't hurt, right?"

"I think it says here that, actually, it can."

She shrugged her shoulders. "Fine, no wine. It does suggest, though, that you be mindful of anxiety and feelings of hopelessness. You need to remind yourself that your mind takes ninety days before it can switch gears and you can picture your life in a different direction."

"Ninety days, huh? They make it sound so easy," I cried.

"Oh, honey, I don't think this will be easy."

"Right now I can't picture my life without him in it. What happened?"

"I don't know. Sounds like he lost his damn mind. I mean, bless his heart."

"I love it when you swear in your Southern accent."

She took my hands. "You can do this. By October 24th, you'll have forgotten that Jackson Montgomery ever existed."

"Ninety days?"

"Ninety days." She smiled.

Day One

♥

Tuesday, July 27

I felt like I was dying. The truck not only ran over me, but it backed up for good measure and crushed me over and over and over again.

I barely slept, and when I woke up, I immediately reached for my phone. Jackson always texted me, *Good morning, beautiful.* All there was this morning was an empty screen.

I sat up, rubbed my swollen red eyes, and remembered what the article advised. I needed to erase Jackson from my life. I hesitated deleting him from my contacts. I had kept every text and voice mail he had ever sent me or left me. I tortured myself and read through the last few texts:

Have I told you lately how much I love you?

I'm such a lucky guy.

Are you up? I can't stop thinking about you.

I loved our late night calls after he would drop me off. *What happened? How could he walk away?* I selected every text and my thumb hovered over the delete button for more than a moment. I reminded myself he'd called me a distraction. In an instant, nine months of happiness was wiped away. I forced myself not to listen to any of his voice messages before I deleted those, too. Finally, I deleted him completely as a contact and blocked his number, not that he would ever use it again, but I wanted this hurt to go away, so I added that step as a precaution. I was going to do as the article said. Ninety days from now, he was going to be a distant memory, a stepping stone to greater happiness, a blip on my radar. I didn't know how that would be possible when my heart was still telling me he was the one, but the ache inside was telling me I had to try.

Next up, social media. I pulled out the tablet my parents had given me as a graduation gift when I'd received my master's degree. My older sisters had all cried foul. Perks of being the baby. I felt like an infant now. I wanted someone to wrap me up in a blanket and hold me until the pain went away. A vision of Jackson holding me in the back of his truck wrapped up in the comforter he had torn off his bed popped in my mind. This had to stop. I couldn't remember those nights star gazing while we planned our future—a future where we were together. *Facebook, I needed to get on Facebook,* I reminded myself.

I knew I was supposed to stay away from it, and I had planned to, but I had to get on it and turn off all the Facebook notifications my phone kept sending me. Just a few days ago I had posted a picture of Jackson and me taking a tour of Cathedral Caverns, this amazing cave not too far away. They took us all the way to the back of the cave and turned off all the lights. I couldn't even see my hand in front of my face. We used the time to . . . well, I shouldn't be thinking about it. What happened between then and now? Does ninety-six hours really make that big of a difference? He had to have been thinking about it even during our date. Did I do something to tip the scales? No. You know what? This was him. All about him, and that was the problem.

I opened up my Facebook account. There are few things I have regretted more in life. He didn't even have the decency to make his change of relationship status private. I was inundated with messages: *What, PB and J have broken up? Say it isn't so. Are you dying?*

Yes, I'm dying. I was stupid and I went against the rules. I clicked on his profile. Why oh, why, did I? His wall was filled with old girlfriends happy at the news and buddies willing to take him out and show him a good time. There were all sorts of congratulations for his job promotion as well. But the one post that struck me the most, and maybe brought me some pleasure, was his grandmother's. I loved Miss Liliana. The fact that she was eighty and on Facebook only made her more endearing.

Jackson Duff Montgomery you better get yourself over to my place and explain yourself. Do you have rocks for brains? I'm cutting you out of my will.

That was always her joke whenever he did anything to her displeasure.

Her post to me: *Baby doll, don't you worry, Nana is going to take care of everything. There are going to be wedding bells, or there will be hell to pay.*

If only she could. Jackson would never go against his dad. I unfriended him, deleted my PB and J photo album, curled into a ball, and went back to bed.

DAY TWO

♥

Wednesday, July 28

DEAR MR. BINGLEY.
All my journal entries have started this way since I was a sophomore in high school and Mrs. Greene, my most beloved English teacher, unlocked the world of Jane Austen to me. She was the reason I decided I wanted to be a teacher. She had this ability to unleash a writer in anyone. She gave me the courage to try out for my first play. And when I got the part, she sat in the front row with my parents.

Men suck, suck, suck, suck, suck! That's right. How could you leave Jane just because Mr. Darcy told you she seemed indifferent, that her affections weren't what they were supposed to be? And so what if her family wasn't rich or well connected? She really loved you, you pompous twit. How dare you leave her with hardly an explanation, especially since you told her things that made her blush in the dark of the cave and you held her like she was your world and you kissed the nape of her neck and whispered, "I love you." I mean, since you danced with her all night at the ball and made her feel like she was important and your intentions were real. Really, how could you?

I hate your guts!
Presley

That was probably enough journal writing for now.

This was my final day of summer vacation. Tomorrow, in-service began, and in eight days school started. I didn't know how I could face it. How could I face him?

My parents were no help, they said I had made a commitment and I had to follow through. As much as they liked Jackson, they had warned me about the complications dating a coworker could cause. Now I was reaping the consequences.

I threw off my covers; I couldn't waste another day in bed. I was a Benson, my dad reminded me. But I wanted to be a Montgomery. No, no. I was getting him out of my head. I had survived one day. Well, sort of. I looked around at all the used tissues and the remnants of the two dozen chocolate-covered strawberries I ate last night. It was *somewhat* healthy. Dark chocolate was practically medicinal and strawberries were a good source of nutrients. So I had a stomachache. It went well with the headache, not to mention the ache in the core of my chest.

Last day of freedom. What do you want to do? I texted Capri.

Sorry PB, David took the day off so he could take me to the new exhibit at the Huntsville Art Museum. Do you want to come?

I didn't need to hear her voice. I knew she was begging me to say no. She wanted to spend the day with her husband. I couldn't blame her. But in my head, I wished them and their cute love-filled marriage to fiery depths.

Have fun. I'll pick you up for the retreat at 8:00 tomorrow morning.

Someone had the bright idea that our training should be more like a retreat. I thought it was brilliant until a couple of days ago. I was looking forward to sneaking off with you-know-who in the woods, maybe taking a dip in the lake under the dark of night.

I hated him.

Showering seemed like a good first step on the ninety-day road to recovery, and probably changing out of my pajamas. It was on days like today that I wished I had a bathtub to soak in. My little apartment only consisted of one tiny bathroom with a shower barely big enough for me. Perks of being a teacher, I guess.

I sat cross-legged on my made bed with my wet hair wrapped up in a towel, trying to decide what to do with my day, my life. You don't know how tempted I was to break my contract despite the ramifications, but I looked around at my tiny apartment that was completely open except the bathroom, and a sense of pride filled me. I was on my own. Maybe I didn't have much now, but it was mine. I had worked hard to get here. Was I really going to let a man take that away from me? A man who so carelessly dumped me? A man I loved with all that I was and am.

I lay back on my bed and begged myself not to cry. I could do this. What choice did I have?

Day Three

♥

Thursday, July 29

DEAR MR. BINGLEY,

Today, I must face him. Remember when you left Jane? You didn't even bother to tell her yourself. You had your sister do it—by letter, I might add. It was cowardly. You should have at least asked her if Mr. Darcy was right. She could have told you then how much she admired you. Jackson is a coward, too. He's afraid of his father and of failing. But you see, he could have just come out and said it. Then I could have told him we would work it out together, because together is better than apart. But he called me a distraction and, worse, he knew how I felt about him. I'm no Jane. There was no question how I felt about him. Now— at all costs—I have to hide my feelings, even the hateful ones. Jane was so lucky that she never had to work for you. I'm determined, though, to get over him. Eighty-seven days from now I'll be saying, Jackson who?

Presley

I closed the journal and placed it in my overnight bag. Running home to Colorado was going through my mind. No. I could do this. I was three percent of the way there. Oh gosh, that was depressing. I headed to Capri's before I changed my mind.

Capri was kissing David on their porch when I arrived. That was uncalled for. I honked the horn. They broke apart. I could imagine the suction sound after that lip-lock. To add insult to injury, David pulled her back for one more kiss. It was going to be one night away, people. I was jealous. A few days ago I would have been oohing and ahhing at the scene, because someone who I won't mention would have treated me the same way if we had to spend almost two days apart.

Capri finally made her way to me. She looked adorable in overalls. Her whole aura screamed she was in love.

I looked down at my outfit. I wore a short, capped sleeve summer dress. The less material the better. Alabama's summers killed me. It was like living in a steamy shower all day long. This Colorado girl was still trying to adjust, if that was possible.

Capri tossed her bag in the backseat and buckled herself in. "Sorry about the long goodbye."

"I'm happy you're so happy." I took off before I changed my mind.

Capri began flipping channels on the radio. "What's up with the country music? You hate it."

"I found a new appreciation for it. Do you know how many songs there are about women shooting, poisoning, and/or running over men with their cars? It's pure genius."

She laughed. "So you're feeling better then?"

"Never better."

"Then why are you wearing his favorite color and looking like a runway model?"

"What? I owned this dress before the mishap. Crimson has always looked good on me. But now that you mention it, I will be buying some Auburn t-shirts when we return. War Eagle!"

"Whatever makes you feel better after what that man-whore did on Facebook. If he wasn't the new vice principal, I would have left him a scathing comment. You should have seen what his grandma wrote."

I bit my lip. "I did."

She smacked my arm. "You're supposed to be staying off Facebook."

"Ouch! I am. I had to get on to turn off the notifications, unfriend him, and delete all of our photos."

"You shouldn't have read his status."

"I tried not to, but I couldn't help it. I couldn't believe he could be so cruel." I had to hold the tears back.

"I was surprised, too. But since you already looked, I should tell you that he deleted the whole thread."

"The damage has been done. Do know what an idiot I'm going to look like walking into in-service today, now that everyone knows?"

"He did you a favor—now he looks like the jerk and you don't have to tell anyone."

"Everyone loves him and now he's one of our bosses, so I'm pretty sure there will be a lot of butt kissing going on."

"Just make sure you stay away from him."

"Oh, believe me, I plan to. But judging from his behavior, I don't think it will be an issue. I'm a distraction he was only messing around with." My voice cracked.

She placed her hand on my thigh. "You look pretty distracting, super model."

"Stop it."

"I'm serious. He can eat his heart out."

"If only he had one."

"We should quit talking about him."

Yeah, we should.

We drove the forty-five minutes to the lake resort with the radio blasting my death-to-men tunes. And when I say resort, I mean a rustic looking lodge with some primitive looking cabins. If the district was that short on money, we should have done this at the school like last year.

Capri and I both looked at each other and cringed.

Capri turned around to grab her bag. "I hope the cabins have air conditioning."

"What? Doesn't everywhere around here? How can you survive in this state without it?" It was only nine in the morning and it was already ninety degrees with eighty-five percent humidity.

"Don't panic. I'm sure they'll have AC."

"You don't sound very confident."

"If there isn't, one of us will pretend to faint from the heat during the motivational speaker's speech. I choose you, since you're a trained actress."

"Okay, just make sure my dress covers everything appropriately when I go down."

"Deal."

"This is why I love you."

She took my hand. "Everything is going to be okay."

I squeezed hers back. "I know. It just sucks right now."

"Eighty-seven more days."

"Yeah. It's right around the corner." My heart wasn't buying it.

Several of our colleagues were pulling into the worn-out parking lot. It had seen better days. I realized I may need to get the suspension on my car looked at when we got back. That end of summer gloom surrounded all of us. Or was it just my end of a relationship gloom?

Several people waved at us and then politely turned to their neighbor, I'm sure to gossip about the demise of PB and J. I thought it was such a cute nickname, like Brangelina or TomKat. Looks like we were destined to go the route of both famous couples—splitsville.

One of our fellow teachers was not shy. Sean Goldman, or Coach as everyone called him, ran up to us. He picked me right up and swung me around. "PB, tell me it isn't so. I was picturing a proposal on the football field this year during halftime. J and I had already talked about it."

"Whoa, Coach." I thought I might puke from the spinning and the info. What did I say to that? We had discussed getting married, but I didn't know he had plans to propose. My heart beat wildly.

Coach set me down and I righted myself. I looked up at his large, looming figure. A once very attractive man, I'm sure, that had let himself go. I was about to inquire further about his explosive piece of news, but Capri saved me.

She grabbed my hand. For a little thing, she sure was bossy. She called it being a Southern girl. "Come on, we want to get a good room. Bye, Coach." She waved.

I followed her, but kept looking back at Coach. "Capri, I was talking to him."

"It was for your own good. You would have only tortured yourself. No contact, remember?"

"You know that's going to be impossible."

"Probably, but we have to do our best to minimize the time around him and his friends."

"He's everybody's friend."

"Not mine or yours anymore."

I stopped and sighed. "I hate that." I felt so empty. *Was he really going to propose?*

Capri pressed her lips together. "Me too, actually, but the man-slut has to go. It's his loss."

"You read the comments on that Facebook post. I don't think he'll be lonely for too long. Maybe this time he'll find some fine Southern Belle with a rich daddy. I bet he wouldn't call *her* a distraction."

"No one is better than you, and I'm not just saying that because you cleaned up my vomit once."

I laughed at her. "I think it's because I hooked you up with my hot Italian friend Anthony Doriguzzi."

Her face turned a shade of red. "I'm married now, thank you very much."

"I know, but I also know that you had a little fun with my friend. What did you say? His kiss was so good you got lost on the way back to our apartment."

She bit her lip. "Yeah, he was amazing, but he wasn't the kind of guy you take home to your momma."

"No, he wasn't." But you know who was? The person I took home to meet my parents over spring break. But he wasn't the same person now, because that man would never have hurt me like this. That man used to tell me all the time that I was the best thing that ever happened to him. *Eighty-seven days.*

I'm not sure there were any good rooms to be had. Each cabin had three bedrooms and one bathroom. They were putting two to a room. Six women and one bathroom didn't seem like a well thought out plan. And though the cabins did have air conditioning, the air smelled like it had been circulating for the last fifty years. To top it off, the rooms had bunkbeds.

"Feels like we're back in school." Capri began to unpack.

"Except, sadly, our dorm room was nicer than this."

"It's only one night."

I looked around the dark, dank room. "Maybe I'll sleep in my car."

She rolled her eyes at me.

"Hey, I'm going to meet Mr. Crandall. He said he found this fantastic one act and he wants to get my opinion."

"Okay. I'll meet you at the lodge. Remember, stay away from the new VP."

"Don't worry, he's the last person I want to see."

Too bad what I wanted didn't always seem to happen. What were the odds that my partner in crime, mentor, and father figure, Mr. Crandall would be talking to the reason I needed a ninety-day program? They were outside the lodge and I was just turning around to avoid them when I heard a voice call out to me.

"Presley, dear. I was looking for you." Victor Crandall reminded me of Mark Twain with his wild white hair, Southern accent, and mischievous eyes.

I closed my eyes and took a deep breath. The article was right, I physically craved Jackson. And I loved him with an all that I was, am, and ever would be kind of love. It wasn't a fairytale kind of love; it was the in sickness and health kind. The kind that had you living in the same house for sixty years until they had to cart you off to a nursing home kind of love. We worked so well together, too. Like last Valentine's Day when we had decided every girl at the school should get a rose. We came up with a plan and talked to a local florist along with some other businesses in the area and we made it happen. All seven hundred and fifty girls were presented with a pink rose. I'll never forget the looks on some of their faces when they were handed a rose. It was priceless. And he was good like that.

I did my best to not look at Jackson while trying to fake happy. "Mr. Crandall, how are you?" I walked toward the men, shaking.

"Fine, fine, fine. I was telling our new vice principal here about my trip to New York and about our plans for the year."

I nodded, only focusing on Mr. Crandall.

"I'm hoping maybe we'll get some more budget money now that we have an in. Right, Presley?"

I forgot how Mr. Crandall hated social media. He felt like it violated the laws of the universe somehow, and maybe he was right, but he really needed to catch up on his gossip. I made the mistake of looking to my right. Jackson caught my eye for a brief second. Gosh he looked good in his jeans and button up shirt. He looked so official. *Focus. Eighty-seven more days.*

I cleared my throat. "We aren't—"

"Administrators and teachers should maintain only professional relationships," Jackson answered for me.

Mr. Crandall's concerned eyes met mine. "Is that so, Presley dear?"

I did my best to keep any moisture from appearing in my eyes when I nodded.

"What a shame. I have found that personal relationships, no matter who we are, should be maintained above all else. I think there will be a mountain of regret on the horizon."

I peeked at Jackson. Surprise was written in his wide eyes.

No one was more surprised by this situation than me.

DAY FOUR

♥

Friday, July 30

DEAR MR. BINGLEY,
   I can't sleep. It may have something to do with that fact that Capri snores, or most likely it's because I saw Jackson several times yesterday. I knew I would, but I wasn't prepared to feel so much hate and love at the same time. I hate him so much for being able to act like it never happened. He stood up, droning on about all the new policies and procedures that they were enacting this year. Only he could make it sound interesting. Everyone but Capri and I gave him their full attention. I kept my head down, doodling on my agenda. Doodling or drawing pictures of Jackson burning in hell, it's all the same thing.

   The day only got worse. They had us do all these team-building exercises like putting together puzzles and getting-to-know-you games. Boring didn't begin to cover it. I'm so glad I was not born in your time period, when women were expected to sit and recite poetry, sew, sing, and draw all day. That is assuming I was born to be a lady. Knowing my luck, I would have been the servant girl emptying out the pots the ladies urinated in.

   I don't know if I can take another day of all the staring and talking behind my back. So we broke up. Can we all move on? Me included? Jackson *obviously has. How can that be? Tell me, Mr. Bingley, is it that easy for men? Do you just decide and it happens? If so, I envy you. Or do I pity you? How can you ever know what real love is, if, on demand, you can turn it off?*

Most confused,

Presley

I decided a walk around the lake was in order. It was still early enough that the sun was barely tickling the horizon. It would be the only time of day when the temperatures were bearable. I threw on some running shorts and a t-shirt before heading out. It felt like a warm shower, not a steamy one...yet. There was a nice path that went around the lake, so I headed there. I enjoyed the peace, and being alone. I loved Capri, and if this was only her and I, it would have been much better. Don't get me wrong, I liked my fellow teachers, some of them like family, but I had needed to be further along on my ninety days to recovery before all of this. Mindy Everly, one of the freshman math teachers, had the gall to ask me if it was okay if she gave Jackson her number. I didn't even bother to tell her he didn't date teachers anymore. I gave her a phony smile and walked away. If he somehow ended up with her, I thought I might feel better about the situation. She talked like she needed her sinuses irrigated and, it's tacky of me to say, but he better like big butts and that's no lie.

I did my best not to focus on Jackson as I watched the sun rise above the tree line. I was thinking of all the fun games I had learned at a workshop I attended last month. I couldn't wait to share them with my students. Games like Red Rover, but you use emotions. Or a twist on Simon Says. I also had some field trips in mind that I wanted to do. Too bad that involved Jackson's approval. This was going to be a long school year. Or at least a long eighty-six days. One day closer to my goal. It felt like forever.

It didn't help any when Jackson came running toward me. Why couldn't he have skipped his morning run? In a panic, I pretended not to see him. I jogged off the path, and headed toward the lake. It didn't matter that it smelled like fish, or that it was tinted green. Anything was better than facing him. I stared out into the murky water trying to get a hold of my emotions. And doing my best not to gag because of the smell. I missed my Colorado mountains and clear crystal blue water. I listened for him to run by, but instead I heard him making his way toward me on the uneven rocky ground. *Please fall and break your leg.*

Didn't he get the hint that I didn't want to see him? "Presley."

I guess not. I didn't answer. He was ruining my plan.

He tapped me on the shoulder. "Hey."

I made a slight turn and acknowledged him. Did I mention he was running shirtless? The chemical craving was unleashed inside my body. He had one of those smooth, rippled chests. I sidestepped to give myself some more space. It didn't help. I wanted to jump into his arms and kiss him like I meant it, sweaty and all.

"Am I interrupting you?"

"As a matter of fact, you are." I stared out across the icky lake.

"Sorry. I just wanted to see how you thought the retreat was going?"

Should I tell him the truth? He was technically my boss now. A few days ago we would have been laughing together at the cheesiness of it all. "I've been to better." So, truth it was.

"Oh. I was wondering, because you looked disinterested when I spoke yesterday."

Why was he looking at me yesterday? "It's your first time. I'm sure you'll get better."

"Was I that terrible?" He sounded disappointed and surprised. I'm sure he was. I had never spoken to him like that.

"Awful, but like I said, newbie. I wouldn't worry about it. Nobody really pays attention at these things anyway." So maybe I lied. People were eating him up yesterday.

"I guess I'll work on it." He kicked a rock.

"Okay. Well, enjoy your run." *Please leave and put that shirt in your hand on, for crying out loud.*

"Why won't you look at me?"

Was that a real question? Out came more lies. "I don't think it's appropriate for teachers like myself to see administrators half dressed. We need to keep it professional, right?"

He stepped closer. "Listen, Presley. I'm sorry things have to be this way."

I sidestepped more away from him, but my courage was bolstered and I turned his way. "Don't be. After you left my apartment, I realized this was a good thing. I mean, our little fling, it wasn't going anywhere."

He narrowed his eyes. "Fling?"

"Yep, fling, temporary. And it got me to thinking. We are so different; it would have never worked out."

His eyes widened.

"You like country music and I like alternative. You run and I walk. And how can someone who loves Alabama be with an Auburn fan?"

"You like Auburn now?"

"Go tigers. I mean, War Eagle. I decided I look better in blue and orange and I think this is Auburn's comeback year."

"If you say so."

"Oh, I do. So really, it's all for the best." I was on a roll now, so why stop? "Especially now that you are, you know, making your way up in the world. I would hate for you to have any distractions or mess around. It's not like you got promoted while we were dating or anything. And if *that* could happen while we were together, who knows how far you could have gone without such a nuisance as me." *Don't cry, Presley.*

His mouth downturned and he scrubbed his hand over his face. His handsome, handsome face. "Presley, I shouldn't have—"

"You're right, you shouldn't have. But like I said, it's all for the best. Now I can move on with my life, maybe go back home where I belong."

He tilted his head. "Are you moving back to Colorado?"

"I'm going to fulfill my contract for the year."

"You probably shouldn't have said anything to me in my position."

"Probably not, but do what you want with that information, Mr. Montgomery. You're good at doing what you want."

"Presley—"

"You should call me Ms. Benson. And do your best to stay away from me. It's the very least you can do."

"You know that's going to be difficult."

"I'm sure someone as smart as you will figure out how to make that work." I stared hard into his surprised brown eyes. "Enjoy your run."

I left him standing there speechless.

DAY FIVE

Saturday, July 31

DEAR MR. BINGLEY,

We talked. I lied, lots and lots of lies. But I was courageous and also told him the truth. Then I cried all the way home after another ridiculous day of team building activities. Capri had to drive us home, I was such a mess. I loved him. I still love him and he hurt me, with no regard to my feelings. At least you had the decency to stay away from Jane for weeks. And you certainly didn't show off your bare chest to her. The chest she used to lie on and sleep. The place where she felt loved and where all was right in the world. I feel ill-used, to use a term from your day. But, like Jane and Elizabeth, I must go on. I will not wallow in misery, at least not in public. I will not let Jackson Montgomery conquer me.

Boldly yours,

Presley

I began to feel anxiety and feelings of hopelessness creep in, so I decided I better do as the plan stated and think of some of the things I liked to do as a single woman. After all, it was the weekend, and Monday I would be back at the school setting up my room and in close proximity to Mr. Montgomery. I decided I should call him that. It would help distance myself from him.

It took me a long time to figure out what to do. One of the things I loved about Mr. Montgomery was that he tried his best to be interested in what I liked and I did the same for him. If I said let's take a ballroom dancing class, he would sign us up without me saying another word.

And if he said, I bought tickets to the rodeo, I would throw on my Daisy Dukes and some boots and go with him. I didn't have to give up any part of who I was to be with him, but now I felt like I was losing a part of me.

A bike ride to the farmer's market it was. I hadn't ridden my bike since the spring, when Mr. Montgomery and I made our way to Willow Bed Park. We lay under a shade tree all day while he read Tom Clancy's *Clear and Present Danger* to me. That Jack Ryan was some character. He was Jackson's literary hero. There was nothing more romantic than the man you love reading to you.

Had I been so blinded by love that I couldn't see that his love didn't run as deep as mine? I rested my head on the arm of my couch. I had to get up. I had to move. I would overcome this.

So, maybe a bike ride hadn't been the best choice. It was the end of July and I lived in Ala-freaking-bama. That's actually a word down here. The only consolation was the amazing strawberries and watermelon I scored. I was making strawberry watermelon lemonade. I placed my treasures in the basket that someone I won't mention bought me, pedaled home, and did my best not to get heat exhaustion. Why did I ever think it was a good idea to move down here?

DAY SIX

♥

Sunday, August 1

I'D ALMOST MADE IT A whole week. I only had twelve more weeks to go. It was doable, right? Except his nana, Miss Liliana, finally made me cave. I was going over to her home to have lunch. She swore Mr. Montgomery wouldn't be present. But she sounded determined to right this crime against humanity, as she referred to it. She was something. She was the feistiest, best person I knew, outside of Capri. They were cut from the same Southern cloth.

I made up a jug of my strawberry-watermelon lemonade to take over, along with some lemon bars. Miss Liliana called that good manners. I loved her. I wished she wasn't related to her grandson.

I drove to downtown Riverton. It was the quaintest downtown area I had ever seen. All the homes were built in the early nineteen hundreds and looked straight out of a Hallmark channel movie. Miss Liliana's was the crown jewel. It stood across from the town square fountain, surrounded by a wrought iron fence. She paid a gardener a pretty penny to maintain the lovely grounds of the vast estate. It wasn't a problem for her. She married into old Southern money. And like she told me, you can't go wrong marrying a Southern lawyer. Mr. Daniel Montgomery sounded like a good man. He died a few years ago from complications after surgery to remove his gall bladder. It left Jackson, I mean Mr. Montgomery, devastated. Almost as devastated as when his mother passed away when he was a sophomore in high school from an undetected heart condition.

From the sound of it, Mr. Jackson Montgomery's mother, Georgia, was a saint and the only person who could tame her beast of a husband. But after she died, he became hardened and bitter. He wanted what he wanted and that's how it was going to be. I had often felt very sorry for my ex-boyfriend. My parents were so kind and they supported my siblings and me in all our dreams, even the unrealistic ones. When I was ten and I wanted to invent a time travel machine, my dad bought me a book on quantum physics. I didn't understand one word of it, but that was love. Maybe I even felt sorry for Mr. Montgomery now. He felt like he would never satisfy his father. That's a terrible feeling no child should ever have to endure.

Well, maybe now his dad would be happy with him. He would reach the pinnacle of education administration, all without his middleclass ex-girlfriend.

I pulled through Miss Liliana's gate and looked around to make sure she didn't have any unwelcomed guests. I knew she promised he wouldn't be here when I arrived, but she was a tricky little thing, and let's not forget determined.

I made my way up the brick walkway with my treats. I was in Southern heaven. The white plantation style home was dream worthy. I rang the doorbell and it played this joyous tune that I knew rang throughout the home. It reminded me of Miss Liliana. I didn't have to wait long for her housekeeper to answer the door.

"Presley." Fiona smiled. "Miss Liliana is waiting for you in the sunroom." Here in the south, they had all sorts of different rooms than I had growing up—parlors, sunrooms, and keeping rooms.

"Thank you. I'll see myself back."

Fiona went on her way and I walked back through the magnificently decorated home. My favorite part was the intricate dark wood crown molding throughout the home. And her furniture looked like it belonged in a museum.

I was filled with sadness as I made my way back. I had pictured many years of celebrating the holidays here, but now that would never happen. *What day was I on?*

Miss Liliana sat prim and proper at her small round table, basking in the sunlight that streamed in through the sunroom windows. She smiled as I entered. "Presley, darling." She started to stand up.

"You stay there. I'll come to you." I added the lemonade and dessert I brought to the finely set table before making my way to her and hugging the little white-haired woman I adored. Her blue eyes still twinkled. "You're looking gorgeous today."

She waved off my compliment. "Poppycock. You, on the other hand, are beautiful. You're looking a little sad, but I intend to fix that."

I sat down across from her. "What's done is done. I've moved on."

"Such a pretty little liar you are."

"So maybe I'm working on it."

"Darling, just leave it to Nana."

"It's past the point of no return."

"There is no such thing. He loves you."

I placed my hand over my heart and rubbed. I felt a piercing pain there. "No. Love doesn't act like that."

"Love does a lot of stupid things."

"Maybe we shouldn't talk about him."

She reached across the table with her soft, aged hand. I gladly took it. "You're hurt. With good reason. My grandson is clearly not thinking straight, but don't give up hope. There is something special between you two."

"Was," I corrected her.

The wrinkles increased in her brow. "I stand by the 'is'."

I gave her my best pressed-lip smile. I hated to argue with her and it would have done no good. "How about we change the subject? Your peonies look lovely."

She gave me a little wink and squeezed my hand.

Day Seven

♥

Monday, August 2

DEAR MR. BINGLEY,

The worst possible thing happened yesterday. And, like always, a man was involved. Men. I'm thinking perhaps Jane would have been better off had you stayed in London. But anyway, there I was having a lovely lunch with one of my favorite people, and I suppose she still is even after what she did. I can't blame her, and I'm even flattered that she loves me so much she'll do whatever it takes to make sure the man in question and I get back together. Even if that means being deceptive and sneaking off to call her grandson to tell him I was "hurt." She failed to mention it was the emotional kind, the kind he inflicted on me.

The jerk came running over and raced through the house. Before I knew it, there he was in his athletic shorts and a sweat-soaked tank top, looking like he had been in the middle of working out. Did I mention how great he looked while panicked? Before he noticed there was nothing wrong with me, or even that I was there, he asked where I was and if I was okay. He sounded worried, beyond worried. Why would he come rushing over like that?

We locked eyes and confusion replaced his worried expression. Miss Liliana smiled like the devil. "I never said she was physically hurt, you ninny."

His head dropped. All I could do was shake my head. My plan for eradicating him from my life is not going as planned. To add insult to injury, Miss Liliana ordered him to apologize and take it back. He stood there looking pained. All he could say was, "I am sorry, truly." For some reason that only made me feel worse, and I wasn't so kind. I said, "Don't be. You did me a favor. I don't want to be with a man who isn't his own man."

For split second I saw a flash of regret in his eyes before he angrily turned around and slammed the front door as he left.

The stupid man made me cry in front of his nana. That did not go how she planned, but she said maybe it went better. How could it be better?

Now I have to go back to work today. How am I going to work with him? How bad would it be to have my teacher's license suspended for a year? Living in my parents' basement bad and waiting tables bad. Okay, so it would be bad.

Curse you, Mr. Bingley, and your kind. Why do you make it so we fall in love with you when you know you have no intention of being honorable and handling our hearts with care? Jackson is just like you. One day we are dancing at the ball and thinking life is grand. Of course we love each other. Everyone can tell. Then, just like that, you close up your estate and never look back. You were not your own man, Mr. Bingley. Shame on you.

Heartbroken,

Presley

I looked at my phone, it was only five in the morning. I lay back down on my bed. I grabbed a pillow for comfort and held on for dear life. One week down, and it had felt like forever. I wasn't feeling better. I would say I ached more. Yesterday hadn't helped. Why was it that he would come rushing to my side because he thought I was physically injured? He had to have known how much he had hurt me in a way that can't be seen, in a way that is felt much deeper. Why wasn't he trying to fix that? Or the better question, why did he do it in the first place? He was better than that. At least I used to think so.

I was going to need some serious latte action, and not the fat free kind. We were talking the kind with whipped cream and a caramel drizzle. Something to look forward to, I guess.

Maybe wake me up when September ends.

DAY EIGHT

♥

Tuesday, August 3

I SURVIVED MY FIRST DAY BACK at school. It could be because there were no students there. Most likely it was because I didn't see Mr. Montgomery. Sadly, I kept waiting for him to pop in and help me rearrange the furniture in my room, especially the couch, or as we used to call it, the casting couch. We might have made out on it a few times. I don't have desks in my room, as we do a lot of role playing, games, practicing lines, and of course, acting. I have a small raised platform we can use when the advanced classes are using the auditorium stage.

I was at least excited to get up my cutout of the New York skyline I had been working on all summer. Against the black backdrop, I put posters and playbills on it of all my favorite plays and musicals, like *Wicked*, *The Lion King*, and *Les Miserables*, to name a few. It took up one whole wall. It looked fabulous, if I do say so myself.

The day gave me the courage to go back and face the staff meetings I would have today. I would sit in the back and avoid any contact with the new VP.

Capri and I found an empty bistro table in the cafeteria as far away from the main action as we could. The cafeteria was the only place large enough for the whole staff. I did my best to keep my head down and to myself, but I swear to you, I could feel him. I knew the instant he walked in, and my head involuntarily popped up. Yep, our eyes met. Neither of us moved. I couldn't read his expression from across the room, but he looked nice in his suit and tie. I wasn't used to seeing him so formal at school. Who knew how long we would have stared at each other.

Capri intervened. "Presley." She nudged me. "Snap out of it."

Eight days and he still had me mesmerized. I shook my head and went back to looking at my pad of paper. I still loved him. And I hated him for it.

Capri rubbed my arm.

"I'm okay," I whispered. I lied. I absentmindedly began doodling on my paper. Mr. Montgomery was going to find himself the tortured subject in my work of art. I only had to decide his fate. Poisoning? Being run over by a car? That could work. I drew my Beetle with some legs under it, wicked witch style, except it was male legs with dress shoes that looked like his.

Capri looked at it and laughed.

Our twosome was joined by Mr. Crandall. "Ladies."

I smiled up at my mentor. "I love the new set of bowties."

He smartly straightened his moss green bowtie. "Thank you." He sat down next to me and peeked at my paper before I could turn it over. He chuckled. "I love you, my dear."

"You probably shouldn't say that out loud. Someone could mistake that for sexual harassment."

He waved his hand around. "I dare them."

"This is why I adore you."

Our beloved principal, Dr. Walters, entered to begin the meeting. He was a stately man in his mid-sixties. He walked with a slight limp from an accident years earlier, but his smile warmed the room. He waved to everyone like he was a celebrity, and he kind of was. He was the rock star of Riverton High. Mr. Montgomery would have big shoes to fill when he replaced him. And I knew it would be *when*, not *if*. Mr. Montgomery possessed the same charismatic qualities as Dr. Walters, and he was almost as popular with the students.

I tried not to watch the two men chum it up like old friends, but I was only eight days in and my body was still craving him. Capri kicked me under the table. She was a good friend.

I was rubbing my leg when Dr. Walters started the meeting. A hush fell over the cafeteria and all heads turned his direction, all but mine. I kept mine firmly down. I couldn't risk eye contact with the enemy, or another kick from Capri.

"Good morning, y'all. This is going to be the best daggum year yet." He'd said that last year, too.

I was happy to see his Southern vocabulary was still intact.

"We have the best teachers and staff not only in the county, but in the state to boot. We have the test scores to prove it."

I smiled down at my death drawing while he praised the school and went over our rankings and standardized test scores. I was lucky to work for such a terrific school. Too bad it was probably my last year. With that thought, I added some more tire tracks to the dead vice principal in my picture.

In the midst of my self-therapy Capri nudged me. "Wow." That came out awfully breathy.

I took my chances and lifted my head just as Dr. Walters was introducing Brad Sutton. Capri's reaction suddenly made sense. I would say wow was a good word for the Greek god that stood next to Dr. Walters. Judging by the fact that Mindy Everly actually took a piece of ice out of her diet Coke and rubbed it on her chest as she drooled, I would say *wow* was the consensus in the room.

He was gorgeous with his jet black, styled hair and olive skin. His biceps were about to burst through his polo shirt. He had this air about him that said he knew full well how beautiful he was. Unfortunately for me, all I could do was compare him to Mr. Montgomery, who sat behind him. Mr. Montgomery was attractive, and he knew it, but he didn't flaunt it.

"We are excited to have Brad Sutton join our staff. He will be filling the vacancy left by Jackson in our social studies department as well as on the field," Dr. Walters informed the rest of us.

"Go Cowboys!" Brad pumped his fist in the air.

There were quite a few in the crowd that reciprocated, including Coach, who beamed at his new assistant. I noticed Jackson, I mean Mr. Montgomery, took note. I detected a hint of longing in his look. I knew how much he loved coaching. Sympathy for him crept in, but I squashed it when his words rang in my head of how I had been a distraction and he had just been messing around with me. I found myself holding back tears. More tire tracks were added to my picture.

Capri nudged me and whispered. "I don't see a ring on Brad Sutton." She said his name with a dreamy sigh.

I narrowed my eyes at my married friend.

"I'm not interested in him, but I'm thinking he would make an excellent rebound for you."

I looked up at him again and perused him. He was gorgeous, but I felt nothing. Not even a little flutter. I shrugged. "The plan said to be careful of rebounds. Besides he's not really my type."

"Someone has to be your first step back into the dating world. Look at him and imagine the possibilities."

I shook my head at her. "Looks aren't everything."

"True, but he's so pretty. He's the perfect person to get back at the new VP."

"I'm not dating anyone to get back at him. I don't want to date anyone, period, right now."

"Okay, be all sensible."

I smiled at her. "Don't worry, I'm sure I will do something reckless in the near future."

"Promise?" She smiled with mischief.

"You know me. I can't help myself."

Dear Mr. Bingley,

I made it one more day. When will this ache in my chest go away? Will I ever be able to look at him and feel nothing? The hate that bubbles up in me when I look at him only means that my love for him is ever-present. It isn't fair.

Until tomorrow,

Presley

DAY NINE

♥

Wednesday, August 4

I'M TEN PERCENT OF THE way there. Too bad I don't feel ten percent over him. I wish they had a rehabilitation clinic for this type of situation. It would be nice to check myself into some place that he didn't have access to. I needed to step up my game. I was going to have to jump on the offensive side. No more defense for me. I was Presley Benson after all. Hear me roar. No more meowing in the corner like a kitten. So what if the love of my life rejected me? That sounded terrible. How about, so what if I wasted nine months of my life? I had so many more to go and I wasn't going to spend them feeling sorry for myself because one man couldn't see how good he had it. That's right, Mr. Montgomery, I was the best girlfriend you ever had or will have.

I took my brave new attitude to school with me. I had to finalize my syllabus before the open house tonight. Tomorrow was the official first day of school. I was going to make this the best school year yet. I would go out in a blaze of glory before I hightailed it back home. Then I'd find a homegrown Colorado man who could keep me warm in the winters.

I was feeling like a lion until I rolled into the staff parking lot at the same time as the new VP. Looked like he bought a brand-new truck. He had been talking about it. I couldn't think about it, because it involved me taking test drives with him, which meant testing out how comfortable the trucks were for making out. If you ever wanted a list of the best trucks for comfort and accessibility for romantic pursuits, I was your girl. And it looked like he bought number one on the list. I hated him.

I reminded myself I was on the offensive so I parked as far away from him as possible and tried my best to rush so there was no chance of any interaction. I imagined myself with a football in hand, running toward the end zone. The place where I no longer cared about the man in the truck who got an A+ when it came to kissing.

I grabbed my satchel and walked as fast as my high heels would take me to the school. The click of my heels against the pavement was interrupted. The defense was trying to intercept. Though I couldn't figure out why. Wasn't he the one who decided we were no longer headed toward the same goal?

"Presley, wait up."

That was a negative. I was proud of myself and didn't turn around. Instead, I ungracefully picked up the pace in heels and a pencil skirt. That's right, I could hustle all dolled up.

"PB."

For a moment, my heart hiccupped. That was a personal foul using my nickname. *End zone, end zone.* I ignored him. I barely walked in the front office doors before his long legs caught up to me. I could hear him walking behind me, but I was determined for there to be no interference.

I was so focused on who was behind me that I forgot to focus on what was in front of me, or should I say who. I ran smack dab into the Greek god and his admirers in front of the attendance office door. So, here's the good news. The floor cleaner the janitors used was top quality. The bad news was that pretty shine makes for some slick floors. Slick floors, plus high heels, plus an ex-boyfriend, equals disaster, or at least embarrassment.

After running into the hard body, I did my best not to slip and fall. I probably should have accepted the inevitable and let my butt hit that floor, but I flailed my arms about, trying to steady myself before the floor and I met. The gasps and squeals of shock rang in my ears as me and my wounded pride tried not to cry out in pain, all while making sure we didn't have any wardrobe malfunctions. Thank goodness, I had worn pretty silk panties, but regardless, I wasn't really wanting to share that fact with anyone, especially the two men who were in a contest to help me up.

As soon as Jackson touched me, I knew it was him. Is it weird that your skin can memorize a touch? It felt much different than the Casanova's firm grip.

"PB, are you okay?" Jackson knelt next to me, and in a gentlemanly move, he pulled down my skirt. His hand glided down my calf like it had dozens of times. I felt paralyzed by the touch. I stared into his deep brown eyes and confusion ran through them. He pulled his hand away. I tried to catch my breath. I didn't want his touch to have an effect on me. He didn't deserve it.

"I'm fine. I don't need your help."

His confusion turned to frustration.

"Presley, correct?" A masculine voice to my right called.

I turned toward the tantalizing sound to find Don Juan flashing a dazzling smile at me.

"Are you hurt?"

"Only my pride."

Brad's smile widened. "Let me help you up." He held out his large hand.

I hesitated until the VP took my hand without asking. That was a no-go and a personal foul. I tried to yank it away while giving my other hand to the handsome helper to my right. Mr. Montgomery wasn't letting go, so both men hoisted me up like I was some cow that need two strong men to pick her up. Oh yeah, I was going to be talked about in the teacher's lounge for eternity.

I did appreciate that most of the women who had been ogling Brad kept to the women's code and averted their eyes. It was a common courtesy. If a woman falls in front of another woman, you are supposed to pretend like you didn't see anything and go about your merry way. I could understand, though, why they were sticking around. Given an up-close view, Brad was pretty dreamy. He had unusual light green eyes that drew you in.

I didn't get a really good chance to stare into them because more awkwardness ensued when both men kept a hold of my hands and each tried to pull me in a different direction. Breaking my teacher's contract was sounding more and more enticing. I pulled both of my hands away. Each man stared at the other. I looked between the two and felt oddly like I had entered some sort of competition.

"Excuse me." I started to limp away.

"Presley, let me take you to the nurse."

I didn't bother looking back at Mr. Montgomery. He had no right to be nice to me. I shook my head and kept on walking.

Brad came after me and landed by my side. "Are you sure you're okay?"

"I might transfer to another school."

He chuckled. It was quite manly. "I hope not."

Was he flirting? Because that was the last thing I needed. I was doing my best not to wince as I walked to my classroom. The stairs were going to be fun.

Brad was in no hurry to leave my side. "Looks like we have morning car line duty together."

I looked up into his smiling eyes. "I hadn't checked the schedule yet. But I figured I would have the honor. I'm still a low woman on the totem pole."

"I guess that makes me the low man. It's not a bad spot." His teeth sparkled.

"Just wait until the rain is coming down in sheets."

"I lived in Houston for five years before here, so I'm used to it."

"In that case, you may enjoy the weather here."

He laughed. "I take it you don't?"

I shrugged. "It has its moments." Why did my mind flash to Jackson and me dancing in the rain? I knew why, but it was annoying and counterproductive. We made it to the stairs. "I'm going down."

"I guess this is where we part. I look forward to getting to know you better."

"Maybe next time I won't run into you."

"I enjoyed that part the most." He walked off grinning.

I rolled my eyes and hobbled down the stairs. No coworkers or men for me, thank you very much.

Dear Mr. Bingley,

I survived one of my most embarrassing moments today—no need to rehash it here—as well as the open house. The open house reminded me of why I was staying. I loved seeing my returning students and my new babies, as I like to think of them. It was a good thing this next event happened after my open house euphoria, or I would be headed back to the mile high city as I write.

I will give you this, Mr. Bingley, at least you had the decency to stay away from Jane once you broke her heart. I know you came back to proclaim your love and propose. I know that's not going to happen in this situation. And if it ever did, believe me, I would not, I repeat, I would not be as easily entreated as Jane. Why she said yes to you right away, I will never know. You didn't deserve it.

Just like Mr. Montgomery has no right to continue to try and engage me in conversation. Which brings me to my story. Like I said, the open house was terrific. I enjoyed seeing my students and talking to their parents. I felt confident about the plans and goals that I've set for the year. The kids seemed excited, especially those that will be involved in the one act competition.

I made it all the way to the end of the evening without even a glance of the heartbreaker. That all changed when I was getting ready to leave. I had grabbed my bag and was heading for my classroom door when two men appeared. The two men involved in the day's previous embarrassment. Two beautiful looking men staring at each other and sizing the other one up. Each man gave the other one a nod of greeting, but the VP had to play his part, so he asked Brad how he was settling in and about the football team. I heard pining in his voice and it pricked my heart. All more reasons to hate him.

I took that as my opportunity to escape. I excused myself and walked between the two men, out the door. It didn't have the desired effect. First, Brad—glorious body Brad—asked me if I wanted to join him and some other of our colleagues for a late dinner. He had no idea how much that pained me. As you know because I wrote to you about this, the previous assistant football coach, my ex, asked the exact same thing last year after the open house. Do you remember how excited I was and how I gushed to you about him? I wrote down every detail, like how our legs touched under the table and how he opened all my doors. I declared him the one *before I barely knew him. That was not going to happen this year. I politely declined the invitation and walked away. I didn't rush in case of another mishap where my butt met the ground. I'm still sore from the morning embarrassment.*

I congratulated myself on my getaway and slight of Mr. Montgomery. So maybe I gave him an evil smile while Brad extended his invitation. I could tell by the way he rubbed his neck back and forth it bothered him that Brad was paying attention to me. And if Brad wasn't a coworker, and the ninety-day plan didn't discourage rebounds, I may have done something I would have regretted and accepted the invite. Instead, I did the smart thing and walked away, or at least I tried.

Apparently, Mr. Montgomery can't take a hint. He came calling after me, and he had the audacity to call me PB again. I ignored him. It wasn't until he said Ms. Benson that I stopped. His formal address pierced me almost more than the use of my nickname. It sounded cold coming out of his mouth. The same mouth that whispered a hundred times that he loved me. The mouth that could kiss me for hours on end. The one that spoke beautiful words of encouragement.

I had reached the stairs and held onto the rail for support while he caught up. I stood there, breathing deeply, begging myself not to cry. He paused and didn't say a word for a moment. We must have looked odd standing there with my back to him. Finally, Jackson's voice appeared. "Would you please look at me?"

It took everything I had to turn around and look at him. Oh, Mr. Bingley, Brad is probably better looking than Jackson, but there's something about Jackson that draws me in and doesn't want to let go. I'm trying. I really am.

I locked eyes with him and glared. He gave out a long, slow sigh. "Can we at least be friends?"

My eyes began to sting, but I refused to let him get the better of me. "No, Mr. Montgomery. And I would appreciate it if you would limit our conversations to school matters only."

He stepped closer. "Presley."

"Ms. Benson, if you don't mind."

He pinched his lips together. "As you wish, Ms. Benson."

How dare he use the line from Princess Bride, *our movie! Sorry, Mr. Bingley, that it isn't* Pride and Prejudice. *Jackson was more of* Westley *than a Darcy or you. Other than the fact you are both cowards.*

Eighty-one more days.

Good night,

Presley

DAY TEN

Thursday, August 5

*D*EAR MR. BINGLEY,
  Wish me luck today.
Sincerely,

Presley

I woke up with that first day anticipation. In fact, I'd hardly slept. I was filled with excitement and unease. Something struck me in the middle of the night about the way Jackson said, "As you wish." I didn't recognize it in the moment because of how upset I was with him, but playing it over in my head made me realize he had put some meaning behind it. But did it really matter? The answer was a big fat no. I was ten days in—double digits, baby! He was going to be a distant memory in no time.

I was such a great liar.

I dressed with care, including a nice pair of flats. No need to tempt fate today. My butt already had a nice bruise on it. It went well with the bruised ego. At least it gave Capri a good laugh. Capri, who needed to step up her game. She was supposed to be my offensive lineman and shield me from the defense. She was failing miserably.

The streets were alive with first day of school traffic. The sleepy days of summer were over. I was sad to see them go, along with what seemed like my own little piece of heaven. Eighty more days, right? Before I felt really depressed about my obliterated relationship, my phone rang and I answered it through my car.

"Hello, Miss Liliana."

"Darling, it's so good to hear your voice."

This woman was going to kill me. "I miss you, too."

"We need to change that. Come have dinner with me tomorrow night."

"Thank you, but I don't think that's a good idea."

"I told Jackson I got you in the divorce."

"Miss Liliana, we were never married."

"Well, you should have been."

I wanted to bang my head against my steering wheel and wail like a child. "I love you, but I need to distance myself. I'm sorry."

"Young lady, I don't accept. We're family. I promise my imbecile grandson won't be here. I expect you at six tomorrow night." She hung up.

Feisty old woman. I adored her, and knowing that she loved me and thought of me as family meant the world to me, but it caused pain. My mom always said you should never count your chickens before they hatch, and I realized now I had raised a whole chicken farm in my head when it came to my future with the aforementioned imbecile grandson. Eighty days and all I would be having was fried chicken. That sounded a little more morbid than I meant it.

I pulled into the school parking lot early. I had to be there before the kids started to arrive to make sure their parents were following the rules and flow of the car line. I didn't mind the duty. For the most part, it was nice to see the kids in the morning and wish them a good day. Especially those first few days when the new freshman had those terrified, unsure looks. It was amazing to me last year how during the course of the first week those faces became more confident, at least for most. Some it took a lot longer. A few of those now sophomores still have those looks today; high school could be daunting.

I ran in the school to drop off my satchel and get my room ready. It was the one downside of car line duty, not being able to greet my home-room students when they walked in first thing. But I set out a welcome sign with a basket full of apples I had brought. Maybe it was a little cheesy, but I thought it was a nice touch.

I ran into Capri in the hall. "Aren't you looking fetching this morn-ing. Is that for the VP or Brad?"

"Shhh." I looked down at my tiffany blue dress. "Neither. Men suck."

She laughed. "Some don't."

"Fine, David doesn't."

She smiled at her husband's name. "Try not to fall again."

"I'll do my best. But seriously, you need to do a better job today of keeping you know who away from me. If not, I may cut you from my team."

"I know too many of your secrets," she reminded me with an evil grin.

"Hey, what happens in Maui stays in Maui. All I'm going to say is, Kai." Kai was a male hula dancer we met on an amazing spring break trip we took our senior year of college. We saved for three years to take it. Best money ever spent.

She blushed. "Fine, brat, your secrets are safe with me."

"Let's go to Hawaii again." I sighed. Maybe I should have given Damon my number, but we promised ourselves what we shared in Hawaii would stay there. Meeting a guy on vacation rarely worked out, but man could that guy kiss. My mom always said you had to live real life with them. That's how you would know if you could build a life together. I thought I had done that with Jackson. Too bad I hadn't known he was only messing around.

"I'm married now," Capri said, like I needed the reminder.

"That's okay. You can help me spot gorgeous, unattached men."

She smirked and pointed down the hall at Brad.

I grabbed her finger. "Not happening."

Brad noticed us and walked our way. Capri laughed. I would have smacked her, but professionalism overruled.

"You ready to head out?" Brad asked me. He was dressed in a polo shirt that barely contained his biceps. I wasn't into guys that had biceps almost the size of their heads.

Capri nudged me forward.

"Yep." I glared at Capri. She was crazy if she thought I would even consider the jock in front of us. He was gorgeous, but he wasn't...he wasn't...It didn't matter. I was getting over the *wasn't*. At least, I was trying.

Brad and I walked down the hall together in awkward silence at first. I felt like I had forgotten how to interact with the opposite sex. My brain was still switching gears, trying to imagine my life without Jackson. I'm not even sure if I realized how firmly I had set my heart and mind on being with Jackson forever. I had thought he felt the same way. I forced myself to smile up at my coworker.

He returned the gesture. "You look nice today. Is it okay if I say that?"

"I think that is well outside of what is considered sexual harassment. And thank you. You look nice, too."

"A woman who knows how to return a compliment. I like it."

I wrung my hands together and looked straight ahead. Uncomfortable was a good word for how I felt. And I hated Mr. Montgomery for those feelings. We were over. His choice, not mine, but regardless, it happened. I wondered when my old self would appear, the pre-Mr. Montgomery version. Maybe the problem was I liked the Jackson version. Loving him made me a better person. I guess I needed to discover the post-Jackson me.

Brad opened the door for me and the August heat hit us. I threw on my shades and hoped my hair survived the steam bath. My mom had already texted me about the brisk morning they were having in Colorado. I was missing home more and more. I took my place at the beginning of the line near the flag pole and Brad dutifully took his place several feet away.

Cars began to line up and students began to file out. I greeted each student, helped open and shut car doors, waved to nervous parents and tried to give them a reassuring smile that their babies would survive their first day of high school. The car line was mostly filled with freshman and sophomores who were dependent on their parents for transportation. It was all going well and good until *he* walked out in his suit and tie looking how I had pictured my future.

The new VP high-fived a girl and boy I had just opened a car door for. "Good morning, Ms. Benson."

I gave him a half smile in return, only because of that whole professionalism thing. I did my best to ignore him, but he made that difficult by standing next to me and following me to each vehicle. I liked that he tried to greet and high-five each student, but he could just as easily do that in the north parking lot. The south was my territory.

Then our hands touched as we both went for the same minivan door to open. I froze and his gaze lingered on me. His warm brown eyes made me want to kick him. He wasn't supposed to look at me like that. And his touch should have felt cold and unwelcome instead of like I had come home. I shook it off and walked to the cars between him and Brad. We didn't need to be doubled up.

I noticed Brad looked inquisitively between Mr. Montgomery and me. Meanwhile, Mr. Montgomery's eyes tightened out of frustration. I could read him well. But why was he frustrated? This was his own doing. I didn't know what delusions he had about what would exist between us when he obliterated our relationship, but he was living in a fantasy world if he thought we could go back to being friendly coworkers. I would behave professionally, but that was all he could expect.

The walk back into the school was more awkward. Why did I suddenly feel like I was always in between these two men? Both reached for the door, and neither seemed to want to let the other open it. So, they each opened one of the double doors for me. I looked between the two men, who stared hard at one another. Were they puffing out their chests? Neither option was good for me. The deciding factor came when Mr. Montgomery said, "Presley." His tone had some underlying pleading to it, so I walked through Brad's door. But I hated the smirk Brad gave Mr. Montgomery. I wanted to feel some self-gratification, but it wouldn't come. It actually made me not like Brad, because Mr. Montgomery would have never reacted that way.

And what did Mr. Montgomery do? "Have a great first day, Brad. Let me know if you need anything."

He was a gentleman and I hated him for it.

"Presley." Brad caught up to me.

I paused. "I'm kind of in a hurry."

"Of course. I just wanted to say I'm sorry."

I tilted my head. "For what?"

"I heard that you and the vice principal used to date and he broke up with you over Facebook. What a jerk."

I stood for a second. That was the rumor going around? I walked off. "That's not what happened."

Brad followed. "Oh. Well, he's still an idiot for letting you go."

"How would you know? For all you know, I'm crazy or I cheated on him."

"Is that true?" He sounded worried now.

I was crazy all right. I stopped and narrowed my eyes. "This is not a conversation I usually have with acquaintances."

His olive colored skin turned a nice shade of red. "You're right. I'm sorry." He walked toward his classroom without another word.

Capri rushed over to me.

"You're fired." I walked past her.

Happy first day of school.

DAY ELEVEN

♥

Friday, August 6

DEAR MR. BINGLEY,

Please don't make me go back to school. I'm not one for wallowing in my misery. I've been trying to rise above the circumstances, but do you know how hard it is to know that everyone is talking behind your back? I've tried my best to ignore the stares and fake politeness. The worst part is that he's coming off as Prince Charming, at least with the women, like he's gotten a pass somehow. Everyone is wondering what's wrong with me, well almost everyone.

Should I be wondering that too?

Still hurt and confused,

Presley

I took a breath and gathered my courage. My mom said it would get harder before it got easier. Why did she always have to be right?

I took another step toward recovery by gathering up anything that had any connection to Mr. Montgomery and threw it in a box that I would deliver to Miss Liliana tonight. I threw his lucky Alabama t-shirt in the box as the final item. Not before breathing it in one more time. It still smelled like him, coriander and cardamom, spicy and . . . I had to stop thinking about it and him. We were over. I threw a lid on the box and shed a tear or two.

I felt like I should get more than ninety days since I had to see him so frequently, but I had to be over him in seventy-nine days. I didn't want to feel like this anymore. My offensive strategy wasn't working. I needed a new coach. Mr. Crandall popped into my mind. Maybe he could give me the secret male way of moving on.

I got to school extra early because Mr. Crandall was always there before anyone. He liked to absorb the energy of the stage. I'd watched him before, walking back and forth across it, breathing it in as if it was alive. Sometimes he would recite Shakespeare as he went. I loved the stage, but he *was* the stage. I wanted to be him when I grew up.

I crept into the auditorium and one spotlight lit the stage. Mr. Crandall stood still, with his eyes closed. He held what looked like the script we were considering for the one act. We still needed approval from administration before we could move ahead with it. That meant Mr. Montgomery would have a say in it. Our lives were too intertwined. I would never date a coworker again. Lesson learned.

I stood at the back of the auditorium and admired my mentor for a moment. I wished I could see into his mind. I'm sure it was fascinating. I bet he pictured the entire play in his thoughts like a movie. He had this amazing ability to block and stage each scene perfectly. I couldn't wait to get going on this year's play.

I wasn't sure how he was alerted to my presence, but when he opened his eyes, he focused in on me and smiled. In that moment, I felt a small amount of peace.

"Presley, dear, what brings you to these hallowed halls this morning?"

I approached the stage. "I need your wisdom."

"You are assuming I have any." He held out his hand to help me up the stage steps.

I smiled warmly. "I'll take my chances."

He gave my hand a little squeeze. "You are as courageous as you are beautiful."

I shook my head at him. I did adore him. "I'm not feeling either at the moment."

"Hmmm. Let's have a seat."

We both lowered ourselves and sat on the edge of the stage with our feet dangling over.

Once situated, he patted my knee. "This too shall pass."

"That's what I wanted to talk to you about. How do I make that happen? And quick."

He chuckled. "There is no remedy for love but to love more."

"You're quoting Thoreau to me?"

"There is wisdom there, and isn't that what you're seeking?"

"I don't want to love more. It's too painful." My eyes welled up with tears.

"Then you have been blessed to know real love."

"I don't know about that, maybe one-sided love."

"Ah, my dear, it is a shame that he has chosen to throw away such a gift, but make no mistake, he loved you. That was apparent."

The tears escaped and fell into my lap. "I thought so too, but if he really loved me, how could he walk away so easily?"

"I'm not a betting man, but I would wager staying away from you is the hardest thing he's ever done."

"You're biased."

"I do love you, dear, but I've been around the block a few times and believe me when I tell you, you're not the only one hurting."

I ran my fingers through my curled hair. "That doesn't make any sense."

"Maybe I'm not the person you should be talking to then."

"He made it clear why he left. He called me a distraction. Said he was only messing around."

"So he's frightened."

"What?" I shook my head.

He took my hand and held it. "Nothing scares a man more than realizing he can have it all."

"I hate to say this, but you're only confusing me more."

He laughed. "It's only fair. Women have bewitched us and confounded us since the beginning of time."

"Then how do you get over us so easily?"

"Dear, we don't. We may do a better job of concealing our feelings, but I assure you, we feel it acutely when we lose the women we love."

"Are you speaking from experience?"

He sighed and looked out into the empty chairs. It took him a moment to speak. "Like our new vice principal, I let the love of my life slip away."

"Were you married?" I had always wondered. He had never talked about a wife and I knew he wasn't married now.

"No, dear. I took the coward's way out and told her we would be better off going our separate ways once we graduated from college."

"Tell me about her." I was intrigued.

A smile appeared on his face. "Connie Weatherly was beautiful like the morning sky, fair and lovely with hair the color of honey, and eyes of blue. She cast her spell upon me." He reverenced her name.

"What happened?"

His smile disappeared. "Along with her beauty, she had brains. She was headed for bigger and better things. She wanted to be a biomedical doctor and had been accepted to Johns Hopkins. I was headed to New York to see if I could make it on the stage. I made it on the stage, as you can see." He patted the wood beneath us.

"Were you intimidated by her?"

"Oh yes. She was a force to be reckoned with, quite like yourself."

"I don't know about that."

"Believe me, you possess those qualities that drive men to aspire to new heights."

"Or leave."

"Only because we're fools."

"Do you regret pushing her away?"

"Every day."

"Maybe you should look her up."

He laughed and slapped his knee. "I'm sure she ended up with someone much better than myself, like I hoped she would."

"I think you're pretty terrific."

"The feeling is mutual." He touched my cheek like my father would. "You know, maybe the more love Thoreau spoke about was the love we should have for ourselves. Don't you dare let Jackson's actions make you think any less of yourself. Just as I, he will come to regret not taking the gift given to him, if he doesn't already"

A tear rolled down my cheek. "I knew you were the person I needed to talk to."

He patted my cheek. "The question is, what will you do when Jackson realizes his mistake and comes seeking your forgiveness?"

"That's not going to happen."

"I wouldn't wager on that, dear."

DAY TWELVE

♥

Saturday, August 7

DEAR MR. BINGLEY,

I'm going to try that more love thing this weekend, so this will be our only communication. Miss Liliana had to cancel last night. Well, I ended up canceling on her. Daniel and Miranda, Mr. Montgomery's brother and sister-in-law drove up from Birmingham unexpectedly. They brought Dallin and Aubrey, their five and six year olds. Miss Liliana insisted I still come and be part of their family dinner, but I knew Mr. Montgomery and his dad would enter into that equation. I love Daniel and Miranda, even if Daniel is a little arrogant and Miranda is the epitome of a Southern Belle. She was forever trying to get me to join the Junior League. She was exactly the kind of woman Mr. Montgomery's dad expects his sons to marry—high-class with a royal Southern pedigree.

Mr. Montgomery wasn't the only person I had to get over. I had imagined myself aunt to those adorable children with the cutest southern accents, and lifelong friendships with their mommy and daddy. Oh well, I guess at least I never have to see Mr. Montgomery, the senior, again. It wasn't much conso-lation. I was willing to endure him to be Mrs. Jackson Montgomery. I'm not *ever writing or saying that title again. I will overcome him.*

Now I'm headed to Chattanooga, Tennessee, for a film festival. Yeah, Mr. Montgomery and I had talked about going to it together, but I didn't need him to be happy or to enjoy the things I loved. Maybe someday I won't want him anymore, either.

Seventy-eight days and counting,

Presley

Day Fifteen

♥

Tuesday, August 10

I HAD AN AMAZING WEEKEND OF self-love that spilled over into Monday. So much so, it inspired me to do something a little crazy. The film festival was centered on how romance films had evolved through the decades. It was fascinating, albeit a little painful to watch movie after movie about falling in love when you're trying to fall out of it, to watch the evolution of how perceptions of love and relationships had changed over the years. It made me realize that Mr. Crandall had come from a place in time where the man was supposed to be the breadwinner and cowboy. The take-charge alpha-male. No wonder he felt inadequate to seal the deal with the lovely Connie.

Sure, I was a little disappointed that my mentor, like Mr. Montgomery, behaved so abominably, but I felt like Mr. Crandall was a victim of his age. And if anyone deserved a second chance, he did. That was, if it was available to him. I broke the rules and went on Facebook after I spent my evening yesterday scouring online to find a Connie Weatherly that went to Johns Hopkins around thirty-five years ago. Mr. Crandall wasn't too forthcoming with information, so I was estimating. If I was right,

Connie Weatherly was now Connie Harris. I searched what she made available in her profile, and as far as I could tell, she wasn't currently married. And she had aged beautifully. Her hair was no longer the color of honey, but she looked lovely in gray.

Don't worry, I didn't look at any of Mr. Montgomery's posts, not that I could anyway. I blocked him from everything, which meant I couldn't creep on him. Who needed to creep on Facebook when I saw him every day at school? You would think when someone breaks up with you, they would do everything they could to avoid you. He didn't need to help in the car line or eat lunch in the teacher's lounge at the same time as me.

Thankfully, Capri and I had lunch at the same time and she was finally stepping up to the plate and shielding me from him. Like today, when she brought large handmade menu looking things that I could hide behind, if necessary. It was obvious what she was trying to do, but I adored her for it even if we did look ridiculous talking behind the large pieces of decorated cardboard. And what were the decorations, you might ask? Auburn of course. Mr. Montgomery loathed the school. I had looked up at the wrong moment to catch a glimpse of his reddened, frowning face.

What did he expect?

But just because I couldn't be in love, didn't mean Mr. Crandall couldn't be. I did something I never had before. I contacted a stranger via social media. I sent the supposed Connie Weatherly a private message over Facebook. It went something like this:

Hello, you don't know me, but I think we have a mutual friend named Victor Crandall. I believe you attended the University of Virginia together. Victor and I teach at the same high school. He doesn't know I'm contacting you. To be honest, I'm not sure how he would feel about it. But I can tell you that he regrets how things turned out with you. I know this may seem completely out of left field, but I was wondering if you might like to get in touch with him? He's against any sort of social media, but if you are interested, I would be happy to provide you with more information. If this isn't the

Connie Weatherly I'm looking for, please disregard this message. If it is, and this has caused you any pain, I apologize. Sincerely, Presley

Then I waited. I did worry about opening old wounds. I kept wondering how I would feel if several years into the future someone contacted me about Mr. Montgomery. I would be over him by then, right? Because it would be well past ninety days. But I had a feeling I would always wonder, *what if?* That was a depressing thought.

Seventy-five more days.

Day Eighteen

Friday, August 13

DEAR MR. BINGLEY,

I'm not a superstitious person, but I have this feeling of foreboding today. I should be happy. I'm twenty percent of the way there. I do feel a little better today, except for this nagging feeling that won't go away, but maybe I'm imagining things. You see, I'm good at that. I imagined a life with Mr. Montgomery. It was a good life, too; never perfect, but always beautiful. Now, supposedly, I only imagine an eighty percent life with him. Still not bad, except it will never happen. I know that. I truly do. So why do I still want to?

Don't answer that,

Presley

I arrived at school decked out in my new Auburn shirt. If God cared about football, I prayed he let Auburn win the Iron Bowl later this year. Nothing upset Mr. Montgomery more. Go Tigers! I meant, War Eagle. I had to remind myself that a tiger was their mascot, but War Eagle was their motto. I wasn't sure why. I should probably look that up. I thought the Denver Broncos had the ultimate football fans, but I was mistaken. It was like a religion here in the South. And they made you choose a team once you crossed the border. So I was switching sides. It probably went against some blood oath in Alabama, but I wasn't staying. I had to move on, even if after ninety days by some miracle I was completely over Mr. Montgomery. I didn't think I could stand watching him become who his father wanted him to be.

And I couldn't stand watching him be who he was now.

After the final car in the line drove away, I hustled into the school to escape both the heat and Brad, who had already asked what my plans were for the weekend. Besides dinner with Miss Liliana, it would be spent planning lessons and loving myself some more. I had already bought face masks, candles, and dark chocolate. It was going to be a good weekend celebrating my single status. I should have started dating myself a long time ago.

Then I came upon a scene as I neared my classroom that made me remember why I was in love with Jackson Montgomery. I wondered why he hadn't been present this morning in the car line. I turned the corner, but stopped when I heard his voice. He was sitting on the steps with Leo Olson, the starting quarterback for Riverton High School's football team. He was the sweetest kid, but he came from a rough home life. He had a lot of responsibility placed on his shoulders, including caring frequently for his younger brother. Leo was in my intermediate class, which I knew he only took because he needed what he thought would be an easy credit.

"Coach J, my family needs me. My mom started a new job and I need to watch Henry after school."

Mr. Montgomery lowered his head and thought for a moment.

Leo looked on with such trust, begging for a solution.

Mr. Montgomery met Leo's eyes. "What school does your brother go to?"

"Columbia Elementary."

Mr. Montgomery's eyes had a spark of hope in them. "How old is Henry?"

"Ten."

"Do you think he could walk a couple of blocks every day to a babysitter's house?"

Leo nodded, but with some hesitation, like he dared not to hope.

"I'll talk to your mom and we'll work this out. How are you doing in your classes so far?"

Leo's eyebrows gathered in. "Um, okay."

Mr. Montgomery cocked his head. "Just okay? What can I help with?"

"Math."

"Bring your math book to lunch, and I'll come find you in the cafeteria." He ruffled his dark hair.

"During lunch? That's when I hang with my girl."

"She can hang out with us, too."

"All right man." Leo bumped fists with Mr. Montgomery. "You're the best, Coach."

"Get to class." Mr. Montgomery smiled. That was, until he saw me staring at the scene amid the chaos of kids trying to get to class on time. "Ms. Benson." He gave me a little nod and stood up.

I turned before he could see in my eyes how much I loved him. How much I wanted him. Could you blame me?

"Presley, I mean, Ms. Benson." He followed after me.

I froze and shut my eyes. I was so close to my room. I almost ignored him, but he was my boss. A fact I hated. "Yes?" I didn't bother looking at him.

"You really can't look at me?"

I turned on a dime and glared at him. "Better?"

He sighed. His eyes moved to my chest.

A few weeks ago, I would have teased him about keeping his eyes to himself. Had it only been a few weeks?

"Are you really an Auburn fan now?"

I shook my head. "After everything, that's all you care about?"

"Presley." He inched closer and reached his hand up like he was going to caress my cheek like he always used to, but he stopped himself.

"Have a good day, Mr. Montgomery." This time I didn't pause. I marched straight into my room, put on a fake smile for my students, and counted the days until I would be over him.

I thought my encounter with my former boyfriend was the reason for the icky feelings earlier that day, but like a lot of things lately, I was wrong. Miss Liliana swore on her love for Nick Saban, Alabama's beloved head coach (all the Montgomery's loved Alabama football), that Jackson wouldn't be present during any part of my visit. I failed to anticipate that the other Mr. Montgomery would cross my path.

He was walking out as I was coming up the walkway. How did I not notice his car? I was in a daze, that's why. I had woken up feeling so ready to take on the world, and I did, but Jackson was still part of that world and it was exhausting.

Daniel Montgomery II was the kind of man who had intimidation woven into the very fabric of his being. He was taller than his six-foot-two son and always wore a dark suit and power ties. Even though his suit was looking a little loose now, his perfectly in-place gray slate hair and chiseled jawline said *I dare you to cross me.*

I was always up for a challenge. While his son and I were dating, I had always done my best to be polite even when he was undeserving of it. Well, I had mostly tried to avoid him. It was apparent from our first meeting he didn't like me. Jackson and I had been washing his truck in Jackson's driveway last October right after we were an "official" couple. It was a warm summerlike day, so I wore cutoffs and bathing suit top. I was soaked from Jackson spraying me with the hose and I had just dumped a bucket of soap-filled water on Jackson. He had barely taken me in his arms to kiss me when his dad pulled up. He took one look at me and disgust filled his features.

Miranda, his Southern Belle daughter-in-law, would never have behaved in such a way. She would have hired someone to wash the car. And she was always impeccably dressed. Sometimes I wondered now if that's what Jackson liked about me. I was the first woman he had dated that didn't fit the mold he was expected to fill. Maybe he knew all along that eventually he would do what was expected of him. I was only a brief dalliance. The thought sickened me. It also gave me a boost of courage when Daniel Montgomery II stopped to speak to me.

"Ms. Benson, can I have a word with you?"

I planted myself firmly in front of him and looked up to catch his cold brown eyes. "Sure, Daniel, what can I do for you?" Oh, that felt good. I had always wanted to call him Daniel. I knew he would hate it, and my apparent sarcasm.

He flexed his fingers and pressed his lips together. I could see the diatribe in his eyes he wanted to spew at me. I dared him with my own to do so. I didn't have to pretend around him anymore.

He pulled it together. He cleared his throat and squared his shoulders. "Don't give my mother any ideas or encouragement of you reconciling with my son. You're doing the right thing staying away from him. He was meant for another kind of life. Not one you have any part of."

His callous words felt like a punch to my gut, but I refused, with all that was in me, to let him know how deep they hurt. "I count myself lucky that you will have no part of my life. I only hope when you're done making your son into who you want him to be that he's truly happy."

"Young lady, I don't know who you think you are—"

I stepped closer and stood as tall as I could. "I'm the woman who loved Jackson with all my heart and supported him in what *he* wanted to do and be. His happiness was my happiness. Too bad you can't say the same. Have a good evening, Daniel." I walked off and headed straight for Miss Liliana, who had taken in the scene from her front door. Her eyes shined with admiration. I shook as I walked toward her. Not only had I lambasted her son, but in that moment I acutely felt how much I still loved her grandson. How sorry I felt for him. I didn't want to feel any of those things, most of all love.

It hurt too much.

DAY TWENTY

♥

Sunday, August 15

"WE ARE TOTALLY DOING IT wrong."

I looked up from my laptop and lesson plan to see Capri fixated on her own laptop. "What are you doing wrong?"

She turned her laptop around for me to see on her kitchen table. "Post coital snuggling should last for at least seven minutes."

I pushed her laptop back toward her. "TMI, Capri. TMI."

She smiled. "We only snuggle for like five before he drifts off to sleep."

"Again, I don't need to know about your sex life. And who came up with the name coital?"

She laughed. "I don't know, but I'm telling David he needs to give me at least two more minutes."

"Don't believe everything you read online."

"Hey, it helped you. What day are we on now?"

"I'm not sure how much that ninety-day article is helping. It's day twenty and I'm not sure I'm any closer to getting over him the healthy way, or any way for that matter."

"You're not curled up in the fetal position, so I would say you're right on track. In seventy days, he will be a distant memory."

"Fat chance, since we work together."

"Hmmm." She pursed her lips. "Maybe you should go against the article's advice and do the whole rebound thing. Just be upfront with the guy that you don't want anything serious and you're getting over a relationship."

"Yeah, that sounds enticing. 'Hey, could we just make out and have completely superficial conversations for the next seventy days until I get over the love of my life?'"

She giggled. "Sounds like fun to me. I think Brad might be a willing victim."

"Uh, no. No more coworkers."

"Fine. I'll think of someone. How about my cousin, Beau?"

"The guy that can eat fifty hot dogs in ten minutes? I don't think so."

"You don't need to be picky."

"If I'm going to have a superficial relationship, I'm going to be very picky, like Chace Crawford picky. Is he single by the way?" I winked, like I actually had a shot at the famous actor.

She went back to perusing her online articles, looking for more ways to tell David how they could improve their already terrific marriage. "Don't you worry; I'm going to find you someone."

David came strolling in and kissed Capri on the cheek before giving me a smile. "How's it going, Presley?"

"Who do we know that's hot and single that Presley could have an un-meaningful relationship with?" Capri asked David.

He narrowed his eyes through his Harry Potter style glasses. He had the hipster look right down to his plaid shirt and skinny jeans. I would never tell him skinny jeans didn't belong on men. Mr. Montgomery felt the same way. And jeans looked so good on him.

"This sounds like something I don't want to be involved in."

"Yes, I would run fast if I were you." I smiled.

"Don't go yet." Capri grabbed his hand to stop him. "You need to read this article about post coital cuddling."

His face turned blazing red.

I did my best to stifle my laugh, but I failed miserably.

He didn't say a word. He disappeared.

"I'll email it to you," Capri called after her mortified husband. "I love messing with him." She grinned at me wickedly.

"You're evil."

She wagged her eyebrows. "I know, darling. Come over to the dark side."

"Maybe you can cast an evil spell on Mr. Montgomery, or one on me to help me forget about him."

She reached across the table and took my hand. "Aww, honey. You're doing better than you think you are." She suddenly sat up straighter, with that aha look on her face again. "But I know something we can do that will make you feel even better."

"No more chocolate, I'm over that remedy for now. And by the way, it doesn't live up to its hype."

"This is much better, and you may even burn some calories. Follow me."

♥

Dear Mr. Bingley,

I did a wicked thing tonight. Something I haven't done in a long time. Something I probably shouldn't have done, but it felt good, at least in the moment. We rolled Jackson's house. I know how immature it was, but I can't tell you the satisfaction it gave me to look at the trees and bushes in front of his townhouse covered in toilet paper. With every roll we tossed and wound, I felt this release of tension. I'm sure he'll think some students did it out of their love for him, but in my heart, I'll know the truth.

But did you know his townhouse is for sale? I didn't, either. I suppose with his big raise and at his father's insistence, he'll be buying a house fit for a Montgomery. I'm sure it won't be the cute fixer upper in downtown Riverton near his nana's. The one with the trellis with ivy crawling up it. I daydreamed about us living there as husband and wife. No. I'm sure he'll buy a brand-new home with no character.

Do you think he misses me at all?

Don't answer that,

Presley

Day Twenty–One

♥

Monday, August 16

I FELT A LITTLE GUILTY THE next morning when I woke up and looked at the couple of packages of toilet paper left over from the night before. But I had to say that didn't last long when I got to school and a harried Mr. Montgomery made it out to the car line right before I was ready to head to my classroom.

"You have some toilet paper stuck to your shoe." I pointed out to him. It was hard to keep my smile inside.

He swore under his breath and reached down to extract the white stuff.

"Bad morning?"

He looked up, stunned. I'm sure he was surprised I was speaking to him. I was, too, but I was only doing it for nefarious reasons.

"You could say that. Some kids toilet papered my house. Can you believe that? And I have a showing at my house this morning."

"You're moving?"

His brows gathered in. "Yeah." He paused "I figured it was time."

"Bigger and better things for you all around." I walked away feeling tossed and used.

Sixty-nine more days. May God have mercy on my soul, or at least my heart. As Capri would say, I was a holy mess.

Day Twenty-Five

♥

Friday, August 20

IT HAD BEEN A ROUGH week. After Monday, I had to stop acknowledging Mr. Montgomery existed, even if it meant being rude. I didn't respond to his good mornings or when he held the door for me. Nothing, nada, zilch. I wanted to call in sick to work, but I was too responsible for that. I had to trudge on. Sixty-five more days. Just over two months. I could do this. Right? *Please tell me I can do this.*

I didn't wear an Auburn t-shirt for casual Friday. Tonight was our first football game, so I supported our cowboys and wore a Riverton jersey. Not the one Mr. Montgomery gave me. I had given all his stuff back to Miss Liliana, even though it displeased her.

I took to talking to Brad during car line duty so I didn't have to speak to the VP.

"Are you going to the game tonight?" Brad closed a car door.

"Yep. Wouldn't miss it."

Brad was dressed up for game day. All the players and coaches wore shirts and ties.

"You look nice, by the way." I figured I could compliment him...in front of Mr. Montgomery.

Mr. Montgomery raised his eyebrow. I ignored him.

"Thanks. I'm nervous about tonight."

"Don't be. Our boys will do great."

"Make sure to tell Leo to watch out for number sixteen on the Eagle's team," Mr. Montgomery inserted himself into our conversation.

"I've watched the films and we've discussed our strategy. We're ready for them." Brad got territorial.

"Great."

I detected the yearning in Mr. Montgomery's voice. I wondered how often he caught practice, even though he wasn't coaching. Then I told myself not to wonder, because it was none of my business. He was none of my business.

"I'll see you tonight." Mr. Montgomery opened the school door for me again.

I smirked, or was that sneered?

Brad followed me chuckling. "Remind me not to get on your bad side. Your looks are lethal."

"I'm going to take that as a compliment."

"Your smile is even more deadly."

I grinned. "Save your lines for someone else."

"You can't blame me for trying."

"I'm on a strict no teacher diet."

He laughed. "Let me know if you ever want to cheat."

I looked him over—and he was pretty delectable—but no way was I going down that road again, even if it was only superficial. "Have a good day, and good luck tonight."

"Thanks." We parted ways.

I had to say, I was a little flattered that Brad flirted with me. It helped my mind remember that there were other men out there, and maybe I could be with one, or heck, even a dozen different ones. Not at the same time, of course, but it gave me some hope.

My day went pretty much as planned from there until my third block. Mr. Montgomery decided to drop in for a surprise evaluation. I seethed underneath. Why didn't he let Ms. Dickson, the other vice principal, do it? The injustice of it all. That sounded dramatic, right? I was a drama teacher after all.

"Ms. Benson, relax and pretend like I'm not here."

If only I could. I had been trying to for twenty-five long days. I nodded, so as to not be completely disrespectful in front of my students. "Okay, guys, let's get in a circle and stay standing."

This was a mostly freshman class, so they were still eager to promptly obey. My twenty students gathered and formed a circle.

"One of the most important things you need to learn about being on stage is to develop an awareness of those that share the stage with you. I know we all like it to be about us." I got a few snickers. "But no matter if your role is large or small, you're part of a cast. A cast must always work together as a team. The object of this game is to count to twenty."

Twenty weird stares erupted, all directed toward me.

"I know it sounds simple, but you can't communicate verbally, and if more than one person says a number at the same time, you have to start over."

Their faces still said this was going to be a piece of cake. I let them believe it would be. I smiled confidently at them. "Go."

I loved watching them trying to communicate with their eyes. Finally, two brave souls said "one" at the same time.

"Ah, see, it isn't that easy. Let's try again."

This time they watched more carefully for body clues and they made it to nine. After four tries, they made it all the way. I loved the look of triumph they each displayed. Even more, when they congratulated each other.

"Now turn around and face the outside of the circle."

"What?" they collectively cried.

"I have every confidence that you can do this."

They all reluctantly turned around.

Mr. Montgomery joined my side. I hated to say I was still drawn to him. My hand wanted to reach out and take his. My lips wanted to touch his skin. I sidestepped away from him, causing him to frown and move closer.

"How can I pretend you're not here if you invade my space?" I did my best to say that through gritted teeth, all while pretending to be a model employee. I'm not sure how well I pulled it off, if I did at all.

He stepped even closer.

Two could play his game. "Mr. Montgomery would like to play." I clapped my hands. "Hannah, Elle, please make room for him in between you." They were on the side farthest from me.

He raised his eyebrow at me and smirked before taking his place in the circle.

I wanted to smack that smirk off his face. I had known, though, he would join in. He was a hands-on teacher. Something I used to deeply admire in him. He could make history come to life, whether it was building replicas of the Nina, Pinta, and Santa Maria, or dressing up as Napoléon, he was fantastic.

Why couldn't he be a loser ex? Probably because I avoided dating losers when possible. But they were so much easier to get over.

"Are you ready?"

My students murmured their agreement. I think they were worried how this would all turn out. Mr. Montgomery shouted, "Yes."

I didn't need his enthusiasm.

He also started them off, giving courage to my students to voice the next number. In fact, several of them did and they had to start over.

"That's okay, we got this," Jackson assured them.

I watched the way my students responded to him. Their confidence levels rose in their faces and postures.

How was I expected to get over a guy like that in ninety days? By remembering he dumped me, and quite rudely, I might add. Did I really want a man who would put his career before me? No. But deep down, I knew Jackson wasn't that kind of man. His father was.

I didn't know how he did it, but he started off and they made it to twenty on their second try, which is unheard of facing away from each other. They bounced almost flawlessly from number to number as if it was coordinated. I was about to call the cheater on it, but something more interesting came walking into my room.

Mr. Crandall and what I could only describe as a beautiful man came strolling in. Mr. Crandall was all smiles. His companion had square shoulders, thick ash brown tapered-cut hair, and a perfectly tanned and strikingly symmetrical face that was looking at me with interest.

And to my surprise, I found myself throwing my attention his way. For one second, I forgot that I had an ex-boyfriend, and that said ex was in my room. That one second felt glorious. It was a start, I suppose.

Mr. Crandall and his associate in tight blue jeans approached.

"Presley, dear, I'm sorry to interrupt your class, but I wanted you to meet someone. This is my nephew, Kaine Larsen. I told you about him. He's going to help us construct our set this year."

Kaine held out his masculine, calloused hand.

I gladly took it, hoping for another second of no Mr. Montgomery related thoughts. I didn't get my wish, since the living, breathing version appeared next to me. Darn him. I ignored him for the moment and greeted the handsome stranger. "I'm Presley, nice to meet you. Your uncle failed to mention how attractive you were." What? What? Why did I say that?

Mr. Crandall and Kaine both grinned. My eyes flew to Mr. Montgomery. I hated that they did, but I had to see his reaction. His eyes were wide, and I noticed that he broke out in red blotches like he did when he was upset. That had rarely happened in all the time I had known him. His reaction, though confusing, gave me courage to own it. That's right, I had said it. I quickly checked for a ring on Kaine. Phew. At least he didn't appear to be married. I kind of wanted to die inside.

A few girls giggled at my boldness.

Kaine gave me a gleaming smile. It only enhanced the package. "I could say the same thing, Presley." He gave my hand an extra squeeze. I didn't feel anything, per se, but it wasn't revolting, so that was a start. I'm sure I blushed at the return compliment.

Mr. Montgomery cleared his throat and thrust his hand out. "I'm Jackson Montgomery, vice principal."

The men sized each other up. It was a tough competition, I'll tell you. One any woman would be happy to judge and get either man. Except me, because I was on my way to forgetting about one, and my plan cautioned against rebounds. But if Kaine had no current romantic entanglements, I would consider going the whole superficial route with him.

"Nice to meet you." Kaine gave Mr. Jackson a firm handshake.

"We are off to make some measurements. Will you be joining us for fourth block?" Mr. Crandall asked me.

"Most definitely." I smiled at Kaine. I usually used my planning period, fourth block, to help out in the advanced class. They would be the group competing in the one act competition late in the fall.

Mr. Crandall's eyes gleamed with mischief. Was he trying to help me the way I was trying to help him? His lost love still hadn't replied to me.

"I was hoping to spend a few minutes with you during fourth block to discuss your evaluation, Ms. Benson," Mr. Montgomery interrupted.

"I'll join you as soon as I can." I ignored Mr. Montgomery and focused on my mentor.

"We look forward to it." Mr. Crandall waved.

The bright spot in my day walked out the door. I turned toward Mr. Montgomery and some gloom crept in. The color in his face had all but disappeared. Did it bother him that I called another man attractive in his presence? Was he remembering how forward I was with him once upon a time, telling him how handsome I found him well before we started to date?

He opened his mouth, but no words came out. Instead, he turned around and took a seat on the "casting" couch where we had won the part of being each other's significant other. I never thought I would lose it to his ambition and father's wishes.

I did the only thing I could do. I went back to teaching my students, who were perceptive. Hannah was doing well on her stage whisper, since I heard every word, and I'm sure Mr. Montgomery did, too. "Is it true Ms. Benson and Mr. Montgomery used to date? I think he wanted to hit that hot guy Mr. Crandall brought in here."

Great. Now my students were gossiping about me.

Maybe, just maybe, I would give them something to really gossip about.

"Did he really warn you against Brad?" Capri whispered.

I looked around the football stands to see who was near us before I answered. We sat up on the top bleacher. It was better to people watch and keep conversations private, but you could never be too careful. "Can you believe it? He had just got done telling me what a terrific teacher I was and how he hoped I would consider staying."

"Please don't move back to Colorado."

"How can I stay?"

"In sixty-five days, you're going to be completely over him, so what difference will it make?" She was putting way too much faith in me.

"It's not that easy. Besides, I don't want to see him moving on with someone else."

"You move on with someone else first. How about Mr. Crandall's nephew?"

I grinned. "He is delicious. I almost channeled my inner-Joey with a, 'How you doin'?'," I said, referencing the *Friends* character.

She laughed. "You should have."

"I had already made an idiot out of myself when I told him how attractive he was."

She placed her hand over her heart. "I'm so proud of you."

"Something in me kind of snapped. I wanted to make Mr. Montgomery feel insignificant, like he made me feel. It wasn't one of my finer moments."

"Are you kidding me? He deserves it. And that's why I may or may not have 'accidentally' tripped one of my students with a cup full of paint in their hands when he came to evaluate me."

It was hard to hide my smile. "I can't believe you did that."

"Why? He loves the color red."

"You really are evil, but I adore you."

"Maybe I felt a little guilty for making my student feel bad about it, even though it wasn't his fault. And I have to say, Jackson took it all in stride. He laughed about it and told Eli he'd buy him a Coke."

"Sounds like him. Why is it the only jerky thing he's ever done is to me?"

"I'm sure you're not his only indiscretion?"

"That makes me sound like his mistress or something."

She wagged her eyebrows. "You're too good for that, and for him. He's going to look back someday and wish he could take it all back."

"I doubt it."

"It's obvious by the way he still looks at you, or when he looks up when your name is mentioned. It's going to take him a lot longer than ninety days to get over you. Mark my words, sister."

Day Twenty-Six

♥

Saturday, August 21

D*EAR M*R. B*INGLEY,*
I survived another week of work. And I'm almost twenty-nine percent of the way to my goal. Can I picture my life without him yet? What choice do I have? Yesterday, when he warned me that Brad was a womanizer and that I wasn't the only woman he had been making advances to, Mr. Montgomery said he just wanted me to know because he still "cared" about me. He doesn't love me. Do I still love him? I do. But I wasn't in denial. Sure, it's hard to believe he isn't part of my daily routine, and I've picked up the phone at least fifty times wanting to call him. Sometimes something hits me funny and I want to share it with him, and I've forgotten he doesn't want to hear from me. And sometimes I want to call him and scream. But I never will. He will never have the satisfaction.

According to another article Capri read, I'm in between the sweaty mania and blurry anger stages. Whatever those are. Apparently I should be feeling this major burst of energy soon that will make me want to run a marathon. I'm not counting on it. Now, maybe I'll take a nice leisurely bike ride and do some Pilates in the park, but I'm only running if someone is chasing me with some blunt force object. The worst part is, according to this article, I haven't made it to the extreme sadness stage. What the heck? I don't want to be any sadder than I already am. I don't care how emotionally advanced it makes me.

Capri needs to quit reading articles on the internet. For my and her husband's sake. I don't know if David will ever look me in the eye again after the whole post coital conversation.

Maybe it's time to try that superficial fling thing. Even if it does mean producing oxytocin and tricking my body into bonding with someone. I wonder if there is an antidote for the dumb little hormone. Maybe then I could sever the bond I feel every time I'm around Jackson.

I think I'll do some research. Or maybe raise some Kaine?

Men still suck,

Presley

DAY THIRTY

♥

Wednesday, August 25

I WAS ONE THIRD THERE. THIRTY-THREE point three-three-three percent. I was still waiting for my marathon burst of energy. But guess what? Even though the past month had sucked, I'd survived. That's right. Take that, Jackson Montgomery! He seemed to be surviving better, or at least he was a good faker. I knew him, and his smiles didn't light up his eyes anymore, even if he always had one plastered on his face. And for being the vice principal, he spent an inordinate amount of time in various classrooms. He was the most hands-on administrator I'd ever known. I didn't think he was ready to give up teaching. Just like he wasn't ready to give up coaching. He spent Friday night's game on the field. From the stands, I could tell it annoyed Brad. The players flocked to Coach and Mr. Montgomery. I can't blame Brad for being bothered by that, even if he is dating Mindy Everly. Or that's her story.

Mindy announced to us on Monday in the teacher's lounge that Brad and she spent practically the whole weekend together. Brad may have been part vampire. She had a few hickeys on her neck. Gross. I'd never understood why anyone would consider that romantic. Men shouldn't leave any marks on you, except the ones that show in your eyes. You know, the happy ones. The mark of a cherished woman. Mr. Montgomery used to shine right through mine. Now it was mainly tears in the middle of the night.

I hadn't cried in a few days, so I'd take that as a good sign.

I was kind of looking forward to the day ahead. We were starting the set design and guess who was going to be there? That's right, Kaine. I was hoping he wasn't evil like the bible version. But I wouldn't mind it if he was a little wicked, in a good way.

According to Mr. Crandall, his nephew was single, but recently out of a long-term relationship. So, maybe he needed a little superficial TLC like me. Was I awful to think like that? I felt like it was a test of the emergency broadcast system. I needed to know if I could be attracted to another man, and not just in the physical sense. There were men before Mr. Montgomery, but Mr. Montgomery was a game changer. He opened my eyes to a whole new world. I would never be able to settle for less after him. Maybe someday I would be able to thank him for that. For showing me how a woman should expect to be treated, minus the horrible way in which he ended it. Before that, he was a real gentleman. He was the kind of man who opened doors, and called, not texted, even though he did that too, but he mostly called. He always had a plan, none of this just hanging out stuff. He was so kind. And he bought my tampons on a regular basis. You can't beat that. He even got the right kind. With the tampons always came chocolate and sometimes a flower, depending on where he bought the feminine hygiene products. He had spoiled me.

I needed to know he hadn't ruined me. I needed to know if other men like Jackson existed. And Kaine seemed like a good place to start.

Capri snuck out of her class for a minute so she could get a peek at Kaine. We stood at the back of the auditorium and watched him and his uncle discuss, what, I don't know, but who cared? We had a great view.

Capri fanned herself with her hand. "My, my." Her southern accent was out in full force.

"I told you."

"You didn't do him justice. Do you think he'll get sweaty enough to take off his shirt?"

"Need I remind you that you're married?"

"David and I are solid. A little eye candy never hurt anyone."

"I don't think any clothing is coming off. Do you know how many parents would complain?"

"Uh, none after they hauled their butts down here to see how fine of a specimen he is."

I laughed. "We'll be sure to send a note home with the kids."

"Send a photo, too."

"You better get back to class."

"If I must. I'm going to live vicariously through you, so don't disappoint me. Forget about what's his name."

"I'm trying."

She squeezed my hand. "I know. And you're doing a great job."

"You're a good liar...and friend."

"I do what I can." She walked away with an evil grin after pushing me forward. She must have known I was considering retreating.

I don't even know why I was nervous. Kaine could want nothing to do with me, and I wasn't looking for any type of entanglement, just a guinea pig. I knew how terrible that sounded, but really, my intentions were pure.

Mr. Crandall was alerted to my presence. "Presley, dear, join us."

I bit my lip and sauntered toward the men. I did my best not to full on stare or grin at Kaine. I could tell I was in his line of focus. I wished I could say that caused some type of physical reaction in me other than nerves. Once upon a time, before I ever met Mr. Montgomery, a man like Kaine would have already had my blood flowing. I wasn't going to give up, yet.

Mr. Crandall held out his hand to me when I approached the stage steps and helped me up.

"Thank you."

He gave me a little wink.

I braved a look at Kaine, who was smiling at me. Yep, still nothing, not even a little flutter or a skipped beat of my heart. "Hi."

"Hey, there." He had a sexy voice.

We did that awkward staring thing for a few seconds before his uncle saved me from probably making a fool out of myself. "We were just discussing the set design. I think for this kind of competition, we will need to make every piece count. They will each have to serve multiple purposes. Do you agree?"

I nodded. I had been thinking the same thing. We only had forty-five minutes from start to finish in the competition, and that included getting your set on and off the stage. It was going to be tricky.

Mr. Crandall smiled at my agreement, but in the next breath unease lined his face.

"Something wrong?"

He scratched his chin and looked at Kaine with a little grimace before addressing me. "Well, it appears we may have hit a little snag. Our new," he cleared his throat, "vice principal has just informed me that our play selection may not be appropriate."

I could see Mr. Crandall brace himself, like he knew the fury boiling inside of me. "I'll be right back." I turned and marched off to find my idiot ex-boyfriend, seething as I went. How dare he. Mr. Crandall and I were careful when we had selected the play loosely based on Beethoven's life. My high heels against the tiled floor reflected the anger I felt, fast and furious.

The culprit happened to be walking my way. He must have noticed my death glare as he approached. His tentative smile turned to pressed lips and narrowed eyes. "Presley, I mean, Ms. Benson." A hint of regret laced his words. He was in for more.

I didn't return the greeting. Without a word, I pulled him into the prop room, our room. The room in which he first told me he loved me. It had been the nearest door. He wasn't the only one filled with regret. Hurt filled my soul as I looked around at all the brightly colored costumes that hung around us, and the memories that now lingered and afflicted pain. I tried to push through the ache in my chest for what used to be. I shut the door and let out a huge breath.

Mr. Montgomery stood there, stunned. His brown eyes were as warm as I remembered them, a month ago. "We probably shouldn't be in here together."

We stood a foot apart from each other.

The desire my body felt for him waned with those words. I stepped farther away from him. "You don't need to keep reminding me about how you feel about me."

"That's not what I meant."

"Isn't it?"

"Presley." He inched closer.

"Please don't call me that."

His brows furrowed. "Why can't we be..."

"Friends?" I scoffed. "If this is how you treat your friends, I would hate to see how you treat your enemies."

"What are you talking about?"

"The play, Jackson, I mean, Mr. Montgomery. How dare you sideline it. You should know Mr. Crandall and me better. You know how we vet the material we use."

His face began to redden. "The subject matter is questionable."

"Are you kidding me? We're talking about Beethoven, who was an extremely conservative individual."

"The play hints at suicide and adultery."

I shook my head. "Did we read the same play? Where is there talk of cheating?"

"His relationship with Julie implies it."

"Only if you have a dirty mind. There is no history to prove that, and the play doesn't suggest it."

"What about his nephew's attempted suicide?"

All I could do was stare at him in utter disbelief at the person he had become. "What happened to you? We used to laugh about this bureaucratic crap. You know this is a non-issue."

"You don't understand the politics of it."

"Apparently, there are a lot of things I don't understand. Like you. Good day. And don't worry, I'll make sure no one sees me leave. I would hate to tarnish your reputation, Mr. Montgomery." I spun around and headed for the door.

He caught my hand and pulled me back.

I froze. In an instant I felt . . . I felt. Yeah, I felt.

"Presley, don't you know I wish things could be different?"

Tears welled up in my eyes.

He pulled me closer. I saw Jackson, not Mr. Montgomery, in his eyes. I saw wanting. The feeling was mutual.

I pulled away. "Don't. Please just don't. You're not who I thought you were."

He let go of my hand and hung his head. "I'll see what I can do about the play."

I hurried out of the room before I lost it.

Day Thirty-One

♥

Thursday, August 26

DEAR MR. BINGLEY,

We touched. I thought he might even kiss me. If I say I wanted him to, will you think ill of me? No more than I already feel. I hate myself for feeling that way. I shouldn't; I don't want to. This is too hard. Now my body craves him more than ever. I think I'll need more time to get over him, but I can't stand that thought. Please tell me how to make this emptiness and pain go away. I beg you.

Now I understand why Jane took you back so easily. Do you men have any idea the effect you have on us? If you do, you should be utterly ashamed of yourselves. But don't fear. I will rise to the occasion. I'm no Jane.

In need of help,

Presley

Day Thirty-Five

♥

Monday, August 30

I NEEDED THE WEEKEND TO DETOX. I wasn't talking about purging alcohol from my body. I had stayed with that part of the plan and hadn't had a drop. No, I was on a strict no men diet. I turned into Capri over the weekend and started searching online how to decrease the levels of oxytocin in your body. That encounter with an unnamed male had me reeling and wanting him more than ever. All I came up with was that, like men, oxytocin sucked. It was a two-faced little hormone. Not only did it make you feel all warm and fuzzy for that special someone, but it can also strengthen bad memories. That's right. It's a double whammy of yucky. And guess what? There's no cure. A man invented it, that's all I have to say.

At least I got the burst of marathon-inducing energy. Maybe I didn't run twenty-six miles, but my apartment had never been so clean, and I did run...to the mall. Let's just say I was looking freaking fantastic today, and for the rest of the week. Who cared if my savings account was now looking a little pathetic? I was looking fine and feeling...well, I was still working on the feeling fine. Fifty-five more days, baby, and I'd be the happiest and healthiest ex-girlfriend ever. That's what I kept telling myself. Someday I was going to believe it.

I walked with a little spring in my step all the way to the car line with my new, pink A-line ottoman dress. I ignored the men already helping kids out of the car, even though they both looked my way and acknowledged my presence with waves and smiles. Mr. Montgomery's was half-hearted. No matter. I ignored it. I was back on offense.

I did my best to focus on the students exiting their vehicles instead of the stares. I knew he was staring. I could feel it. I was proud of myself for not acknowledging him, but I wanted to. That oxytocin was wicked stuff. It should be an illegal substance.

I fist bumped, high-fived, and even hugged a few kids with a big smile on my face. I was a drama teacher, after all. I could fake happy like no one's business.

After the last car, I headed for the school's entrance a little brisker than normal. I was avoiding the defense at all costs, even in my brand-new peep-toe pumps. Let's just hope I didn't make a date with the floor again. The bruise from the last time had barely gone away, but my injured pride was still alive and well.

"Ms. Benson."

Noooo. I was almost to the goal line, aka the door. Didn't he get the I-hate-you vibes from the car line? I looked for someone, anyone, to pass the ball to, but not another player was in sight. So, I did what any good quarterback would do. I was going to run the ball in myself. I picked up my pace and ignored the opposing team. Note to self, wear tennis shoes from now on and start training for that marathon. Mr. Montgomery was a better athlete than me. He caught up to me and pushed the door shut that I had just opened.

I glared at him, completely ignoring the fact that he was my boss. "Excuse me."

He pinched his lips together and breathed in deeply. His eyes begged me to not be angry with him.

"I need to get to my class."

He dropped his hand. "I wanted to let you know that the play has been approved."

"Thanks." I reached for the door. I wanted to say it should have never been sidelined, but that meant being in his presence longer, and that dumb little hormone inside of me was clambering for him.

"Have a good day."

"I will." I threw open the door in defiance and marched myself, albeit cautiously, to my classroom. I ran into Mr. Crandall on my way. "Good morning."

He tilted his head. "Are you sure?"

I ran my fingers through my hair and huffed. "Positive."

"You're a good actress."

I half grinned. "Thanks."

"I heard the good news. Looks like you still have some sway after all."

"It had nothing to do with me."

The little glint lit up his eyes. "You're mistaken there, dear. I think you would be surprised at the power you still hold over our new vice principal."

I shook my head. "I only made him see reason."

"Are you so sure? I guess you were unaware that Dr. Walters told me to find a new play. Jackson made him reconsider."

I stood up straighter. "I wasn't aware."

He smiled. "Why do I feel like there will be a twist in the plot?"

"What do you mean?"

"I mean, we're in for an interesting semester. Good luck, my dear." He walked away.

"Wait, wait. You can't say something like that and leave."

He waved to me from behind and kept on going, chuckling as he went.

DAY THIRTY-SIX

♥

Tuesday, August 31

DEAR MR. BINGLEY,
The only twist that was going to happen was the one where in fifty-four days I would be completely cured of the man who went to bat for us. Speaking of bats, I heard a great country song this morning while I was getting ready. It was about a cheated-on woman bashing in the taillights of her ex's truck with a bat. I should have started listening to country music a long time ago. It would have clearly directed me away from charming men raised in the south.

Jane should have read up on gentleman who earned five thousand pounds or more a year. Oh, but wait, she couldn't have because you male chauvinist pigs back then only let men be published. I'm sure you painted yourselves in the best light possible. Just like everyone at Riverton High thinks my ex is a saint. I suppose he is, as long as you come with the right credentials and you never date him.

I guess that is the hardest part for me. Reconciling the man I dated with the man who broke up with me.

Today, though, is a new day.

Wish me luck,

Presley

With the play selection approved, we moved forward with auditions. Mr. Crandall and I sat with the advanced class during fourth block and read through the entire play. We had each student read several different parts to get a feel for who would be best in each role. It was exciting, as was Kaine's vision for our set. He was building a piano into a wall that could be turned around depending on the scene. I wasn't sure how that was possible, but he seemed confident in his abilities. It was kind of sexy.

Speaking of sexy, Kaine came strolling on stage at the end of fourth block, the last block of the day. He looked ready to work in his jeans, t-shirt, and work boots. I was still waiting for my heart rate to increase or something whenever I was around him. It didn't seem right that a man as good looking as he was didn't cause any sort of physiological response in me. It was a crime.

Whether he made me swoon or not, he smiled at me when he walked on stage. I gave him one in return, along with all the girls in the class. I inwardly laughed at all the heads coming together and blushes. That would have been me, too, at that age. Heck, it would have been me last year before some other gorgeous man crashed into my life.

Harper, who we were considering for the female lead, raised her hand. "Do we really have to kiss if we get the part?" She shyly looked at Leland, who we were considering to be Beethoven. Her attraction to him was apparent. Leland's head popped up, but I couldn't tell how he felt about her or the fact that they could be kissing on stage.

"Yes," I answered for both Mr. Crandall and myself. "But don't fear, we'll walk you through the process."

Harper's face turned a cute shade of pink. She whispered something to her friend and they both smiled. I took it my answer was to her liking. I watched Leland do his best to look at Harper without appearing that he was. Oh, the games we played. We start young, don't we? I wished I could say it changes, but I don't think it ever does.

As soon as the bell rang, Harper made a beeline toward me. "Can I talk to you, privately?"

"Sure." I put my arm around her and walked her to the backstage area. "What can I do for you?"

She bit her lip and looked down at her shoes. "Um. I've never...you know..."

"Kissed someone?"

She looked up, her cheeks were burning red. "Yeah."

"That's nothing to be embarrassed about. I didn't kiss anyone until I was eighteen."

"Really? But, you're so pretty."

"Looks have nothing to do with it. If they did, you would have been kissed by now."

She smiled at the compliment.

I placed my hand on her seventeen-year-old shoulder. "You shouldn't feel pressure to kiss anyone unless it feels right for you. If you get the lead and you don't want your first kiss to be on stage, we can stage a kiss."

"No, I want to."

I raised my eyebrow. "What if it isn't Leland?"

She blushed again. "Can we do that stage thing then?"

I laughed. "We'll see what we can do."

"Are you going to show us how to kiss on stage again with Mr. Montgomery?"

I had to hold back the tears. I shook my head. "No." I couldn't believe it had been a year. We had shared our first kiss on stage before we ever started dating. All it took was that one kiss and I was his, whether he was ready or not. He was cautious about dating a coworker. We should have both thought twice about it, but when he kissed me, it was like I was fused to him. I thought he felt it, too. He'd kissed me longer than necessary, to the cheers of my students. And I'd never forget what he said, though I wished I could. He quoted from *The Princess Bride*—it was how it became our movie—"Since the invention of the kiss, there have only been five that were rated the most passionate, the most pure. This one left them all behind." He said that after many of our kisses. And now I hated him for it because it was true.

"I heard you broke up. See you tomorrow." She walked away, not knowing how much she had just killed me inside.

Yeah, tomorrow. Tomorrow was September. And then I could say, next month my plan would be complete. The ache would be gone and I would have moved on.

That thought motivated me to walk back out to the stage and make Capri proud. I was going to do something totally superficial. "Kaine."

He was putting on his tool belt. For some odd reason, that kind of did something for me. Anyway. He gave me his attention. "Yes, ma'am."

Nice touch, but I was on to Southern men now. I walked toward him. I needed this to be a more private conversation.

He smiled as I neared.

I planted my feet firmly in front of him and took a deep breath. "I need you to kiss me."

He shook his head and his not quite buckled tool belt hit the floor, making a loud enough sound that I jumped. "Sorry about that." He bent down to pick up his belt."

It brought me to my senses. "No. I'm the one that's sorry. Forget I asked." I turned to go crawl under a hole and die.

"Hey, you didn't let me answer."

I turned back around to see him grinning.

"I take it you need a warm body to show your students kissing technique?"

I grinned. "Something like that? But, really, forget about it."

"What if I was willing to help you out?"

I rubbed my lips together. "Are you?"

His baby blue eyes shined. "I could be persuaded to, but maybe we should get to know each other better first. How about dinner Friday night?"

Oh gosh, oh gosh. I wasn't expecting that. "Completely superficial, right?"

He laughed. "You are one interesting woman. I can do superficial."

"Fantastic. It's a date then."

What just happened there?

Day Thirty-Seven

♥

Wednesday, September 1

DEAR MR. BINGLEY,

It's September and I have a date. A date with an attractive man. Maybe, probably, the most attractive man I've ever had a date with. I know what you're thinking. You think this is a rebound and I'll regret it because no one can live up to Mr. Montgomery. But you're wrong. I've been upfront about my intentions and Mr. Montgomery isn't the end all. You must have thought you were or you wouldn't have come back to Jane and proposed so quickly. You really were a pompous twit.

No matter what you think, I'm not rebounding or using Kaine to help me get over Mr. Montgomery. I'm simply exploring my options. I'm throwing my line back out into the vast ocean of men. It's natural and normal, healthy even. Yes, yes, I'm doing it for my health.

Good day to you,

Presley

My phone rang on the way out my door to work. "Miss Liliana, you're up early this morning."

"I didn't sleep at all last night."

"I'm so sorry. Are you sick?"

"Very."

"Can I do something for you?"

"Don't go on that date."

I fumbled my phone and almost dropped it. "How did you know?"

"Darling, you live in the South now, where secrets never keep."

It wasn't a secret, but I wasn't broadcasting it either, unless you counted Capri.

"Regardless, this won't do. You won't find a better man than Jackson."

"You do remember that he broke up with me?"

"I know. He's an imbecile, and I'm trying to correct his grievous behavior, but you're not helping by dating someone else."

"I'm not dating anyone. I'm going on a date."

"Darling, please reconsider. Jackson—"

"Jackson, what?"

"Oh, dear, I wasn't supposed to say."

"Miss Liliana?"

"Jackson doesn't think he's good enough for you."

"Jackson was the one who told you? And what does he know?" My blood was boiling.

"Now I've upset you."

"Of course I'm upset. It's none of Jackson's business who I date. He lost his right to care when he told me he had only been messing around with me."

"You know he doesn't really believe that."

"He has to, because if not, I could never forgive him for the way he's treated me. Love doesn't act that way."

"Darling, please think about it. He's under more pressure than you know. There are things you don't know."

"He let me go." A tear ran down my cheek. That's all I needed to know.

"It was an awful thing to do, I know, but don't go past the point of no return. You'll both regret it."

"Miss Liliana, I love you, but he pushed me away, and in fifty-three days, he'll be a distant memory."

"Fifty-three days?"

Crap, did I say that out loud? Only Capri knew of my plan. And I knew how ridiculous it sounded, even if it was scientifically proven. "Never mind. I hope you have a good day. Let's have lunch next week."

"Presley, please don't do anything you'll regret."

"I won't." I wasn't going to regret going out with Kaine.

That wasn't the way I wanted to start my day. It didn't get much better. Miss Liliana was right about living in the South. The intrigue of my going on a date was beyond me, but when I walked into the school, I felt like I was on display. Eyes were following me and heads came together. Except for Coach.

"PB." He bounded up to me on my way out to the car line.

"Hey, Coach."

"I feel like I've hardly seen you this year."

"I know, things have…"

"You mean Jackson?"

I nudged him and he laughed. "I guess I didn't get you in the divorce."

He patted his belly. "There's enough of me to go around."

"I'm sorry I've been avoiding you, well not really *you*."

"Don't worry, I get it, especially now that you've moved on to Crandall's nephew."

I stopped dead in my tracks. "Don't tell me you're buying into all the gossip."

He grinned. "So you're not going out with him?"

"We're going on *a* date Friday night."

"Now I'm offended. We play at home that night."

"Sorry."

"That's okay, you can bring him to the game."

I started walking toward my destination again. "I don't think that's a good idea."

He followed after me. "I think it's perfect. Jackson needs to see what he's missing out on."

"This isn't a revenge date."

"Don't get in a tizzy, I know. But someone needs to smack some sense into Jackson and judging by the way he was acting last night, I would say this would do it."

"Hold up. You're not on Jackson's side?"

"Hell, no, girl."

I laughed.

"You're the best thing that ever happened to him. He hasn't been the same since he went all administrator on us and let you go. I need my man back and you need to help me."

"I had no idea the budding romance you two had going on."

"It's complicated." He batted his eyelashes like a woman in one of those old silent films.

"Does Marie know?" Marie was his wife.

"She encourages it. The more time I spend with him, the less I get in her hair. So help a guy out and give Jackson a wake-up call."

"As much as I love you and Marie, I'm not using someone just so you can rekindle your bromance."

"Girl, that's just cold."

"He doesn't want me back anyway."

"I know you're smarter than that. I expect to see you at the game Friday night." He jogged off without another word.

After all my morning conversations, I especially dreaded going out to the car line to face Mr. Montgomery. Who knew one date would cause so much disruption? Did everyone think I wouldn't move on? That I would pine endlessly for him? I wasn't that kind of woman. My identity had never been wrapped up in a man. Sure, I loved who we were together, but I was still me.

My saving grace came in the form of the best friend ever. She ran up to me as soon as I walked outside. "I thought you might need some backup today."

I breathed a sigh of relief. "I love you."

"I know." She locked arms with me and we looked like we were off to see the Wizard of Oz.

I wished I were in Kansas, because Kansas was next door to Colorado, and this girl could have used her mom right about now.

Brad and Mr. Montgomery acknowledged our presence with head nods. And perhaps Mr. Montgomery's eyes lingered longer, at least according to Capri.

"I think Jackson is looking a little forlorn," Capri whispered in my ear.

"Forlorn?"

"Yeah, it means pitiful and sad."

"I know what it means; I have a degree in English. It just sounds funny coming out of your mouth."

"Excuse me for trying to save the English language. I found a great article online with words we should be using in our everyday speech."

"I apologize; I didn't realize what a crusader you were."

She smacked my arm. "I do what I can for mankind."

"You rank right up there with Mother Teresa."

We both laughed. Under the circumstances, I needed it. Especially when Capri was Capri.

"You forgot to tell me where Kaine is taking you Friday." She grinned evilly at me. Did I mention that she said that way too loud? Both Mr. Montgomery and Brad looked my way with interest. I could see Mr. Montgomery's red-spotted skin from where I was. And, unfortunately, our eyes locked. Why was I always looking for his reaction? I needed to get over that. We were over.

"Well?" Capri demanded.

I shook my head, trying to get Mr. Montgomery out of it, and focused back on Capri in all her evil glory. She was getting way too much pleasure out of this. "Uh, I don't know yet."

"You should have him take you to that new Chinese bistro that opened up on Market Street." Now she was going overboard. She knew Mr. Montgomery hated Chinese food. It was one thing we never agreed on.

Again, I met Mr. Montgomery's eyes. Dang it. I needed to quit doing that. His chin lowered to his chest. I looked away. He didn't have a right to be disappointed.

"I've been wanting to try that place, so maybe." I gave a half-smile to Capri. Growing up, you always dream of those moments when you can exact revenge on your ex, but in reality, it never feels as good as you imagine. I couldn't take pleasure in causing Jackson pain. And I could tell he was bothered. So maybe he still had some feelings for me. I wasn't sure if that made me feel better or worse. I was going with worse.

"Well, that was fun," Capri remarked on our way back into the school.

"You're wicked."

"Wicked good. But dang it, I forgot to mention that Kaine was an Auburn fan and you should watch the season opener with him on Saturday."

I rolled my eyes at her. "Get to class. And by the way, thank you."

She reached back and grabbed my hand. "You're my girl. And you got this."

I sure hoped so.

Day Thirty-Nine

Friday, September 3

D EAR MR. BINGLEY,
Today is the day. I'm going on a date with Kaine. He called me to firm up plans last night. It was so weird giving him my number. Even weirder when he called me. He's taking me to the miniature golf course. I wasn't sure if we could eat there, but he wants to show me some of his handiwork. Oh, and then we're going to the game. He's a huge football fan like everyone else around here. Capri thought it was a fantastic idea. So much so, she's dragging David to the game. David is the only person in Alabama who wasn't born with the football gene. He would rather be home reading a book or gaming online with his buddies. Capri never wanted to talk about that part of David's life. It was their dirty little secret. She did make David learn football lingo so he could pretend, but he was awful at it. It was a source of entertainment for me. Like when he called an interception an intervention. Jackson and I laughed about that for days.

I need to quit thinking about him. I'm trying.

Wish me luck,

Presley

I was slipping on my new red pumps before work when my mom called. "Hi, Mom. It's early for you."

"I wanted to wish you luck and see if you were still going through with your date?"

"Was that a question?"

"You seemed hesitant when we talked a couple of days ago."

"I did?"

"I know you better than you know yourself."

I laughed at her and walked out into the partly cloudy day. "Be that as it may, I'm going out with Kaine tonight."

"That's an interesting name."

"I suppose so, but it fits him."

"Is that so? Should your dad and I be worried?"

"No, Mom. I don't think he's making any deals with the devil to kill me."

"In that case, what do you want for your birthday? It's only a few weeks away, you know."

"You mean it isn't coming on a day other than September 25th?"

"Well, aren't you sassy this morning."

"I love you, Mom. I just haven't wanted to think about it. I'm now officially over the national average of when women get married, and I'm the only person in our family who won't be married before twenty-seven."

"Honey, twenty-seven isn't old. Everyone gets married in their own time. It isn't a competition."

"I think Nikki, Jen, Erin, and Michelle would all disagree with you, especially since they've each teased me about it."

"Your sisters love you."

"Sure they do. I've been getting a lot of texts using the word spinster."

"You will be the cutest spinster ever."

"Thanks, Mom."

She laughed. "I'm teasing you. Any guy would be lucky to have you. And maybe things will work out with Jackson."

"That's not going to happen."

"Are you sure? Because I kind of had a feeling about him."

I paused before I opened my car door. "What feeling?"

"I shouldn't say."

"Mom."

"Okay, it's just when you walked in with him over spring break, I felt like someone punched me in the arm and said, 'That's him. Presley's going to marry him.'"

I held back the tears. I had felt the same way. "Does Dad know you're hearing voices? You may want to get that checked out." I had to respond with humor. If not, I was going to lose it.

"It will all be okay, honey." She knew me so well.

"I wishaand I was showing fourth block a series of hilarious videos about stage kisses to hopefully help them feel more comfortable about actually doing it. I was hoping they would psych me up, too, since I was going to have to demonstrate. Again, I should be thrilled. In another life-time, I would be downright ecstatic that kissing Kaine was in my future, but all I could think about was last year. Talk about excited. You've never seen someone so ready and willing to kiss another person. I'll never forget his grin before our lips met or the wow in his eyes when we parted. I had felt it too. It was like nothing I had ever experienced. He said he had felt the same.

These thoughts weren't helping me.

It didn't help, either, that Mr. Montgomery showed up to fourth block and sat out in the auditorium.

"Don't mind him, my dear. He's here to evaluate me today." Mr. Crandall informed me.

"But I'm teaching this block today."

His grin was a little impish. "Silly me, I forgot."

I narrowed my eyes. "Sure you did."

"Just helping the plot along." He walked off smiling to himself.

No matter. I wasn't going to let Mr. Montgomery phase me. "Every-one take a seat on the stage. We're going to have a little fun today." I waited for my students to get situated on the stage. It took longer than it should, but I reminded myself I was dealing with teenagers. "I know everyone is nervous about stage kisses."

"Not me," Leland called out.

The class laughed, but I noticed Harper blushed. I wondered how she was going to feel when Mr. Crandall and I cast those two as our leads.

"Everyone settle down. Thank you for your honesty, Leland. But before we get to the videos, let's go over a few rules of kissing etiquette." I held up my finger. "Number one, no tongue."

The class snickered.

"Number two, hygiene is a must. Brush your little pearly whites religiously. Mints and gum aren't a bad idea. Number three, keep your hands where they belong."

That was met with more snickering.

"And last but not least, keep your sick germs to yourself. If you're not feeling well, don't infect your classmates." I smiled out across my attentive audience. "Are you guys ready to be entertained?"

There was a murmur of agreement.

I turned on the videos of over-exaggerated stage kisses, or almost kisses. We also watched a video about complete strangers kissing. It was awkward to say the least, but it got several laughs. Mr. Montgomery had joined us on the stage and was laughing, too.

I tried to ignore him, but as always, found it difficult.

The videos ended and I headed up to the front of the class again. "So the good news is none of your kisses will be this bad. Or at least we hope not."

More laughs and some razzing among the boys.

"Remember, if you aren't comfortable kissing on or off the stage, you don't have to."

"Are you going to give us a demonstration?" One of the senior girls asked.

"Yo, Coach J, show us how it's done with Ms. Benson," Leland suggested.

Mr. Montgomery and I locked eyes in that most uncomfortable way. And to my shock and horror, he began to walk toward me.

I dropped his gaze and focused back on my class. "Not today." I was flustered. "Um, Monday, I have a special guest to help me out."

Mr. Montgomery stopped dead in his tracks.

"Rejected," the boys shouted out.

Mr. Montgomery stared at me, his face a few shades redder than normal. What was he thinking? I wouldn't kiss him even if he begged me to. Maybe that was a lie, but I would like to think I would be strong and say no. I wasn't a Jane.

"Oooo," some of the girls giggled. "Is it the guy that's working on our set? He's hot."

I ran my fingers through my hair. I hadn't bargained for this. "Settle down. It doesn't matter who."

Mr. Montgomery's eyes disagreed with that statement.

I couldn't even agree with it myself, but dang if Mr. Montgomery would know. "Your homework over the weekend is—"

There was a collective groan.

"Have fun." I grinned.

They cheered and dispersed, leaving me alone with Mr. Crandall and the man who wouldn't go away.

"Have a nice weekend." Mr. Crandall waved and scurried off the stage. Traitor.

That left me to ignore Mr. Montgomery and push the TV cart back to the closet where it belonged.

"Let me get that." Mr. Montgomery rushed forward.

"I've got it."

He grabbed a hold of the cart and stopped my forward momentum. "Presley..."

"What?"

His eyebrows gathered together. "It doesn't need to be this way between us."

I rubbed my face in my hands. "Says the man who did the leaving. Do you have any idea how much you hurt me? Any at all? Do you even care?"

He swallowed hard and struggled to speak. "I'm sor—"

"Don't you dare say you're sorry again. And quit talking to Miss Liliana about me. It isn't fair to her or me. And don't concern yourself about my love life."

"Love life?"

"That's right. What, you didn't think anyone would want me after you?"

He stepped closer. "How could you think that?"

"Oh, I don't know. I'm beginning to see there are a lot of things I should have thought about or maybe not thought about. The question is, how could you?" Against my will, tears sprung up. I wiped them away as quick as they came. I had to wipe furiously.

He lowered his chin to his chest and breathed out heavily. "If you think for a minute this is how I wanted things to turn out, you're mistaken." He walked off, leaving me standing there speechless.

I didn't feel like leaving my apartment after my run-in with Mr. Montgomery. For a moment, I had felt better for tearing into him and telling him how I felt, but when that wore off, all that was left was intense sadness. Maybe that was good. Maybe it meant I'd hit that terrible stage of extreme grief, and once I passed it, I could move on. But the pain was so real I wasn't sure how to overcome it.

I dug in deep and called on my inner Elizabeth. I sat up on my bed. I was almost halfway to my goal, I reminded myself. I was a lion, not a kitten. I could roar instead of meow. I was on offense, not defense. I was a Benson. I could do this.

I placed some cold spoons—I had put them in the refrigerator earlier—over my eyes to get rid of the puffiness from crying. It sounded odd, but it worked. I had a large supply of them, just in case.

Capri called as I lay there looking like an alien with metal over my eyes. "Are you okay? I heard you and Jackson had it out on the stage today."

"Is nothing sacred at that school?"

"I'm afraid not. But good for you."

"You should see me now."

"Spoons?"

I laughed. "Yeah, lots of them."

"Try and forget about him and have fun tonight."

"I've been trying to for the past thirty-nine days."

"Hang in there and let loose. Make me proud. We'll see you at the game."

"Save us a spot." *Meow, I mean ROAR.*

Day Forty

♥

Saturday, September 4

DEAR MR. BINGLEY,

Why didn't you tell me not to go on my date with Kaine? I fear I despise you even more. It was the most awkward night of my life. Even more awkward than when I came out of the bathroom at senior homecoming with my dress tucked into my spanx. You remember that? I wrote a book about it to you. Well, hold on. You are in for another story.

It didn't even get started off on the right foot. He was late, for starters. I forgave him for that because he looked fantastic in tight fitting jeans and his Auburn t-shirt. But that didn't last long. I know my expectations are high—Jackson raised the bar. The bar should have always been as high as it is now, but honestly, Jackson set the standard. It was simple things like opening my door. Last night, I stood at his truck door waiting for him to open it out of habit. Kaine had already gotten in the driver's side. He gave me a what's-up look through the window when I just stood there. I realized then my night wouldn't go as planned, but I was ROARING not meowing, so I proceeded.

He took me to the miniature golf course and I thought we would be playing a round, but no, he just wanted to show me the windmill he built there. I did say superficial, so I have no one to blame but myself, and Jackson of course, but more on him later. The windmill was nice. I even complimented him on it. That was a mistake. You see, he and his fiancée, or should I say ex-fiancée, broke up over said windmill. My second mistake was to ask him why. We took a seat on the AstroTurf near the windmill and there I was treated to the whole sordid affair, which was more like the tale of a man who still wanted to be a boy.

As it turns out, thirty-year-old Kaine wanted to be twenty-year-old Kaine, which didn't sit well with his beautiful ex, Sandra. She really is beautiful. I saw several pictures of her on his phone. That was a real treat. Apparently, Kaine quit his lucrative job at a tech firm in Birmingham so he could pursue his dream of building things. The windmill was his first and only paying job. Yeah, the school wasn't going to pay him. That was all volunteer.

Mr. Crandall took pity on his errant nephew and is letting him crash at his place until he gets his life sorted out. I couldn't muster up any sympathy for him, even when he cried. Yes, that happened. I basically told him to man up and go get his engineering job back and be a grownup. I told him that though we women can certainly stand on our own, we don't want to take care of boys. For all our independence, we want to know a man can take care of us if needed. When he got done sniffling, we left for the game where I bought him a Coke and a hotdog. I felt like I was taking my own nephew out.

I haven't even gotten to the highlight yet. I know you're thinking, what could be worse? Let me tell you. No sooner had we settled in near Capri and David, a man a showed up. Now this man, unlike Kaine, didn't leave his girlfriend for carefree fun and no income. No, this man left her because she wasn't good enough for his new administration position or his dad. Both idiots. I can't say which one was worse. You men are a piece of work. And guess who got to sit in between the two jerks? You're right for once, Mr. Bingley, it was me.

Jackson had the audacity... no, first I should say that David and Jackson have been keeping in touch. They've been keeping their friendship hidden from Capri and myself. Yep, guess who's been playing online games with

David? You would think he should be studying or something. Didn't he tell me that's why we had to break up, because he had been messing around? So maybe it was all a lie. He was just done with me. He obviously hates me because he asked David to move over and he sat right next to me. Doesn't he get what his body does to my body?

I scooted as close as I could to Kaine, who was on the phone with Sandra trying to work it out. You think I'm kidding. I wish I was. Do you know what it's like to be on a date with a man who talks to his ex for most of it? I don't know how many times I heard the phrase, "Baby, I'm so sorry, please forgive me." My favorite was, "I fished your engagement ring out of the toilet."

Capri, David, and the other jerk all looked his way. Capri even laughed.

Then Mr. I-smell-and-look-fantastic leaned in and whispered, "How's your date going?" I don't believe in physical violence, but I've never wanted to hit someone so bad in all my life. I wanted to smack that smirk right off his face.

I couldn't take any more. As soon as our team made a touchdown, I got up and left amid everyone around me celebrating, well everyone but Kaine. He was still blubbering on the phone. I had a feeling he and Sandra were going to work it out. I don't even think he noticed that I left.

Capri grabbed my hand on my way out, but I only nodded that I was okay. But Jackson couldn't leave well enough alone. He followed me out to the parking lot, where I had no car. I wasn't a damsel in distress. I could walk home and did. Jackson kept calling after me, offering me a ride, but I ignored him. And maybe I gave him a nice hand gesture. Not my finest moment. He still followed me home in his new truck. He acted like a creepy stalker, slowly following behind me. I paid him no attention. I hated him for caring enough to make sure I made it home safe, but not caring enough to take care of my heart.

So it's Saturday, and I've lived through yet another humiliating event, and now my heart and my feet hurt.

Fifty more days.

I need some serious help,

Presley

Day Forty-Two

♥

Monday, September 6

THE WEEKEND DID NOT GO as planned. And from now on, I was sticking with the plan. No rebounds, superficial or not. I didn't care if Chace Crawford did ask me out, the answer was going to be not only no, but heck no. Men were terrible, awful people. But the problem was, I needed one to demonstrate how to stage kiss.

I had to use five spoons on each eye to even look halfway decent for school. It was a rough weekend. I used up all that leftover toilet paper from rolling Jackson's townhouse blowing my nose and wiping away tears. I didn't even know I could cry so much. We should have had today off since it was Labor Day, but the powers that be had decided it was better to have a longer Christmas break, so they got rid of some smaller holidays. I knew then that I would regret that decision. I could have really used a day off.

I had lain in Capri's lap most of yesterday while she stroked my hair and we watched what felt like fifty episodes of *Gilmore Girls*. She informed me that when Jackson returned to the game on Friday night, she had slugged him in the arm. Also, Brad and Mindy broke up. Or

117

more like, it came out that Mindy had made up their exclusive relationship. I guess this all played out on Facebook. I was thinking maybe Mr. Crandall was right. Maybe I'd stick to my social media hiatus. Except I was still waiting to see if Connie was going to ever message me back, though I was beginning to think love wasn't a worthy pursuit.

Riverton High School was becoming more and more like an episode of *General Hospital* or *Pretty Little Liars*. I figured, why not add to the drama of it all? I decided to ask Brad to be my willing victim.

Before I could get to the car line, Mr. Crandall met me in my room. "My dear, I'm so sorry about my nephew. I fear not only was he a charlatan to you, we have now lost our carpenter."

I set down my satchel and smiled. "I love that you still use words like charlatan."

He gave me a quick squeeze. "You are a remarkable young woman. I'm sorry I tried to intervene in your and Jackson's relationship."

I stepped back. "What do you mean?"

He grimaced. "I knew my nephew was considered what you young ladies call hot and I knew if I brought him around, he would be attracted to you. I had no idea, though, what a pansy he was."

I laughed. "I haven't heard the word pansy in forever."

He rested his hand on my cheek. "Regardless dear, I'm sorry I tried to make Jackson jealous. Though I'm sure that part of the plan worked."

"And what was your full plan?"

"To see you happy again."

I plastered on a big fake smile and pointed to my pearly whites. "See? Happy."

He patted my cheek. "Not quite, but I admire your tenacity."

I sighed. "I better attend to my duties. I'll see you fourth block."

"I'm looking forward to it." He dawdled off. If only he were thirty years younger.

I walked at a snail's pace to the car line. At least the mornings were cooler. I loved this time of year here. The humidity was down, but it was still warm. That's my kind of weather.

The men had beaten me to the line this morning. It didn't bother me. It was easier, this way, to slight Mr. Montgomery as I walked past him to my self-appointed spot in the middle.

"Good morning, Ms. Benson." Mr. Montgomery grinned at me.

I didn't even bother scowling or returning his greeting. So what if he was my boss?

I turned my attention toward the hard body at the end. "I heard it was a nail-biter, Friday."

Brad walked closer and opened a car door. "It was a close one." He sounded terrible.

"Are you sick?"

He rubbed his throat. "Too much yelling."

That made sense. "I have a proposal for you."

He was intrigued. He walked closer, with a baby-I'm-all-yours look. It did nothing for me. "Name it."

"I'm teaching our advanced drama students how to kiss on stage during fourth block and I need some willing lips to help me demonstrate."

Brad didn't meet my eyes. He looked above me first and smirked at Mr. Montgomery. Normally, that would have irked me, but after the weekend I spent bawling in my apartment, I applauded it.

"So what do you say?"

Brad moved in and leaned toward me. "My lips will be primed and ready for you."

I pushed him away. "Don't get any ideas."

"Just wait, darlin', you'll be wanting more."

I was going to gag, but he was willing, able, and he had good breath. And...I turned to see Mr. Montgomery seething. His ears were bright red. I gave him my own smirk before opening a car door.

On my way, back into the school, Mr. Montgomery took the liberty of gently grabbing my arm. "Hey."

His touch made my body sing and then cry. I froze in place. "I need to get to class."

"Don't kiss Brad."

I whipped my head up and glared at him something fierce. He should have withered under my gaze. "Is that a directive, Mr. Montgomery, because I don't remember you having a problem with me kissing a fellow teacher last year?"

"I wish you would quit calling me that."

"I wish for a lot of things, too."

"So do I." He pulled me closer. His brown eyes penetrated mine.

"Isn't there an unspoken rule about you fraternizing with me?"

He dropped his hand and stepped back. He ran his fingers through his hair and blew out a large amount of air.

My body cried.

"I'm not telling you that you can't kiss him, but he doesn't deserve the honor."

I raised my eyebrow. "And you do?"

"Maybe not, but at least I would never disrespect you by talking about it. He's the kind of guy that kisses and tells."

"It's a simple kiss, nothing more. I've learned my lesson. I'm done dating coworkers." I hustled away before my body acted of its own accord. *Forty-eight more days.*

Capri and I kept our heads together during lunch, deep in private conversation.

"By the way, Mindy hates you."

I shrugged. "I'm not too upset by that."

Capri laughed.

"Do you think this is a bad idea?"

"Heck no. I think it's brilliant. You get to kill two birds with one stone. Upset Jackson and live out every woman's fantasy in this building."

"Even yours?"

"No."

"You're not convincing me."

"I love David, even if he was seeing Jackson behind my back. Who knew he was a closet gamer, too?"

"I guess there were a lot of things I didn't know about him." I popped a grape into my mouth.

"Ah, honey. It's his loss. And you get to kiss Brad."

"Sadly, I don't even care."

She sat back and narrowed her eyes. "Then kiss Jackson. Show him what he's missing."

I shook my head. "No way. I'll have to start my ninety days over if I do that. Besides, I hate him."

She reached out and touched my arm. "And you still love him."

"Yeah." I rested my head on the table and held back the tears I had been wanting to cry since Mr. Montgomery touched me earlier.

"You're almost halfway there." Capri tried to be encouraging.

"I don't know if I'll make it. Are we sure that website was legit?"

"Uh, yeah." She was affronted at my insinuation. "The toughest part is almost over, I promise."

I lifted up my head and blew some hair off my face. "Really?"

She patted my head and grinned. "I swear."

I sat up and sighed. "I guess I should go brush my teeth or something."

Her wicked smile erupted. "Make it count."

I walked out of the teacher's lounge to the stares of my fellow teachers. Some of the looks were dirty, like from Mindy. I gave her a fake smile, she turned and pouted. Coach gave me a thumbs up and made me smile. He was hoping this would fix Mr. Montgomery. I knew it wouldn't. Not only were we over and never getting back together, he was trying to be someone he wasn't. Don't get me wrong, he made an excellent vice principal—even though I would never admit that out loud—but the suit and tie wasn't him. He wasn't meant to be his father's protégé. And until he came to realize that, he would be lost to everyone, including himself. But what did I know?

Third block went way too fast. I almost backed out. I think the only reason I didn't was because Mr. Montgomery asked me not to kiss Brad. I know how childish that sounds. I had lost all dignity. I felt like something in me had snapped. I felt out of control. I could see why the plan cautioned against alcohol and rebounds. That really would be a holy mess. And now here I was off to kiss a coworker. So my life had become a B rated movie.

I popped a mint in my mouth and weaved in and out of students on my way to the auditorium. After this little episode, I was going to lay low. Capri was right, I had to stay on track and that meant getting my life under control again. I had been blindsided, but at the end of the day I was still me. And *me* didn't go out with men like Kaine or Brad. I didn't toilet paper my boss' house, eat bags of chocolate in one night, or spend money on clothes like it was going out of style. That was hurt Presley coming out. I had to find my equilibrium again. Right after I kissed Brad, of course.

Mr. Crandall started class by handing out field trip slips. The theater in downtown Huntsville was putting on *Fiddler on the Roof* and we had been invited to a special daytime performance. I was excited about it. The cast was also making themselves available for a Q&A session afterward. The best part was that when it happened I would be cured of my ex. That was the plan anyway. It was a good thing, too, because I had always envisioned myself walking down the aisle to "Sunrise Sunset." And we all know who I pictured myself walking toward, in white.

I shook my head. *Forget about it, Presley.* I was trying. I really was.

Mr. Crandall started spouting off the rules of theater etiquette, right down to dressing up. "There is nothing I hate more than to see sloppy manners and dress at the theater." He stood tall. "Don't disappoint Ms. Benson or myself. We reserve the right to exclude you."

He was a softy and I wasn't buying it, but the kids did, and that was the most important thing.

Mr. Crandall clapped his hands to conclude his speech and it was like that act magically made two men appear at the side auditorium doors. If I didn't know better, I would say they had raced each other to see who could get there first. And if I wasn't mistaken, they scowled at each other and maybe even gave each other a little shove as they walked in.

Surprised, I looked at Mr. Crandall for his take. His eyes twinkled and he gave me a mischievous sort of grin.

I bit my lip, not sure what I should do. It was one thing to kiss Brad; it was another to kiss him in front of the man I was still in love with. It was against my will to still love him, but nonetheless, I did. I stood taller and reminded myself I was an actress, and I could rise to this awkward occasion. What could be more awkward than my date with Kaine? Please tell me nothing.

"Looks like some guests have arrived." Mr. Crandall chuckled and displayed a wide grin. He was trouble and he knew I was in for some.

"Is she going to kiss both of them?" Some girls giggled.

"I'll kiss her," some hormone crazed teen boy offered. Looked like I may need to use my role-playing skills and let him down gently—and inform him I would never do jail time for him. And that the thought of kissing a teenage boy made me want to vomit, as it should.

I kind of felt like throwing up now as Brad and Mr. Montgomery made their way up to the stage. Mr. Montgomery looked like he wanted to push Brad off into the orchestra pit.

Then to add more to the fun, Capri came running in. "Presley—" She stopped when we all stared at her. Her eyes drifted toward the men who were now standing close to me. "Looks like you already know."

Oh, my gosh. Could this get any worse?

Capri grinned in her evil way. "I think I'll stay and watch the show."

So the answer was, yes, it could get worse.

I closed my eyes for a brief second and breathed deeply all while try-ing not to look like I was. I could do this. It was nothing. I was teaching a technique, nothing more, nothing less. I opened my eyes and focused on my students, who were being the most attentive students in the history of school. Oh geez.

"Last week we talked about the rules of stage kissing. What were they?"

"No tongue," Leland shouted out. I knew that would be the one they remembered first. Laughter rang through the auditorium.

"Very good. What else?"

"Keep your hands to yourself."

"Good breath."

"No kissing while you're sick."

Mr. Montgomery cleared his throat and interrupted my students. "Well, I guess Mr. Sutton is out then." He patted Brad on the back.

Brad stepped away from him. "I'm not sick. This is a side effect from coaching." His voice sounded worse than this morning, giving me some pause.

"You don't want to get Ms. Benson sick now, do you?"

Brad's lips curled up into a smart aleck grin. "Don't worry, I wouldn't do anything to *hurt* her."

Mr. Montgomery's jaw clenched at the slight and maybe he turned a tad red out of guilt. He hung his head in defeat and stepped out of the way for Brad.

Why did part of me want him to fight for me, not physically, but in that I-would-move-heaven-and-earth-so-we-could-be-together way.

As Brad neared, I felt ill. My lips weren't ready to be touched by anyone else's but the man who was staring at me and begging me with his eyes not to go through with it. He didn't deserve to ask. I wasn't even sure why he cared. Didn't he tell me six weeks ago that he was done with me? That I was in his way? He hadn't meant to, but that cemented my resolve to go through with my lesson.

I turned my attention back toward my eager students. "I'm happy to know you listen to me sometimes." I smiled at them. "I've asked Mr. Sutton here to help me demonstrate the how-to's of stage kissing."

There were smatterings of oohs, ahhs, and whistles.

"Settle down. This is a demonstration. Mr. Sutton and I are only friends." We weren't even that, but I was kissing him momentarily, so friend sounded better than warm-bodied willing victim. "The purpose of a stage kiss, or any kiss for that matter, is to show or evoke emotion. A kiss can convey love, lust, regret, even friendship. But you don't just kiss someone. The story starts before lips ever come into play. Mr. Sutton, if you would please stand next to me."

Both Brad and Mr. Montgomery moved closer. I caught Capri enjoying the show from the front row. Mr. Crandall also seemed enthralled. I couldn't look into my ex's eyes. I didn't want to, but I had to look into Brad's eyes. They gleamed with macho pride. It was getting him nowhere, I assure you.

I hated to, but I pulled Brad closer to me. I felt like my whole class leaned forward to catch the action. "Now see, when I place my hands on his chest and look up at him and smile, I'm saying I adore him."

Brad smirked.

I'll give him that his chest felt nice. "Now, if he brings his hand up and rests it on my cheek and gazes into my eyes, he reciprocates the emotion."

Brad wasn't a quick study like last year's willing victim.

"That's your cue," I whispered to a dense Brad.

"Oh yeah." He clumsily rested his large hand on my face. It was rough and felt all wrong. He smelled wrong, too. He smelled woodsy like pine. It wasn't bad, but it wasn't delicious like someone else I knew.

I trudged on in the uncomfortableness of it all. "Now, he could do a couple of different things with his other hand. He could stroke my hair or maybe rest it on my other cheek so he's cupping my face." I met Brad's unusual green eyes. They were beautiful, but they did nothing for me. "That's your cue again."

He grinned before he stroked my hair, but it was more like petting and he pulled on it. I tried not to wince.

We were just getting this over with. "Now, you just don't go in for the kill." I felt I had to say that because I could see in Brad's eyes that's all he wanted to do. He had no finesse. He was no Mr. Montgomery. Last year, I hadn't even needed to explain. He knew how to romance a woman with his eyes and touch. *Shake it off, Presley.* I let out a breath. "Mr. Sutton is going to lean in, but not kiss me." *Like ever, please.*

He leaned in and hovered an inch above my lips. He licked his lips. Then coughed. "Sorry."

I did my best not to cringe. Maybe he was sick. I knew I was. "The moment before the kiss actually conveys more emotion than the actual kiss itself, so make it work. The hesitancy mixed with desire is what the audience is looking for. You're telling a love story without using words. Just one kiss can captivate or turn off your audience, so make it count. And by that, I don't mean kiss for a long time; even the briefest kiss, if done right, can show how your character feels." It was do or die time. Dying almost seemed like the good option here. "Don't forget, brief," I whispered to Brad.

He smiled before his lips landed on mine.

I felt like I needed to plug my nose and down the bad medicine. It was awful. Not only did he apply too much pressure, but the jerk tried to slip his tongue in my mouth. That was a no go. I pushed him away and did my best to hide my disgust. I was an actress, after all, playing my part. Before I could say a word, Mr. Montgomery appeared in my line of sight. He looked ready to hit Brad and come to my rescue. And that did it. I couldn't hide my feelings any longer. I pushed Brad out of the way. "Excuse me." I marched right past Mr. Montgomery whose eyes were now warmer as I passed by him. "I hate you."

DAY FORTY-THREE

💜

Tuesday, September 7

DEAR MR. BINGLEY,

Oh, Mr. Bingley. Whatever happened to my nice little life? The one where I was just a nice girl who loved a boy and everywhere we went people would say, "Don't they make a nice couple?" And people thought I was nice. Now people say things behind my back, like, "No wonder he broke up with her. Well, she's certainly getting around. I heard she made Mr. Crandall's nephew cry. I would cry, too, if I went out with her." So maybe it was mostly Mindy and her friend, the evil librarian Stella, but it hurt.

And to add insult to injury, Brad called in sick to work today. He has strep throat. Yay, me. I'm popping vitamin C and ginseng like it's going out of style. It was a good thing he didn't show up to school after his little stunt. I can still picture his smug face after he kissed me.

Are there any gentleman left? Are the Kaines and Brads of the world it?

So, I'm back on track. Now we know why the plan cautioned against rebounds. Not that either man was even close to that. But now I know I'm not ready. This wound caused by Mr. Montgomery is deep and it's barely begun to heal.

If only I had an aunt and uncle that would invite me to stay with them in London. At least Jane had that going for her. Maybe I'll consider teaching abroad for a year or two. That could work. Let's make it an all-girl school with an all-female staff. Even better.

Wishing for myself back,

Presley

DAY FORTY-FOUR

♥

Wednesday, September 8

I HAD JUST GOOGLED HOW LONG the incubation period for strep throat is. I was pretty sure it was psychosomatic, but my throat hurt and felt a little raw. I was sure it was nothing. I have an amazing immune system. I didn't even get the flu last year after Mr. Montgomery did—and we swapped lots of germs. It was thoughts like those that weren't helping me along in my ninety-day quest. He finally did me a favor yesterday and today and didn't do car line. I had a nice surprise when Coach took Brad's place.

I think Coach needed a ninety-day plan to get over Mr. Montgomery, too. He made an interesting observation, though. He said, "It's never good when you try and balance everyone's expectations. You'll always lose yourself."

That's how he saw his friend, Mr. Montgomery.

"I guess mine were too much, so I had to go."

"PB, that's what I meant about him losing himself. He's not the same without you."

I didn't think I had unrealistic expectations of him, or at least not ones I didn't think he had for us.

It didn't matter now. I checked my glands to see if they were swollen before my second block class filed in. I couldn't tell if they were or not. Again, I was probably fine.

DAY FORTY-FIVE

Thursday, September 9

DEAR MR. BINGLEY,

I'm halfway there. And I haven't seen Mr. Montgomery in two days. I can't tell you how helpful that has been. I think there have been some district meetings he's had to attend. But whatever the reason, it has been a welcome relief. I firmly believe if this was the case all along, I would have progressed much quicker. I may even be over him by now. Okay, we know that's a lie, but it would have been better. Capri's online reading habits have finally paid off. That and she and David have upped their post coital snuggling. He still won't look me in the eye.

Now, if I can just figure out a way to stay away from him. I could ask Dr. Walters to reassign my car line duty. I'll take it next semester, even though it's colder and usually wetter. These are good thoughts. I need to keep exploring, but my head kind of hurts.

I'm not getting sick.

Nope not me,

Presley

Oh my gosh, I felt terrible. I barely made it through the day. Remember that truck that hit me when Mr. Montgomery broke up with me? It came back to finish the job. My mom told me to look in my mouth to see if there were any white looking pus things. I didn't see anything, but it's kind of hard to look down your own throat. She suggested it was just stress and to rest.

Yeah, resting was good. I didn't even bother with dinner. Not that I could have anyway. I was having a hard time swallowing. I probably should have gone to urgent care, but I was stubborn, if you couldn't already tell. And it wasn't like ten percent of my students were out sick today. But sleep sounded so good. I couldn't ever remember being this tired.

I slipped into some sweats and crawled into bed. I surrendered and fell into a deep sleep.

Day Forty-Six

♥

Friday, September 10

I ACHED AND FELT LIKE I had a hangover. And why was it light? Where was I? And who was making that awful sound? Was that my name being called? *Am I dreaming?*

"Presley, are you okay? Open the door."

I stirred and tried opening my eyes. I must have been dreaming, because Mr. Montgomery was calling my name and he sounded worried.

"Presley, please."

I got one eye open. It was too light. I normally woke up when it was dark. What time was it? I tried to reach for my phone. My strength was gone.

"Presley, please. I'm coming in."

What? How? My brain was running slow, but a huge oversight came to mind. He had a key to my apartment. I forgot to get that back. I wanted to yell at him to proceed with caution and it wasn't in his best interest, but my mouth and body weren't cooperating with me. I was still trying to remember what day it was.

I heard the deadbolt and door lock turn and before I knew it, Mr. Montgomery rushed through my door. "Presley, are you here? Are you all right?" He was panicked.

I rustled under my covers. It was the best I could do at the moment.

He rushed forward and landed on my bed. He tore the comforter off my face. "Thank goodness. I've been worried sick. We all were."

The light hurt my eyes. I squinted at him. "Why are you here?" Every word burned.

He reached out and caressed my cheek. "You're burning up."

I realized I was shivering, even with sweats on and being buried under my blankets.

He set me more on fire when he began kissing my head and cheeks.

My self-preservation side kicked in. "Stop. Why are you here?"

He sat back. He was full of smiles. The kind that shone in his eyes. The kind he had lacked for the last several weeks. "You didn't show up to school this morning or call."

Oh crap! I sat up, even though it expended way more energy than it should have. "What time is it?"

"Nine."

I had never slept through an alarm or been late to work. My eyes welled up with tears.

"Hey." He wiped away a tear with his thumb. "Don't cry. It's okay."

I pushed his hand away. "No, it's not."

"I'll call the school right now."

"Please just go."

He shook his head. "No can do." He fished his phone out of his pocket and called the school and Capri. Why she hadn't come instead of him, I didn't know.

I reached for my own phone and saw several missed calls and texts from Capri and the school.

"I'm going to take her to the doctor," came out of his mouth.

That was a negative. He wasn't taking me anywhere. And I wanted my key back. If he could give me my heart back, too, I would more than appreciate it.

He hung up and smiled right back at me in his suit and tie.

"I can take care of myself."

"I'm well aware of that fact." He smirked.

"Good. Now give me back my key and leave."

"No, ma'am. Do you still see Dr. Gammel?"

I pulled my legs up toward my chest and turned away from him. Did he know how much he was killing me? "Go. If you ever cared about me, leave now."

He did the opposite and took me up in his arms. I didn't have the strength to pull away. "PB, I know I've screwed up, but this morning when you didn't show up and I thought the worst, I was kicking myself for ever letting you think that I didn't want to be with you. I can't pretend anymore that I don't love you."

Tears of hurt and anger flowed. I did my best to pull away.

"I know I'm ticking you off, and you have every right to be mad at me, but I'm not leaving."

I was livid, but too tired to fight. But believe me, I would be as soon as I felt better. "Aren't you worried about your precious career?" Okay, I still had some fight in me, even though talking set my throat on fire.

He gave me a pained stare. "I deserve that. But the only thing I'm worried about right now is you. Let's get you to the doctor."

"I can take myself."

"You're in no shape to drive."

"I'll call Capri."

"She's got a class right now."

"We'll go after school."

"Dr. Gammel closes early on Fridays."

"I'll go to urgent care then."

He shook his head and smiled. "You're stubborn, but I can be stubborn, too."

I pulled up my covers and shivered. I had never felt so sick.

"I'm not leaving." He folded his arms. "I can watch you in bed all day, which suits me just fine, or we can go help you feel better and then I can watch you in bed all day."

"I hate you."

"I know. But I love you and I'm going to take care of you."

"You don't love me."

"I've done a poor job of showing it, I'll give you that, but Presley, I've loved you since the moment our lips first touched, hell, maybe even before that."

Was he trying to kill me? Well, guess what? I wasn't a Jane and his declarations of love weren't going to change my mind. But I really did need a ride to the doctor. Death felt like it was knocking on my door. "Fine, I'll go to the doctor, but after that you're leaving."

"We'll negotiate after." His eyes were dancing.

I crawled out of bed and headed for my bathroom on shaky legs. That was a bad call. I looked in the mirror and death had come knocking.

"I'm calling Dr. Gammel's office. I'll get her to work you in," Jackson shouted.

I didn't bother replying. I knew she would do anything for him. Dr. Gammel was like a second mother to Jackson. Wyatt Gammel was Jackson's best friend growing up and his mom, Sylvia Gammel, was a top-notch doctor and cookie maker. Jackson loved her. She was a lovely lady. I had only ever had to see her once in an official capacity. I had to update some of my vaccinations before I could start teaching. Unofficially, we'd had dinner at her home several times.

I ran my fingers through my hair. It looked like something was living in it. I had to lean on my sink for support. I definitely couldn't drive myself anywhere. But Jackson was the last person I wanted to play my chauffeur. How dare he come in here and, for one, use the key I gave him. Okay, he thought I was dead, so I'll give him that one, but he had no right to say he loved me or to act like it. It wasn't changing my mind. Ninety days or bust, baby! But first, I needed to get myself checked out. I could roar later.

I brushed my teeth and hair. It was all I could do. I wasn't even going to bother to change. And the only reason I brushed my teeth was for Dr. Gammel's benefit.

I walked out of the bathroom holding onto the wall for support. If only I hadn't kissed Brad. This was all his fault. Actually, no. It was all Jackson's fault. I glared at him.

He was a Boy Scout anyway and came to my aid. He put his arm around me and helped me walk. "Wow, can you give some looks. I had no idea."

"We don't need to talk."

He laughed. "Man, I've missed you."

"I need to grab my bag."

"I can just carry you. You're shaking like crazy."

"Don't even think about it."

He gave me a crooked grin. "So you're still mad?"

I tried to pull away, but he pulled right back. "I know I have a lot of making up to do."

"Don't waste your time."

"I'm not giving up."

"You already did."

He stopped and kissed my head. "I know. It was a huge mistake."

"We're not getting back together, and keep your lips to yourself."

"I'm not afraid of getting sick, if that's what you're worried about. I'm already sick over what I've done to us."

He knew I couldn't care less if he got sick or not. "Silence is golden."

"Okay." I could hear the smile in his voice. The jerk kissed my head again.

We made the arduous trek out to his shiny new truck. Every step took way more energy than it should have.

"Let's take my car." On top of everything else, I couldn't stand the thought of riding in the number one rated make out truck.

"My legs are too long for your car."

"You poor thing."

He laughed and swooped me off my feet. "I want to show you my new truck. When you're feeling better, we can test it out again."

"Put me down, Mr. Montgomery."

"Please quit calling me that." He hurried us to his truck.

I gave up. I was just going to ignore him. But it was hard as every part of me wanted to curl up against him and soak him in. I missed him, his touch, his kisses. He was not going to waltz back into my life like nothing had happened. He treated me like an option and so, by choice, I was done with him, no matter what my body said.

He deftly opened his truck door with me in his arms. He'd had practice. He could even do it while we were making out. He gently placed me in the leather seat. I shivered even in the warmth of the cab, where the sun had heated it nicely. I wrapped my arms around myself.

He touched my warm cheek. "Dr. Gammel will have you feeling better in no time. Then you can punch me like I know you want to."

I almost laughed. If I believed in violence, I definitely would have, but I didn't believe men or women should hit each other. I turned from him and closed my eyes.

He hustled around and jumped in. While he drove, he reached over to hold my hand like he always did, but I pulled away. He blew out a large breath. "I'm sorry. I wish I could give you a good explanation right now, but I can't."

I felt too ill to respond. If I could, I would have said, "That sounds like a bunch of crap." Instead, I leaned against the window. I didn't want to be the angry crazy person anymore. He knew how I felt, so I left it at that.

Like the gentleman he was, he turned the radio dial to my favorite alternative station, even though it was far from his preference. I didn't mention I had found a new appreciation for country music. I didn't mention anything on our ten-minute drive to the doctor's office. He prattled on about things like how they got a sub for my classes, and Capri would call me later.

Then we pulled into the parking lot and it was like a thought struck him. "Did you change your phone number?"

I shook my head no.

"Huh. When I call, it just rings and rings and rings. You might want to get that checked."

"I blocked you." I spoke into the window.

"I guess I deserved that. I suppose that's why I can't see you on Facebook or access any of the pictures you had of us."

The fact he was looking for them bothered me, but I didn't make mention of it. "I deleted everything."

"Really?"

I turned to look at him. "What did you expect?"

"That it wouldn't be so difficult."

I turned away from him.

"I know how terrible that sounds."

"Do you?" I held back the tears.

"Presley... I don't know what to say. But our time apart has been hell for me, in more ways than one."

I opened the door. I couldn't listen to his unexpressed excuses any longer. And I needed medication. My body ached and my throat felt like it had gone through the food processer along with my heart.

Mr. Montgomery hurried around. "I would have gotten that for you."

"I don't want your help." I felt like I oozed out of his car like slime. "Don't touch me."

He backed away, but stayed close as we walked toward the office. "I'm sorry you don't feel good. A lot of kids and teachers called in sick today."

I didn't acknowledge his attempt at small talk. I still couldn't believe I slept through my alarms and phone calls.

He opened the door for me. "Dr. Gammel said to put a mask on as soon as you get in. I'll check you in at the front desk."

I nodded.

He went to touch me, but decided at the last second it wasn't a good idea. That was a good choice. Not like I could have done anything.

All my energy went into standing upright. And to top it off, I felt nauseous. I wasn't sure if that was illness or the situation. I wanted to be back in bed.

I dutifully grabbed my mask and placed it over my mouth and nose. I found a chair and curled up into it. There were a lot of people in the waiting room. Almost all of them looked miserable like me.

Mr. Montgomery checked me in and then came and sat next to me. "The nurse will call you back soon." He braved it and rubbed my arm.

I can't tell you how soothing his touch was.

I don't know how long I waited, but it was torturous. It was like having your favorite dessert of all time placed in front of you, and then someone telling you not to eat it. And if you took even a little nibble, you'd want to eat it for the rest of your life, and no other dessert would ever compare. You don't know how hard it was not to taste him.

When my name was called, he helped me up. "Do you want me to go back with you?"

I gave him a dirty look before I walked away from him. Was he crazy? For one, I hated him, and for two, he was not looking at the scale. I'm pretty sure my steady diet of chocolate had netted me a few pounds. I was pleasantly surprised it was only two.

Once the nurse had me back in a room, she took my temperature. "Oh my, 103.5."

No wonder I felt like I had been dropped in the tundra.

"Have you taken any medication in the past twenty-four hours?"

I shook my head no.

"Are you allergic to any medication?"

"Sulfa."

"I'm going to run a strep culture."

I almost gagged when she swabbed my throat.

"It doesn't look pretty in there."

I could imagine.

She trotted off and I lay back on the examination table and waited.

Dr. Gammel knocked on the door ten minutes later. She walked in and took a look at my pathetic state. "Hi, sweetie."

I liked her. I sat up slowly. "So what's the verdict?"

"Definitely strep, but let's take a look at you."

She approached with her stethoscope. She was a lovely lady. Tall, with a willowy figure. She exuded charm. It looked like she had stopped denying the inevitable and was letting her hair go gray. It suited her well. "Breathe in and let it out." Next she felt my throat and swollen glands. Next were my ears. "Everything else checks out okay. How have you been?" Her tone was one of concern.

I stared into her kind eyes. "You know?"

"Jackson is an idiot."

I smiled. "Agreed."

"But I love him like a son. He came with you, right?"

"I didn't want him to."

She laughed. "I'm sure he insisted."

"Something like that."

"He's a good kid. A little misguided as of late. It's not my place to say, but I do hope you two work it out."

"Not happening."

"Good for you. Keep him on his toes." She wrote out a prescription and handed it to me. "Twice a day for ten days, should do the trick. But if you aren't feeling better in a few days, come back in. After twenty-four hours, you shouldn't be contagious. Make sure you throw away your toothbrush after that time and get a new one. Any questions?"

I took the white piece of paper. "No. Thank you."

"Feel better, sweetie, and give him a run for his money." She helped me off the table.

First, I needed to feel better. I checked out and paid my copay before I headed back to the waiting room to an eager Mr. Montgomery.

He jumped up and met me, anxious to help me in some way. "I'll carry your purse."

"I got it."

"Okay. What did the doctor say?"

"Strep." I showed him my slip of paper.

He opened the exit door for me. "We'll stop at the pharmacy on our way home. I'll drop you off while they fill your prescription and then go back and get it. Then I'll come back and make you lunch."

We hit the warmth of the outside. "You don't need to do that."

"I want to."

"Let me rephrase. I don't want you to."

"Too bad. You're stuck with me."

"How does the district and your dad feel about that?"

I didn't need to physically hit him. He stopped and placed his arm over his gut like I had punched him.

"That's what I thought." I kept on walking.

He followed. "Presley, I'll work it out. We can work it out."

"There is no we anymore."

"Not if I have anything to say about it."

Day Forty-Seven

Saturday, September 11

I WOKE UP IN A FOG. I vaguely recollected that Mr. Montgomery had taken care of me the day before, even going as far as buying every flavor popsicle imaginable and cleaning my small apartment. I did my best to get rid of him, but I mostly slept. And now it was light again and I heard his voice. I was sure I had kicked him out, but it didn't have much weight, considering I was incoherent most of the day.

I think my fever had finally broken. I was sweating and no longer had the chills. I smelled like I needed a shower. But I lay still as the voice became clearer. It belonged to him.

"Thanks for coming up and taking care of him."

Did he get a dog?

"We can't risk him getting sick."

What? Who?

He laughed. "She's mad as hell at me. I can't wait until she wakes up and sees I stayed the night."

What! I stayed still so I could continue to eavesdrop.

"Honestly, had I known she was this sexy mad, I would have ticked her off a long time ago."

Jerk.

"No. No. I know. I feel terrible about what I did to her."

You got that right.

"I'm not sure if she'll ever forgive me, but I have to try."

You can try, buddy, but it isn't happening.

"Okay, man, keep me posted. I'm not sure where I'll be. If I'm lucky, here."

Your luck has run out.

He hung up and I heard him walk my way. The floors creaked in my apartment.

I still pretended to sleep. I didn't want him to know I had been privy to his conversation yet.

He approached my bed and sat on the edge of it. He stroked my hair. It was heavenly in that hellish sort of way. "Presley, I'm so sorry. I didn't mean for us to get so messed up. You're beautiful when you're angry, though. And I have a feeling you are only going to get more beautiful this next little while. Someday I'll tell you everything. Like how I know about Capri's and your plan to get over me in ninety days."

What the heck! How?

"David told me all about it." He laughed softly.

David was so, so dead. I was going to say the word coital whenever I could around him from now on.

"I know I'm only in for more of your wrath, but I'm going to do my best to make sure that doesn't happen. I love you and I know you still love me, even if you won't admit it."

Oh, his ego.

"PB, get ready for the fight of your life. May we both win." He kissed my head.

I was going to be ready all right. He wasn't going to know what hit him.

Day Forty-Eight

♥

Sunday, September 12

DEAR MR. BINGLEY,

What am I going to do? Mr. Crandall was right, there has been a twist in the plot. Like a major dun-dun-dun moment. Mr. Montgomery is just like you. He arrived on his stallion and has declared he still loves me. This can't be happening, because I still love him and I mean to get over that as soon as possible, or at least in the next forty-two days.

Oh, and get this. He knows about my ninety-day plan. David, Mr. Montgomery's secret friend, ratted me out. But I know he knows and he doesn't know I know, so I'm one up on him. Even though it meant I had to lay in my bed and pretend to be asleep when I had to pee something fierce and I smelled awful—hadn't showered in two days, wearing the same outfit, sweating out a fever, awful. It was worth the pain. When I did pretend to wake up, there he was, smiling and calling me the most beautiful thing he had ever seen. He was such a liar. I had a mirror and the reflection was none too pretty after lying in bed all day.

I promptly kicked him out. He left all right, but not before kissing me. And did I mention that he didn't leave the key to my apartment?

I don't know what he's playing at. Who was he talking to on the phone? It doesn't really matter, because I'm getting over him. No man is going to treat me the way he had and then come strolling back into my life like nothing ever happened. That's right, Mr. Bingley, you don't know how lucky you were you got a Jane.

Unfortunately, I think my rejection has only fueled his desire. I could see the excitement in his eyes when he left. Well, Mr. Montgomery, hold on, because this girl is roaring. I am getting over the oxytocin and I am overcoming the urge to jump back into your arms and test out your new truck. I can live without your kisses and your touch.

So, there you have it. If I haven't mentioned it in a while, men suck! Most determined,

Presley

My phone buzzed as soon as I set my pen down. I was sitting crossed-legged on my bed, still resting, but at least I had showered. Also, antibiotics and Advil were wonderful inventions. I reached for my phone on my nightstand. My phone had been overly active the last couple of days with people checking on me. Capri, my mom, and Miss Liliana were the main culprits. But now I could add a new one to the list.

Good morning, beautiful. I added myself back into your contacts while I watched you sleep. Have I mentioned how beautiful you are?

I rolled my eyes, but kept reading.

I'm sure you'll delete this and block me again, but I wanted you to know that you don't need to worry about car line duty anymore. Coach is taking your place. I figured you wouldn't want to be around Brad. PB, I know you think the obstacles in our way are insurmountable, but I'm willing to climb any mountain for you. Get some rest. Call me if you need anything. Love you, J.

Yep, deleted and blocked. I threw my phone on the bed. I rubbed my face with my hands. This was definitely not part of the plan. And why did he think all of the sudden his dad and the school district were going to be okay with his decision? If anything, I'm sure his father hated me more after our little run-in at Miss Liliana's. As for the district, I'm not sure if they really had an issue as long as it stayed on the up and up. But I'm sure they wouldn't exactly be jumping for joy about it, either. Not that they had to worry, because it was so not happening.

DAY FORTY-NINE

♥

Monday, September 13

THOUGH I WAS NO LONGER contagious and was feeling more like myself, I felt sick about going back to school. From talking to Capri, I knew there was already a rumor going around that Mr. Montgomery and I were back together. I was going to squash that as soon as possible. I'm sure that would only add to the, "she's really going through men" comments. I wasn't going through any men. And let's get this straight, Mr. Montgomery dumped *me*. The other two bozos were serious lapses of judgment. Hard lessons learned that I wouldn't be repeating.

I walked out of my apartment with knots in my stomach, somewhat ready to face the day. The morning was cool and the sun was making its appearance. I breathed in deeply, relishing the fall weather that hung in the air. It had a calming effect. That moment of peace was interrupted when Mr. Montgomery pulled up in his new truck, grinning like he knew exactly how much it was going to irk me to see him there. He came to a stop and hopped out.

I took a sip of my caffeine-boosted coffee and stormed toward my car, doing my best to avoid him.

He wasn't having it. "PB." He followed after me laughing.

I kept on going.

"You know, if you wouldn't block me from calling you, you could have told me by phone you were all right."

I stopped and spun around. "So this is my fault?"

He gave me his you-know-you-would-rather-be-kissing-me grin.

As true as that may be, it wasn't ever happening. I glared at him.

His grin turned into a smirk. "We won't assign blame. But, really, how are you feeling?"

I huffed and turned back toward my car.

"So, you're better?"

"Never better. Now you can go." I opened my car door.

He closed it and leaned against it.

I was torn. Smack him or kiss him? Gosh, he looked good in his dark suit. But I was Elizabeth, not Jane. "I thought I made myself clear about where we stood."

He crossed his arms and grinned. "Crystal clear, but that doesn't work for me."

"I hate to break it to you, but this isn't all about you. Even though that's exactly how you've acted."

He stepped toward me. The amusement gone from his eyes. "I'm sure that's how it looks to you, but if I was the only consideration, I would have never broken up with you."

"You don't know what a comfort that is to me. Excuse me now. I need to get to work." I reached for the car door.

He took my hand and held it against his heart.

My first instinct was to pull it away, but his eyes got to me. They always had. They burned with yearning. He held my hand firmly against his chest. "This is true love—you think this happens every day?"

I pulled my hand away. "Don't quote the *Princess Bride* to me."

"Why? You used to love it."

"That's before you told me you were only messing around with me. Do you know how used I've felt? You don't get to say the things you said and then expect to walk right back into my life like you didn't throw me away. How could I ever trust you again? As far as I'm concerned, I'm not even sure what we had before was real." I threw open my door.

His hands fell to his side and his head dropped. "My love for you is real. I'll do my best to prove that to you. To earn your trust back."

"Please don't." I slid into my car and shut the door. I drove off, shaking and doing my best not to cry. I watched him in my rearview mirror, running his fingers through his hair and looking like he just lost his best friend. I felt the same way.

DAY FIFTY

♥

Tuesday, September 14

DEAR MR. BINGLEY,

I made it to day fifty, but I feel like I'm at ground zero. Everyone at school, including the students, are now gossiping about us. "Are they or aren't they?" is the big question. I'm not sure why. We definitely are not. I don't care that he came and sat next to Capri and me during lunch or that he left me the sweetest get well card on my desk. He was a jerk for toying with my emotions. And guess what? The principal, Dr. Walters, has asked to meet with me before school this morning. I'm probably going to get fired because of all the intrigue I've caused, kissing teachers and now Mr. Montgomery coming on to me. It isn't fair. He should be the one to go, but I know how it works. I'm the peasant, and he's the prince.

Capri told me not to worry about it, but I saw the look of dread in her eyes. Being fired is going to look terrible on my resume. Maybe they'll let me say I resigned. I love my job, but maybe moving home would be the best thing right now. I could do with some miles between Mr. Montgomery and myself. I don't think he understands the restraint it has taken to not fall right back into his arms. But he doesn't understand the hurt he's caused. Hurt like that doesn't just go away. Only in books and in movies is it erased so easily.

Wish me luck. This could be a very short day.
Sick to my stomach,
Presley

I dressed more conservatively than I normally would. I wore a well-fitting black pant suit. The only cute things about it were the red pumps I paired with it. I straightened my hair, hoping that made me look more serious. I couldn't believe, on top of everything else, my job could be in jeopardy.

My stomach was tied in knots on my drive over to the school. I tried to brace myself for the worst. I probably shouldn't have bought all those new clothes. I think I was going to write my own internet article called, *So You Think You Want a Boyfriend, Think Again.*

The school was eerily quiet when I walked in. There was hardly a soul in sight. I hoped it stayed that away in case I had to walk out unemployed. I headed for the administration offices. Not even the secretary was in yet. But Mr. Montgomery was. I figured since I saw his truck in the parking lot he was already there. He and Dr. Walters were talking in the principal's office. Or at least they were until I arrived. The door was open and they were alerted to my presence. Both men were standing near the door and turned my way.

Mr. Montgomery's smile added flutters to my churning stomach. I wish he didn't have that effect on me, but what can I say. He was handsome and charming, even though he was a class A jerk.

Dr. Walters gave me his attention, too. His lips pressed together and he gave me a nod of acknowledgement before turning back toward Mr. Montgomery. "We'll talk later, Jackson." He gave me his attention. "Come on in, Presley, and shut the door behind you."

Foreboding consumed me.

Mr. Montgomery walked toward me. "Good morning."

Even if I had wanted to talk to him, I couldn't have. My mouth had quit working. At least my legs were still functioning. I made my way toward Dr. Walters' office.

Mr. Montgomery touched my shoulder and gave me another small smile.

That's all I needed, for him to touch me in front of Dr. Walters. Then it hit me—his plan was to get me fired. This way, he could keep his job and try to pursue me. I had his number. And if he thought that was going to work in his favor, he had another thing coming. I was headed home to Colorado. I ignored him and walked right into the principal's office.

Dr. Walters stood behind his desk, now near his chair. "Please have a seat." He pointed to the leather chairs in front of his desk. He waited to sit down until I was situated.

I sat at the edge of my seat, both literally and figuratively. My breathing had become shallow.

Dr. Walters leaned his elbows on his desk and folded his hands together. "Thanks for coming in early to meet with me."

I nodded. My mouth still wasn't wanting to work.

He leaned forward. "I'm happy to see you're feeling better."

Oh no. Another mishap to add to this ridiculous school year. I leaned forward, too. "I'm so sorry I didn't call in. You see, I slept through my alarm. I was running a fever of over 103 and—"

He grinned. "No need to apologize. I'm well aware of how ill you were, and how seriously you take your job."

I sat back some and let out a deep breath.

"It's why I wanted to talk to you. I feel like I have done you a great disservice."

I tilted my head. "Why?"

He relaxed his arms and settled them on his desk. He sat back, too. "When Steve informed us he was leaving, I knew Jackson would be the ideal candidate to replace him. I also knew of Jackson's relationship with you."

I bit my lip. "We're not dating anymore if that's what you're worried about," I interrupted him, desperate to keep my job at least for the school year.

His mouth downturned. "I know. That's where I fear I overstepped my bounds."

"Overstepped your bounds?"

He clasped his hands together. "I worried that your relationship with Jackson would impede his ability to secure his new position. I also worried about the ramifications it would create with the staff here if your relationship continued."

I sat up straighter and my posture stiffened.

"I suggested that Jackson reevaluate his priorities." His face reddened.

My eyes stung. "I see."

"I know that sounds cold, and I apologize. I didn't know how deeply he felt for you. To his credit, he refused to discuss his relationship with you. He felt that should remain between the two of you. That being said, central office expressed their concerns as well when interviewing him."

"Again, he broke up with me. And I've accepted that and moved on." That was kind of a lie, but I was in the process of it.

He swallowed hard and gave me a wavering smile. "There have been mistakes all around."

I shook my head.

"I realize it's not my place to intervene in your personal life."

I narrowed my eyes.

"I know that sounds hypocritical in light of what I just divulged, but I'm trying to correct my misdeed."

"If you're going to fire me, please just tell me." I couldn't take the suspense anymore.

He chuckled. "Goodness, no."

I perked up, though I was still unsure of the direction he was going.

"It seems I have something else to apologize for." His watered down blue eyes sparkled. "You're an excellent asset to our school. You possess a talent for teaching that goes beyond your years."

"Thank you." I blushed.

"You see, I asked you to meet with me so I could shed some light on your situation with Jackson. I regret that I played a part in the demise of your relationship. My only excuse, and it is a poor one at that, is that I didn't know the extent of Jackson's feelings for you until last week when you didn't show up and all attempts to contact you were fruitless. Jackson's emotional state spoke of his love for you. I recognized in him my own actions and feelings once upon a time when my wife failed to contact me on a business trip and her phone died. I was a wreck until I knew she was safe and sound. Our new vice principal could not be calmed until he knew you were okay."

I tucked my hair behind my ear.

He gave me a small smile. "He also informed me that he had every intention of pursuing a relationship with you…" He looked me squarely in the eyes. "Even if that meant he would lose his job."

The fluttering was back. "We're over," I stammered.

"Well, so you know. I told Jackson that I felt I could trust both of you to maintain a professional relationship while at school. I see no issue if you would like to rekindle your romance. I told the superintendent the same thing."

I wasn't sure what to say. Thank you? That seemed inappropriate, considering he told Jackson to basically break up with me. "Like I said, we're over. I should get to my classroom now." I stood up.

He stood up as well. "Please accept my apology. I've been around so long and I've seen my fair of share of problems that personal relationships have caused in the workplace. It skewed my view of the situation. I hope my mistake won't cause your view to go permanently askew."

I didn't feel like it was askew at all. I'm sure Mr. Montgomery didn't mention to him *how* he broke up with me. And let's not forget the fact that he chose his job over me. I get we weren't married, but when someone said they loved me, I took that to mean I was the priority in their life. That's how I used to feel about him. "Apology accepted." I guess. What else was I going to say? Maybe I should thank him. He helped me to see how easily Mr. Montgomery could be persuaded to drop me from his life. So I did. "Thank you." I started to walk out.

"Presley."

I turned around. "Have a good day. And if you do change your mind, I suggest you and Jackson not use the prop room anymore." He grinned and sat back down.

Oh. My. Gosh. I was going to die. Now I wished he would have fired me. I couldn't believe he knew we had been making out in the prop room. *I wonder if knows about the casting couch, too?*

Day Fifty-One

♥

Wednesday, September 15

"THANKS FOR HELPING ME."

I pulled the perfectly shaped green apple out of the homemade caramel Capri had made. "I'm happy to."

"My momma thanks you, too."

"I'll make sure to buy one from her at the craft fair this weekend. I promised Miss Liliana I would take her."

Capri grinned at me from the other side of the counter. "She still trying to get you and Jackson back together?"

I rolled my eyes and set the apple down on the parchment paper. "Her and everyone else I know."

"Not me. I still think he's a man whore."

"You're the only one."

"I know." She grimaced. "David has defected to the dark side."

I already knew that. "Where is David? I've been meaning to ask him how that post coital thing was going for you guys."

She snorted. "Now who's evil? And by the way, he's helping Jackson move tonight."

My head popped up. "Really? Where to?" I didn't realize his house sold already. Not that I would. I had been trying my best to avoid him.

She shifted uncomfortably. "He's moving in with his daddy."

I dropped the spoonful of caramel I had been holding.

"I don't think he wanted you to know. I had to terrorize it out of David."

"Did you threaten ten minutes of post coital cuddling?"

"You don't have to pretend you're not upset by the news."

I grabbed some paper towel to clean up my caramel mess. "It doesn't matter to me where he lives."

"You're such a liar."

Yep, I was. Not that it already wasn't a forgone conclusion, but his moving in with his father sealed the deal. We were never getting back together. His dad hated me and was part of the reason he broke up with me. It only proved to me that Mr. Montgomery had never been truly serious about me. I took a swipe at the warm caramel. "In thirty-nine days, it won't matter anymore."

"Maybe he had to do it."

Her tone confused me. I looked up to make sure I heard her right. "Are you defending him?"

"Of course not, but I'm just saying, maybe he has money problems, or he couldn't find a new house, or who knows. It doesn't necessarily mean he's giving up on you."

"He doesn't have money problems. He just bought a new truck and he's always been careful about his money. And he comes from money."

"True. So maybe he's having your dream house built and he's waiting for you to come around."

"I guess he'll be waiting a long time then."

"Are you sure?"

I grabbed another apple and plunged a stick in it with fury. "Very."

DAY FIFTY-THREE

♥

Friday, September 17

DEAR MR. BINGLEY,

I'm in desperate need of a weekend. This week has been tortuous. It's one thing to try to get over someone you're in love with when they aren't in love with you. It's a whole other ballgame when they decide they really are in love with you. It doesn't help that I'm losing allies as quickly as he's gaining them. Just today, Dr. Walters "invited" me to head up a committee with Mr. Montgomery where we would offer a fifth block every Wednesday. This extra block, one time a week, would allow students to explore everything from a chorus group to how to get a book published. Mr. Montgomery and I have been tasked to reach out to the community to get local gurus to come in and teach the students. Mr. Crandall suggested I take my planning period to do that instead of helping him out. All three men agreed that was an excellent idea.

Capri and my dad are the only ones in my corner now. Dads were currently the only part of the male species worth knowing, in my estimation. My dad got that Mr. Montgomery had hurt me to the center of my being. That you don't casually toss me about or toy with my emotions. Why was everyone else so quick to jump on his bandwagon?

I get that we were good together and forgiveness is a beautiful thing. I fully intend to forgive him someday, for my own well-being. That doesn't mean we should get back together. And besides, he's living with his dad. Does that seem weird to you, Mr. Bingley? Mr. Montgomery has always been close to his father and valued his opinion, even if it was to his own detriment—to our detriment—but he never struck me as the type to live with his dad. I always got the vibe that he needed the space from his father, that although he loved his dad, he recognized his faults.

Maybe it's nothing more than his townhome sold quickly and he's building a new house or something. But why didn't he choose to live with Miss Liliana over his father? That's another thing. I would think Mr. Montgomery the elder would see living with your parent as a sign of weakness, that he would be embarrassed to admit his son had moved home, even if it was for a legitimate reason like timing.

It's none of my concern. I need to move on. Thirty-seven more days.

Heaven help me,

Presley

It was a rainy Friday, so I decided against going to the football game that night. I knew that made me a fair weather fan, but I needed a night to unwind from the week and to gear myself up to see Miss Liliana the next day. I knew I would be barraged with pro Mr. Montgomery propaganda. I headed to my favorite café for a little food and some self-indulgence.

Station 33 Café was a little place in downtown Riverton near the old railroad station that had been turned into a quaint museum.

I took my laptop and a book and headed to my little piece of solace for the evening. It was a damp, drizzly night that gave me a little chill. Fall was in the air. I grabbed a small table in the corner of the cozy, low-lit café and set up my laptop while I looked over the menu, both the main dishes and desserts. I was treating myself tonight. Not like I hadn't been. Those couple of extra pounds hadn't gone anywhere.

I ordered the pork tenderloin with applesauce chutney. While I waited for my dinner to arrive, I connected to the wi-fi to catch up on the music and entertainment scene. One of my favorite bands of all-time, Imagine Dragons, was coming to Nashville, which was about an hour and a half from here. And the concert was on my birthday, no less. I had been trying to win tickets through their website. No luck. And the show was sold out and had been for months. It was still fun to dream and watch their concert footage online. But before I could get to that, I had a notice pop up that I had a message from Connie Harris on Facebook.

My fingers went to work at lightning speed to log in to my account. I had wondered if I would ever hear from her. I felt first date anxious to see how she had responded. I eagerly read the following note:

Presley,

I can't tell you how surprised I was to receive your note. I am indeed the former Connie Weatherly that once knew Victor Crandall. His name is a like a whisper from a time long ago. I will admit, it is sometimes a name that howls like the wind. And sometimes I wish I could forget he ever existed.

Ouch.

He is the one "what-if" in my life. And now you have presented me with a possible answer to my question. The problem is, it should have come from him. I assume that since he didn't have the courage to contact me himself, he is still the coward that let me go all those years ago. If that is the case, then no, I would not like to reconnect with him. If, however, he is willing to reach out to me of his own accord, then I would very much like to speak with him.

Sincerely,

Connie

I sat back for a moment and stared at the screen. I felt a little underlying anger throughout the message, but I could hardly blame her. I could commiserate with her. I was in the making of my own what-if scenario. As depressing as it was, I knew I would always wonder.

In the midst of contemplating if I should tell Mr. Crandall what I had done, I heard familiar voices, actually two voices I knew well. My head popped up to see the two Mr. Montgomery's talking to Geena, the owner. She and the younger Mr. Montgomery used to go to school together and I'm positive she had a crush on him. Too bad for her that I recognized the same look of disgust on the older Mr. Montgomery's face when she tried to cozy up to his son. I guess owning a café wasn't a good enough profession for him, either.

I situated my laptop the best I could and kept my head down so I wouldn't be seen. I thought he would have gone to the game; that's the only reason I chose our favorite place to eat tonight.

"I haven't seen you around here in forever," I heard Geena swoon.

"I've been busy," Jackson responded. I could hear in his tone he wasn't interested in a conversation with her.

"Son, let's order so we can leave." Yep, his dad was the boss. And his tone said stay away. I was familiar with it.

I tried to focus on my screen, but all the words were jumbled up. My senses were drawn to the man who was now looking at me. I felt it before I looked up and saw him grinning. I was caught. He whispered something to his dad, causing his dad to look my way. And the look he had given Geena had nothing on the glower he was giving me at the moment. Before it would have devastated me, but now I sat up straighter and glared right back. I would not be intimidated by him.

The staring contest gave the younger of the two men cause for concern. He looked between the two of us and sighed. His father's look only became more hardened the closer his son got to me. I wasn't backing down and kept my sights focused on senior. He finally gave in and walked to the counter to order.

I wish I could say it gave me some satisfaction, but it only hurt.

"Hey there," the younger Mr. Montgomery's smooth, sexy voice rang in the air.

"Hey."

He slid into the chair across from me.

"Are you following me now?"

He grinned and shook his head. "No, but that sounds like fun."

"This is a table for one."

"I always thought of this as our table."

"Why aren't you at the game?"

He rubbed the back of his neck. "My dad um, he had...he wanted some company tonight."

I raised my eyebrow and noticed Jackson's arm. He had a cotton ball and some medical tape placed in the fold of his arm, like he had given blood. "I hear you're spending a lot of time with him now."

He reached out to take my hand, but I pulled it back. He flexed his fingers like his dad does. "I didn't tell you I was moving in with him because I didn't want you to get the wrong impression."

"You don't owe me any explanations."

"Presley, can't we at least try again? Let me take you out tomorrow night."

His father interrupted us. I'll admit his glower had more bite up close and made me want to wither in my seat. "Jackson, our food is coming up."

I guess they got preferential treatment, since I was still waiting on mine. Jackson's shoulders dropped. "Think about it." He gave me a hopeful smile.

Our heads both turned to his father. He now looked like his head might explode. But I noticed he had lost some weight and he, too, had a cotton ball taped to the inside of his arm like his son. I guess the family that gives blood together stays together. The older Mr. Montgomery looked pale from donating.

I almost said I would go out with him, just to tick his dad off, but I was reminded that he was under the influence of his dad and that never worked out in my favor. I tucked some hair behind my ear and turned to focus back on my laptop. "I'm busy."

"That's too bad." I heard the resignation in his voice. "I would say I'll call you later, but I assume you still have me blocked."

I nodded.

"Jackson," his dad's voice had even more edge to it now.

I guess Jackson didn't care. He kissed the top of my head. "Good night. I can be patient."

Warmth encompassed me. That oxytocin was a killer, and so was Jackson. I watched him walk away with my heart.

Day Fifty-Four

♥

Saturday, September 18

"I'M THINKING OF DOING A silver and gold theme this year for Christmas." Miss Liliana perused a booth filled with sparkly ornaments.

It was too early for Christmas in my book, but Miss Liliana took her Christmas decorating seriously, and to her it was never too early.

"That would look lovely."

"I want this to be a memorable year." Her voice had a hint of emotion to it. Before I could ask about it, she took my hand. "You're out of sorts, darling."

I set down a snow globe I was considering for one of my nieces. "Who, me? I'm right as rain."

"Poppycock. Neither you nor Jackson have been right since his lunatic decision."

I shrugged. "I think we've both moved on fairly well."

"I admire your zeal, but you're not fooling anyone."

I gave her a little laugh. "I'm doing my best."

She patted my hand. "Give him hell, darling."

I tilted my head. "I'm surprised to hear you say that."

"After what he did to you, I would expect no less, but don't go so far that you can't come back."

I looked back at the table to find anything to be interested in.

"Presley?"

I had to look up and into her imploring eyes. I rubbed my lips together. "I can't go back to him after what he did."

She took my hand and, for an eighty-year-old woman, she had a lot of get up and go. She hauled me over to a private area. I felt like maybe I should stand in the corner, her look was so stern. "Darling, I understand that he hurt you and said some very unkind things, but it's not anything that you can't work out."

I sighed deeply. I was tired of defending myself. "How can I trust him with my heart again after he decided there were other things more important to him? And that's fine, I wasn't his wife so that was his choice to make. But I wanted to be his wife, and I can't be with a man who won't choose me over his career, or even his family. The funny thing is, I would have never asked. I would have tried to support him in both, but what he did was telling. And him moving in with his dad speaks to where his heart truly lies. And it isn't with me."

She adjusted her diamond tennis bracelet. "I'm disappointed in the role my son has played in this whole fiasco, but..." Her eyes misted.

I reached out for her arm. "Are you okay?"

She placed her hand over mine and composed herself. "Yes, darling. No need to worry your pretty head. There are circumstances that need to be taken into consideration. Don't be like my son and judge without looking into someone's heart."

"What circumstances?"

She squeezed my hand. "It is not my place to say. Well, I think it is, but for now, I have promised not to. Please don't ask me to break my word." She pointed at my heart. "Take a good look in here before you walk away for good." She gave me a wink. "In the meantime, don't go easy on him."

DAY FIFTY-SIX

Monday, September 20

SO MUCH FOR THAT RELAXING, no Mr. Montgomery weekend. I was thinking about him more now than ever. It was kind of ticking me off. I was just over a month to my goal and I kept getting sidelined by the defense. I was going to have to try harder, but I would be seeing more of him this week since he had lined up some visits for the cowboy path program, as he was calling it. He emailed me through the school's email system. That, I couldn't block him from.

I couldn't stop thinking about the mysterious conversation I'd had with Miss Liliana. What circumstances was she talking about? And why did I even care? Oh, yeah. It was a crazy little thing called love. But I could overcome that, right?

Then there was the Connie situation. Her message left an impression on me in more ways than one. I wagered she still carried some of the pain Mr. Crandall caused her. I wondered if she only wanted to talk to him so she could tell him off. Or did she still hold a place for him in her heart? Would she consider rekindling their old flame? And how was Mr. Crandall going to feel about me meddling in his life? Would he still be afraid and let the chance go?

How was I going to feel about Mr. Montgomery thirty-five years from now? Surely I would have met someone by then and we would be ridiculously happy with children and, who knows, maybe even a grandchild. Would sixty-two-year-old me still have a place in my heart for him? I couldn't let that happen.

I left for school early so I could talk to Mr. Crandall in private. I figured I should tell him sooner rather than later so I could quit thinking about it. I had more pressing matters, like how I was going to get over Mr. Montgomery in the next thirty-four days.

I found Mr. Crandall in his usual spot, pacing the stage under the spotlight. He rubbed his chin as he went.

I was almost to the stage before he opened his eyes and looked at me. "Have you returned for more advice?"

I laughed. "Not today. In fact, I have some for you."

"Curious." He reached out his hand to help me up the stage steps.

"Do you mind if we sit down?" I wasn't sure how he was going to take the news, so I thought being closer to the ground was a good option.

Without a word, he helped me sit on the hardwood floor before he joined me. "Are you enjoying your mornings free of car line duty?"

"I enjoy not being around the men in the car line."

He laughed deeply. "Yes, dear, you have caused quite the stir. But who can be blame these besotted fools?"

"Do you mean Mr. Montgomery and Brad?"

"Those are only the ones willing to try." He winked.

I leaned back and narrowed my eyes. "What have you heard?"

He patted my leg. "Not heard, but seen. You turn heads, my dear."

"Uh-huh."

"So modest. But I did see something else that may interest you."

"What's that?"

"In an attempt, I'm sure, to get over you, our Mr. Sutton and the librarian were using our prop room."

"What? No! Stella and Brad?" I couldn't wait to tell Capri.

He chuckled. "Oh, yes, they were quite embarrassed when I walked in on them."

I placed my hand over my heart. "I wonder if Mindy knows. I thought she and Stella were best friends."

He raised his eyebrows. "I think I will steer clear of the teacher's lounge and the library."

"Good thinking. He does get around. I can't believe I let him kiss me."

"That did more good than harm. I think it gave our vice principal a well-earned kick in the pants."

I wasn't touching that comment. "Well, I'm here to kick you this morning."

His eyes widened. "Is that so?"

"Yep. It's long overdue."

"Well, dear, my curiosity has been piqued."

I took his warm, soft hand. "Remember the last discussion we had right here?"

"Of course. I see that I'm right and Jackson has finally come to his senses. The question is, will you?"

My muscles tensed for a moment. "I'll address that at another time. I wasn't talking about Mr. Montgomery or me. I was talking about you and the lovely Connie."

I felt him go rigid.

"How would you feel about speaking with her again?"

He dropped my hand and stood up. He began to pace the stage again. His reaction surprised me.

I jumped up and followed him back and forth. "Mr. Crandall?"

He gazed toward me with his ashen face. "What's done is done."

"But it's not done. Not for her or you."

"And how would you know that?"

I bit my lip. "Maybe . . . I contacted her."

"Dear, why would you do such a thing?"

I stopped and stood my ground. "Because I love you and thought you both deserved a second chance, if it was available. I don't think you gave yourself or her enough credit back then. See, when a woman gives you her heart, all she wants to know is that you will cherish it and give her yours in return. We don't care about the size of your paycheck or your profession, only that you come home to us every night. You misjudged her."

He stood stunned for a moment. "Does she want to . . ."

"Talk to you? Yes. But only if you have the courage to contact her yourself. I think it's safe to say you kind of ticked her off."

He laughed for a second. "I'm sure I did. She was fiery, like you."

"You're going to have to join Facebook. It's the only way I know how to get a hold of her. She wasn't forthcoming with any other contact information. I think she wants you to work for it."

"That sounds like her."

"So, will you?"

He blew out a large breath. "You've certainly given me something to consider."

"Mr. Crandall." I narrowed my eyes at him. "I can't guarantee that it would be a happy reunion, for all I know, she only wants to scream at you. But she said you were her only what-if in life. If you cared about her at all, the least you can do is answer that question for her."

"I will let you know, dear." He walked away, muttering to himself.

I walked out of the auditorium and ran into Capri. She was bursting with excitement. I was pretty sure I knew why. She pulled me to the art room. "You will never believe what I just saw."

Maybe I didn't know.

"I should have recorded it."

"Tell me."

I wasn't ever sure I had seen her smile so big. "I just saw Mindy rip off Stella's necklace in the parking lot and then Stella slapped her."

"Nooo."

"Yes! Jackson and Coach had to break it up. And guess who it was over?"

"Brad." I grinned. "Mr. Crandall told me he caught Stella and Brad making out in the prop room. Now I'm going to have to disinfect it."

"This just gets better and better. I'm pretty sure Jackson was directing all three to Dr. Walters' office."

"That's embarrassing. I bet some kid filmed the whole thing. Watch your Facebook feed."

"We should write a book. You can't make this stuff up. We'll call it, Tales of a Man Whore. Or The Witch and the Evil Librarian and the Man Who Tore Them Apart."

"Those sound like bestsellers. At least I won't be the one people are talking about anymore."

"At least for the next few days, but I'm pretty sure everyone is tuned in to see if you will or won't. I even think Lonnie in the math department is calculating the odds on it."

"Please tell me you're lying."

"Sorry, sister."

"At least find out what the odds are of me rejecting his advances."

"I'm pretty sure they're slim. Everyone thinks he'll win you over."

"Little do they know, I'm almost two-thirds of the way over him."

She arched her eyebrow. "Is that so?"

I dropped my head. "No. But I'm almost over the extreme sadness stage, so I feel like I will gain a lot of traction in the final third part of the plan."

She hugged me fiercely. "I'm still rooting for you. Unless, that is, you change your mind."

I pulled away from her. "Not you, too."

"I'm just saying that I won't think less of you if you decide to get back together with him. I promised David I would tell you that."

"He's a traitor."

"Yes, but I love him. And he says Jackson's been pretty torn up about the situation. And according to David, he has so many balls up in the air, he can't focus on you the way he wants to."

I would hate to see my state if he had more time to "focus" on me. But that statement alone made me wary. I'm not a woman who needs or even wants constant attention, but I wasn't going to be someone's afterthought. "I'm sure his dad will make sure he doesn't have time for me, especially since he's living with him now."

She pursed her lips. "Something seems off about that. I asked David why, and all he would say was that Jackson hoped it was temporary. And here's an interesting tidbit that David learned by accidentally overhearing a phone conversation. It looks like Jackson's dad is taking an early retirement."

"That makes no sense at all. He is his job. Maybe the board got tired of him and ousted him."

Capri shrugged her shoulders. "I don't know, but maybe you can ask Jackson during your visits on Wednesday."

"Ha ha. No."

Students started filing in.

Capri gave me a wicked grin. "I can't wait until lunch. Maybe by then someone will know what the outcome is from the cat fight this morning."

"Something to look forward to."

"You know you want to know as much as me," she called out to my retreating figure.

She was right.

DAY FIFTY–EIGHT

Wednesday, September 22

DEAR MR. BINGLEY,

There is so much intrigue going on at the school right now. I don't know where to begin. I feel like my life is an angsty drama on the CW. First of all, Mr. Crandall has promised me that by this weekend he will have a Facebook profile up and running and will reach out to Connie. I'm holding him to it, even though he looked like he needed to sit down when he told me. It's kind of cute to see him so nervous. I guess I'm glad to know not only women get that way when it comes to affairs of the heart. This is the least dramatic thing going on right now.

I told you Monday about the cat fight in the parking lot over the resident would-be Greek god who, in my estimation, is a total loser. I have it on good authority that not only is he causing problems with the women at school, parents have called and complained about his teaching practices. Sounds like he's unprepared for class, goes off on unrelated tangents, and he gives the answers out to his tests before he gives them. So now he's on probation, but my source, aka Capri, says that's just a nice way to say don't plan on teaching here for much longer and this would be a good time to explore your options. I still can't believe his lips touched mine. We'll chalk it up to a minor breakdown, which I deserved after having my heart stomped on.

As for Mindy and Stella, they are both on unpaid leave, and if they ever hope to come back, they have to attend anger management courses and have a psych evaluation. So maybe I've taken a little more pleasure in that fact than I should have.

That leaves me with my own saga. Word on the street is the odds that I fall for Mr. Montgomery's advances and pleadings are twelve to one. I get that Mr. Montgomery has some pretty serious stats on his side: charming, handsome, kind, intelligent, successful... you get the picture. But I shouldn't be underestimated. I'm a lion, not a kitten; my roar is greater than my meow.

And like David said, he hasn't really put that much effort into winning me back, not that it would matter. But he does seem very preoccupied. I think it has something to do with his dad, but I'm not sure why I care. He does look a little stressed and his eyes have been tired the past couple of days. Yeah, I still notice. And yes, I want to ask him why. And yes, I have to spend an afternoon with him. And yes, I'm kind of dying over it.

Thirty-two more days.

I got this... I think,

Presley

I may have skipped lunch, I was so nervous about spending the afternoon with Mr. Montgomery. Which was sad because I had never felt more comfortable around anyone in my life, not even Capri—don't tell her. But now I wasn't sure how to be around him. Obviously, since it was on school hours and school related, I would act professionally, but it was hard to be so guarded around someone who knew everything about you. Someone I had been so vulnerable with. I guess that's how you're supposed to love, and why it hurts so much when it ends and even more, when it doesn't have to, but you feel like it should.

And I'm not going to lie and say I haven't entertained the thought. But like I said, his words said let's give us another try, but his actions said something completely different. Mr. Montgomery was not Jackson. I didn't know where Jackson went. Jackson walked out my door fifty-eight days ago.

I walked up to the front office, taking deep breaths as I went. It was one afternoon. I could do this. Roar, baby, roar! I stood up taller and walked with purpose to the click-clack of my heels against the tile floor. I was happy to report that my butt and floor didn't meet again. I stood outside the office and waited for Mr. Montgomery to appear. I felt like every staff member that walked by gave me that look that said they knew who I was meeting with and they were calculating the odds in their head. I wouldn't be surprised if there had been some money thrown down as a wager. I would teach them to bet against me.

Mr. Montgomery walked out looking handsome, albeit a little tired, and suddenly I felt like a kitten. I wanted to purr. No. No. I'm roaring.

"Presley." Dashing looks with a charming smile did not help the situation.

"Mr. Montgomery." That was me roaring.

He sighed. "You're not going to give up calling me that, are you?"

"No, sir."

He frowned. "Shall we go?"

I noticed his umbrella and then looked outside to see that it had started to rain. "Can you just tell me where we're going first and I'll meet you there. I want to get my umbrella."

He held up his umbrella. "I got us covered. It doesn't make sense to take two vehicles."

I internally debated about whether I should try to win this argument or just take off. That was my first mistake.

Dr. Walters came out. "Good, good. I'm looking forward to getting this program off the ground. I have my A players on the case." He pushed us both forward. What could I do at that point?

I noticed Mr. Montgomery smirked.

Fine.

We walked out the door and Mr. Montgomery immediately opened his umbrella and kept the rain off both of us. "This is cozy."

"Don't get used to it."

He chuckled. "I miss you."

I looked around. "Aren't we working? That wasn't very professional."

"I'll behave until four."

"I think we'll be back to school by then."

"You never know about these things. We could find ourselves at dinner, or if the weather clears up, our favorite spot in the park. I have a Tom Clancy novel in my glove compartment, just in case."

I moved as far away from him as I could without leaving the protection of the umbrella. "I think asking me out is outside of professional."

"I'm just giving you some possibilities to explore." He closed the gap between us.

"I don't know if you remember, but you gave me one already when you broke up with me." I picked up the pace to his car. So much for being professional.

He hurried alongside me. "I wish I could forget, that we both could. I've regretted it every day since."

"Like I said before, it was for the best." We had reached his truck and I reached for the passenger side door handle.

He placed his hand over mine.

A massive dose of oxytocin flooded my system. I felt his touch from the inside out. I jerked my hand away.

He positioned the umbrella so we couldn't be seen. He used his free hand to tilt my chin up. Our eyes met and it was as if I was looking into my own soul. That's how connected I still felt to him. Forget any hormone, it had nothing on the emotional connection that had existed between us. I thought I knew him on every level. "That's almost as big a lie as the one I told when I said you were a distraction."

Those words burned. I turned away from him. If not, I was going to fall for those soft brown eyes and the invitation on his lips, asking for mine to meet his.

"I'm sorry. I know that doesn't fix this."

"We're going to be late."

He backed away and opened my door for me, but not before breathing out a heavy sigh.

I climbed in and buckled my seatbelt, wishing to be almost anywhere but with him. He clouded my judgement. He made me feel things I didn't want to anymore.

I was glad when he got in and decided to get down to business, or so I thought. "The first person we're meeting with is Carla Rodan. She's a local author, but has had some national recognition. I mentioned to her that you had written some screenplays in college. She's looking forward to discussing those with you."

I looked out his window. "You didn't need to do that."

"Why? You should be proud of them. I know I am. I thought maybe you would have written the one act. I loved your idea about what if Marilyn Monroe had stayed Norma Jean."

I loved that idea, too. I was fascinated with her life. I had thought about finally putting my research and notes to good use, but I had been too wrapped up in him all summer. And I didn't want to overstep my bounds with Mr. Crandall. Then there was the whole fear factor of sharing your work. Mr. Montgomery was one of the few people I had ever let read my work. "Maybe someday."

"You should. You've got a real talent."

That was a matter of opinion. I had some professors that loved me and some that thought middle school kids could write better than me. Art in any form was so subjective. "Thanks."

We drove to downtown Huntsville where Ms. Rodan had an office. Though downtown Huntsville was small compared to large cities like Denver or Atlanta, it made up for it with its charm. Mr. Montgomery and I had spent our fair share of time exploring the cute shops and older homes. During Christmas, the downtown district homes opened for tours. Lovely doesn't even begin to describe how fantastic they were. Not only that, but there was a huge park called Big Spring where they deco-rated all the trees for Christmas. It was Southern charm at its finest and I was going to miss sharing it all with the man sitting in the driver's seat. He made the festive experiences better by holding my hand and telling me stories of the history of the place he grew up in. From harrowing tales of jail breaks to the scientific breakthroughs that were discovered right here. He made the city come alive to me.

I looked through the window out into the water soaked landscape and wiped the moisture out of my eyes before my emotions were exposed.

Mr. Montgomery pulled into a metered space outside of Ms. Rodan's office. "Sit tight. I'll pay the meter and then come around and get you."

"You don't have to open my door."

"But I want to, and I know you don't want to get wet." He gave me a sexy know-it-all grin.

"Fine." He played to my vanity and won. Good hair days were hard to come by here with the humidity. The rain only made it worse.

He paid the meter and hustled over to my door with his umbrella out. He opened my door and his eyes fell to my bare heeled legs.

"Definitely unprofessional."

He chuckled. "I'm just admiring your shoes."

"Right." I stepped out onto the pavement, flattered that he still liked my legs.

He reached for my hand.

"What are you doing?"

He dropped my hand. "Sorry. Habit."

I didn't say anything more because I totally understood it. I'd had the urge to fall back into old patterns when I was around him. Like holding his hand when he was driving or kicking my legs up on his dash so he could admire them. Or flatten the cowlick that always stuck up in the back of his hair.

We dashed to the cover of the awning in front of the office building. Mr. Montgomery promptly opened the door for me. I walked in while he shook out his umbrella before joining me in the small entrance area that smelled like mint. We both looked at each other wondering where the pleasant smell came from. The closer we got to Ms. Rodan's suite, the stronger the smell became. We opened the door to suite 104 and walked in to find an eccentrically dressed woman in a Mumu with lots of bangles draping her arms. Her red hair was curly and big. I would say she was in her fifties and had seen some sun in her day.

"Right on time." Ms. Rodan clapped her hands and her bangles and bracelets chimed.

Mr. Montgomery held out his hand. "It's a pleasure to meet you. I'm Jackson Montgomery and this is Presley Benson."

She didn't take his hand, but she smiled between the two of us. "Intriguing."

Mr. Montgomery and I both looked at each other with raised eyebrows. I had a feeling this was going to be more interesting than I thought.

"Well, sit down, sit down. I made tea." She dispensed with any usual pleasantries. I guess she figured we knew her name. She pointed to a small couch and chair. There sat a tea pot with cups on a coffee table. The mint smell now made sense.

She took the chair, which forced me to sit next to Mr. Montgomery. He grinned as he waited for me to be seated first, like the gentleman he was. He needed to get over that, at least for the next month. I was still roaring.

Once we were situated, she served us tea and cookies. It wasn't a bad way to spend an afternoon away from school. Except for the whole being next to your ex-boyfriend whom you were still in love with thing.

Jackson started us off. "The reason we asked to meet with you was to—"

"I know why. You stated that clearly on the phone," she cut him off. "And I'm happy to come and share my knowledge with your students. Name the time and date."

I looked around her walls, which were filled with accolades from the *New York Times* bestseller list to local awards. I was impressed.

She eyed me in a discerning manner. "I want to know more about you."

I tucked my hair behind my ear. "Me?"

"There is something about you. Like a character from a book come to life. Tell me about yourself."

I set my tea down, perplexed by her interest in me. "There's not much to tell. I teach beginning and intermediate drama."

She pointed to Mr. Montgomery. "He already told me that. The question is, why did they choose you for this project?"

I wasn't sure why that mattered to her. I shrugged my shoulders and looked at Mr. Montgomery to reply.

"I know the answer he'll give. I have no doubt you're capable and insightful. But I don't think assignments like these are usually given to the drama department, if I'm correct."

"I suppose not. But Mr. Montgomery and I worked together with the community before he became vice principal, so I assume—"

"Never assume anything." She was obviously pushy. "Like, I don't assume that you've always called your vice principal here Mr. Montgomery. It sounds stilted coming out of your mouth. Something you're uncomfortable saying."

"Uh...Well." I reached for my tea again and took a sip. I hadn't bargained for this.

She gazed at me. I swore she was reading me like an open book. "So, tell me, why the formality?" She whipped her head to leer at Mr. Montgomery. "Please tell me in this day in age she's not required to call you that at school."

He cleared his throat. "Of course not. I prefer Jackson."

She turned back toward me. "Don't worry, I note the underlying sexual tension you two have going on. I write about this stuff all the time.

You two have all the classic signs. Except I can tell you're torn about it, Presley. Which only adds to the deliciousness of the story."

I choked on my tea.

Mr. Montgomery patted my back. "Are you okay?"

No, I wasn't okay. Who did this lady think she was?

She handed me a napkin. "I'm making you uncomfortable." It wasn't a question. She knew she was, and dare I say she was doing it on purpose.

I took the napkin and dabbed the spot of tea on my blouse I had spluttered out. "Should we email you the times we have available?" I set my tea down. I was ready to move on.

She grinned. "I like your spunk. Jackson, why don't you move on to your next appointment and I'll keep Presley here with me."

Oh, no, no.

"This is a team effort." He was trying to save me. Praise heaven.

"Oh, I'm not going to bite. I promise you, she'll be in good hands. I think she may even enjoy it, so go on now." She shooed him.

Mr. Montgomery and I turned to each other. His eyes said he would do whatever I wanted him to. Before I could answer, he reached into my bag and took my cell phone out. "I'm putting my *new* number in."

I knew he didn't have a new number, but I knew what he was doing. If I stayed, he wanted to be able to check on me.

Carla was no dummy. "Look at that. He knows the password to your phone. I take it you blocked him." She stood up. "I'll see you out, Jackson."

I swallowed hard, not sure I should stay. I was afraid this might be a Hansel and Gretel scenario and I was going to be her dinner.

"Come, come. Your precious Presley is safe with me. We're going to have some girl time."

He handed my phone back to me. "I'll be back in an hour." It was a warning to our odd hostess.

I nodded.

"It's like a scene out of a book. You two are fantastic. Now off with you."

Mr. Montgomery reluctantly left my side and I fought off begging him to stay, or just following after him. I would have, except I was curious and I figured if this chick was completely off her rocker like I was guessing she was, then we should know that before we let her near our students. And I had noticed that Mr. Montgomery made sure I had my pepper spray in my bag. So he was a decent human being who worried about me.

Mr. Montgomery narrowed his eyes at Carla and made slow deliberate steps toward the door.

The Cheshire cat grin she directed toward him was somewhere between amusing and frightening.

Mr. Montgomery gave me one more glance before the door was shut on him.

"Now that he's gone, we can finally have some fun." She sashayed over to me and sat down next to me. She tossed her hair back. "Sorry about all the theatrics. I don't get a lot of visitors, and I just couldn't help myself. You two are too cute for words. His adoration and your rebuffs make this author's heart sing. Tell me how long ago you two broke up."

I arched my eyebrow at her.

She took my hands. "Oh, come on now. We're all friends here. And you aren't fooling anyone."

I took a deep breath. "Fifty-eight days ago."

She cringed. "It's bad when you know down to the day."

I laughed. "Yeah."

She squeezed my hands. "Let's not talk about him yet. Tell me about these screen plays you've written and your fascination with Marilyn Monroe."

I leaned away, surprised.

"He likes to talk about you."

"She's fantastic and the kids are going to love her," I gushed to Mr. Montgomery on our way back to the school.

"I'm just glad I didn't have to avenge your death."

I laughed. "She's definitely different, but she's lived an amazing life. When she lived in Canada she met her husband, who's from Iran, and then they moved to Kenya where he worked for the UN. Her mysteries are based on her time there. She gave me some of them to read and I can't wait. And after telling her my ideas for my Marilyn play, she was so intrigued she agreed to read it. And if she loves it, she'll pass it along to her agent."

He grinned at me. "Wow. I haven't seen you this happy since Baskin Robbins brought back pink bubble gum ice cream for the summer."

I rolled my eyes. "This is better than ice cream. I'm going to go home and get my outline out and polish it before I start writing."

He reached over and rested his hand on my thigh. "Will you let me read it?"

"Mr. Montgomery…"

"It's past four. Please call me Jackson."

I pushed his hand away. "I can't."

He stopped at a stop light and turned my way. "Whether or not you take me back, don't you miss our friendship? I miss talking to you the way we just were. Hell, I've picked up the phone to call you a million times. Can't we at least start with that?"

I thought for a moment. I realized how light I felt sharing my thoughts and day with him.

"Let's go to dinner. I promise I'll keep my hands to myself. I just want to talk to you."

I wanted that more than anything, but…

His phone rang. "Hold that thought." He answered his phone.

He knew I was possibly going to say yes. I had a major internal debate going on. My brain was saying to roar, but my heart was purring like a kitten. Going to dinner with him went against the number one rule in the plan. The rule I could never keep under the circumstances, but I had tried distancing myself. But the inner dialogue was for nothing.

"I'll be right there. I need to drop Presley off at the school first. Don't start in on her."

I didn't have to ask who it was. His dad was a good reminder to listen to my brain.

Mr. Montgomery threw his phone down in his console. "Can I get a rain check?"

"No." I watched the cars speed by. I looked at anything but him.

"If only you understood."

I whipped my head toward him. "You're right. I don't understand. So tell me why. Please."

He reached out to touch me, but pulled back and flexed his fingers. "I can't right now."

That's what I thought. Thirty-two more days to go.

DAY SIXTY

♥

Friday, September 24

HALLELUJAH, IT WAS FRIDAY AND tomorrow was my birthday. My mom and dad had already sent me their gift and I couldn't wait to use it. They got me a spa package. I wasn't supposed to mention it to my sisters, but I was thinking about it, since the brats sent me a whole box full of stuffed animal cats. They called it the "spinster litter." They redeemed themselves with the layer of chocolates and chick-flicks beneath the furry creatures. Not to say I wouldn't be cuddling up to them on the couch. Who else did I have?

I got to school to find that several of my students had decorated my door with birthday cards. I loved my job. I peeked inside the sweet notes, but left them up so I could admire them all day. Even though it wasn't technically my birthday, it sure felt like it.

I walked toward my desk to put my satchel up and there I found a single pink rose lying on top of a sealed silver envelope. I knew instantly who it was from. Jackson, I mean Mr. Montgomery, believed one rose was more romantic than a full bouquet. I had to agree. There was something sexy about a man handing you a single flower, like he picked that one especially for you.

I was torn on what to do. Open the card? Throw the card and the rose in the trash? I couldn't do it. I sat at my desk and picked the rose up and smelled it. I loved that fragrance. I set it down to open the envelope. My hands were shaking. I pulled out the beautifully scripted card that wished me a happy birthday. I opened it and out fell a piece of paper. An expensive piece of paper—a ticket to my favorite band ever. I felt like Charlie from *Charlie and the Chocolate Factory* when he opened his chocolate bar and revealed the golden ticket. Except, I couldn't accept the ticket—in the pit no less. It was worth at least two-hundred dollars. What was he playing at? You don't buy your ex an expensive gift like that. You don't buy them gifts at all.

His message made it worse.

Presley,

Happy birthday, beautiful. May all your wishes come true. I know you made all mine. I love you.

Jackson

My eyes welled up with tears. I placed the ticket back into the card. I couldn't accept such an extravagant gift. I hated him even more for breaking up with me in the first place. Just when I thought I was over that extreme sadness phase it smacked me in the face again.

I picked up the card and decidedly walked myself upstairs. I mean, what was he thinking anyway? You don't go to concerts by yourself and you don't spend money on your exes like that. I didn't even like him to spend that kind of money on me when we were together. Though it would have been fantastic if we were still a couple and could have gone together. But I couldn't think like that.

I walked out the front school doors to the car line. He was still hanging out there every morning, according to Coach. I think he wanted to keep an eye on Brad, who was now trying to keep a low profile and wouldn't make eye contact with me. I wasn't complaining.

Both Coach and Mr. Montgomery grinned at me like they knew they would be seeing me.

I stopped a few feet from the men. "Can I speak to you?"

"Anytime." Mr. Montgomery joined me.

"Happy birthday," Coach yelled.

I smiled at him before facing Jackson and pressing my lips together. He was looking too sweet and handsome to lambast. I handed him the card. "Thank you, but I can't accept this."

He didn't even flinch. He knew I wasn't going to take it. But he wasn't taking it back either. "If you don't go, it will be a waste."

"You can go."

"You know I was never a big fan."

"Well, regardless. I can't accept."

"Why do you have to be so stubborn?"

I noticed how tired his eyes were again. It made me pause for a second before I answered. "Why would you buy me something like this when we aren't together?"

He lowered his voice and stepped closer. "I wish we *were* together. But I bought that ticket for you several months ago when they announced their tour dates. I was planning on surprising you. Surprise."

I breathed out heavily. "That was sweet, but you only bought one?"

"Do you know how expensive those tickets are?"

"Which is another reason I can't accept."

"Please go. I know you want to."

My stupid grin came out.

He smiled wide. "Go enjoy yourself. I want you to have a terrific birthday."

"Fine. But I'm going to pay you for the ticket."

"Not a chance."

I ran my fingers through my hair. "I don't feel good about this."

"You will once you get there." He pushed the card back toward me. "Have a happy birthday. I need to get back to the car line." He gave my hand a little squeeze and walked away.

His touch and gift had me feeling all sorts of things I shouldn't. I walked back into the school and headed to Capri's classroom. Maybe she could talk me out of going. I shouldn't go, but I really, really wanted to.

"There's the almost birthday girl, looking sexy in her Auburn t-shirt."

Yeah, I was still wearing that shirt to bug the guy who bought me the nicest birthday gift ever. "Thank you. I have a problem." I handed her the card.

She wiped some charcoal off her hands before she took the envelope. Her eyes popped out when she read the card and beheld the ticket. "Wow. He wants you bad."

I swiped them out of her hand. "He said he bought the ticket before we broke up."

"Only the one?"

"Yeah. I tried to give it back."

"Are you crazy? I'm so jealous right now. You have to go."

"By myself? I've never gone to a concert alone."

"You can't pass this up. You're on the floor. Do you know how freaking amazing that's going to be? You could get some of the band's sweat on you."

I rolled my eyes. "When you put it like that, of course I should go."

She smacked my arm. "What reason is there not to?"

"I don't know? Maybe that my ex bought the ticket for me and accepting it kind of sends the wrong message."

"I think you've made it clear you don't want him back." She narrowed her eyes at me. "Or do you?"

I looked down at my cute Keds. "I would be lying if I said I hadn't thought about it, but I'm still on the ninety-day plan. It just sucks that he can be so dang nice!"

She pulled me in for a hug. "I know. Heck, even I like him. But it was whorish what he did to you."

"Is that a word?" I laughed through my tears.

"If it isn't, it should be." She squeezed me tighter. "Go. Maybe you'll even meet some fabulous guy there."

"No rebounds. I learned my lesson. And how can I even think about dating anyone else when I'm having such a hard time getting over Mr. Montgomery."

She released me and grinned. "I can't believe you're still calling him that."

"I do it mostly for fun now."

"And you think I'm the evil one? Honey, it's your birthday, enjoy it. And on Sunday, I'll have David make you a cake since I want it to be edible."

"I love you."

"I know. Now go forward and use your ex-boyfriend for all he's worth." She pointed toward the door and laughed.

What could go wrong with that, right?

DAY SIXTY-ONE

Saturday, September 25

DEAR MR. BINGLEY,

Wish me happy birthday. You've been with me longer than any boyfriend. I still don't like you, but I bet, like Mr. Montgomery, you would have given Jane a concert ticket for her favorite band. I suppose it would have been for a Regency musicale or a parlor band, or perhaps the opera. Either way, I'm sure she would have been delighted.

But it would have probably confused her like it's confusing me. I've hit the twenties and I feel nowhere near over him. You know I've tried. And I'm admitting this to no one except you, but I'm worried I won't be able to. Yes, I've roared and avoided him as much as I could. I've mostly stuck with the plan. You know I couldn't follow the most important and number one rule. I had to stay here. And it's not my fault that he decided he wanted me back and that he has free reign of the school and can basically be where I am, except the bathroom.

What am I to do? He has me feeling like a kitten, and no matter that I call him Mr. Montgomery, he has lots of Jackson moments, and I have to stop myself from dragging him into the prop room and reliving our glory days. I *physically ache for him. I give myself huge kudos for being able to resist him. So maybe that's key, if I keep holding out, it will eventually get easier.*

At least I don't have to worry about him tonight. I do feel weird going to a concert by myself. But I'm also excited to see my favorite band.

So wish me luck and safe travels and probably lots of caffeine so I don't die on my way home late tonight.

The birthday girl,

Presley

I rocked a kicking outfit with sky high leather boots that my feet would regret later, and a mini-skirt that said I was still in shape despite my chocolate-heavy diet. And my hair was on point in a sexy messy bun.

After my twenty birthday calls from family and friends, I made my way up north for the concert of a lifetime. At least, that's what I was counting on. I blasted Imagine Dragons on my ninety-plus minute drive while downing Pepsi. I was starting the caffeine early. The concert didn't start until eight and it was going to be at least three hours, which meant with parking and the traffic, I didn't expect to get out of Nashville until close to midnight. Then I had the long drive back to look forward to. And I've always been more of a morning person than a night owl. Ask Mr. Montgomery. I can't count how many times I fell asleep on our dates, either on his or my couch or at late movies in the theater. I once even fell asleep during the symphony. His dad's company was a big corporate sponsor, so we went several times.

Speaking of his dad's company, I wondered how his dad was feeling about being booted out. I wasn't buying the whole early retirement thing. He was the kind of guy that wouldn't leave until you dragged out his cold, dead body. I spent way too much time on the drive thinking about things I shouldn't be. It wasn't helpful on my road to recovery.

I sang at the top of my lungs and danced in my seat all the way up. It was a party for one and a warm up to the main event. I was wishing it was a party of two. Single was fun, and I could do it, but being a couple was better. Sharing these kinds of moments with someone always enhanced the experience. And not just any someone. *The* someone.

I cranked up the music louder and tried to forget about him.

Downtown Nashville was alive with traffic and pedestrians. It took me a while to find a parking lot that didn't require my life savings and a pint of blood. I had a feeling I might be walking back to my car in my socks. The things we do for fashion.

I got through security and had my ticket scanned before I made my way into the enormous arena. There was already a large crowd on the floor. Being in the pit meant standing room only. It was a mix of old and young. I hoped later in life I would still pretend to be cool and make my kids go to concerts with me. I noticed a few embarrassed teenagers trying to distance themselves from their parents. Life goals.

I felt strange being alone. I was probably the only person there not with someone. That was okay. I was embracing singledom. Sort of.

I felt my phone buzz in the small purse I had strapped across my body. I plucked it out of the bag and was surprised to see who was calling me. I had forgotten to block him again. I stared at the phone and debated long enough that he hung up. But he called right back. I answered. "You're lucky I didn't block you yet."

He laughed. "Well, happy birthday to you."

"Thanks."

"Where are you?"

"Um, where do you think?"

"I know you're at the concert, but where are you standing?"

"Why?" I had to practically yell and plug my other ear just so I could hear him. The crowd and noise were growing rapidly.

"I'm here."

I fumbled the phone and barely saved it from hitting the concrete floor. Surely I'd heard him wrong. "Stop joking around. Why are you really calling?"

"Boo."

I jumped and turned around, and this time he caught my phone. He grinned up at me while slightly bent over with my phone in his hand. I was stunned. Like someone had tased me.

He stood up and handed me my phone. "Happy birthday, Presley."

I couldn't breathe. This wasn't in the plan. But there he was, in a tight t-shirt with my favorite pair of jeans on, wearing a smile that melted my heart. I was supposed to be roaring, not drooling. "You...you...said you only bought one ticket."

His smile took a mischievous turn. "I never said that."

"Yes, you did."

"No. I said, 'do you know how expensive the tickets were?'"

This was not happening. "You tricked me."

He stepped closer. His smell was intoxicating. I had to tell my hands to stay down. "I wanted to be with you on your birthday."

I backed away. I was going to maul him. I shook my head.

He took my hand and held it up to his heart. "I've been planning this night since the spring. It's not exactly how I imagined, but here I am."

Words weren't forming as I stared into his sincere brown eyes. In dramatic fashion, the lights lowered and intro music began to play for the opening act. I pulled my hand away and turned away from him. I couldn't think. The lion and kitten inside of me were in a major battle. Kittens are stronger than you think, is all I'm going to say.

Mr. Montgomery stood next to me. We were hovering near the outside of the main crowd. "You're upset."

"You're a genius." I didn't bother looking at him.

"You're anger only adds to how incredibly sexy you look tonight."

"You lied to me."

He had to lean in so I could hear him. Not good. Oxytocin struck again. "The only lie I've ever told you was that I thought we should break up. You don't know how sorry I am for that. But let's forget about that tonight and celebrate your birthday. I don't expect anything from you. I only want to be with you on my favorite day. The day the world gave us you."

I nudged him. He was making it hard for me to be mad at him or remember why I was trying so hard to get over him. "You know how cheesy that sounds, right?"

"I've been practicing it all day. Maybe it was in my delivery. Let me turn on my Barry White voice and try again." He cleared his throat, ready to turn on the charm.

"Please don't." I laughed.

"Come on, baby, you know you love it." He dug down deep to get that Barry White sound.

"You're ridiculous." He had me smiling from ear to ear.

He peered into my eyes. "That may be, but I love you."

I had to sever the connection. It was too much. He was too much. I faced forward and tried to focus on the opening act I hadn't heard of play. I had to take lots of deep breaths and hold my own hands.

He leaned in closer and whispered in my ear. "You don't have to say it back right now, but I know you still love me." He kissed my bare shoulder.

Fire, fire. I was burning in an unbearable hell. I gave him a little push with my hip.

He chuckled.

I did my best to ignore him. I tuned into my inner rocker chick. I jumped up and down and tried to sing along to songs I didn't know. It's what I would have done even if the man I loved hadn't showed up. The man who watched me all night instead of the concert. He was the man who wouldn't let me ignore him.

Imagine Dragons finally took the stage and I thought the night couldn't get any better. They played several of their hits and some of their new material. But then...oh, then they sang my favorite song, "Every Night." The song that I felt was our anthem. I was sure they wouldn't perform it. It wasn't a song that was ever played on the radio, but it was one of those songs that spoke to me. That put into words all the emotion I felt for the man who took me in his arms.

"Our song," he whispered in my ear. When I didn't pull away like I probably should have, he drew me closer. His hand glided up and down my back as we swayed to the music like we were the only ones in the crowd.

I felt like I had been watered after a drought. I clung to him like a hurt child would to his mother. Tears spilled over onto his shoulder where my head rested. For those few minutes, I belonged to him. We were us. It was the best birthday present I could ask for. I didn't care that I was crying in front of thousands of people, most were probably too intoxicated to notice anyway. It didn't matter that everything I had done up to that point to get over him was all for nothing, because I had to face the reality that I was nowhere near over him. All that mattered was that all distance had been erased and I felt like me.

He ran his hand up my neck and through my hair. "Let's get out of here. I want to be alone with you."

Yes, yes, my heart sang. But my brain and inner lion kicked in. I stepped away from him and met his hopeful eyes. The same eyes that had told me he was telling the truth when he said he needed to quit messing around. "I need some air." I weaved in and out of the tight knit crowd, wiping my eyes as I went, looking for an exit.

Mr. Montgomery followed after me. "Presley, wait up."

Who was I kidding, he's Jackson. Calling him Mr. Montgomery had done no good. I still loved him. I walked out as fast as my sore feet would allow me to. I had known I would regret the high-heeled boots, but I had more pressing matters to worry about right now. Jackson followed me outside into the cool September night. An eerie fog had settled in. It matched my foggy feelings. I wrapped my arms around myself for comfort and warmth.

Jackson put his arm around me. "Presley?"

I pulled away from him. "Please don't touch me right now." I kept on walking.

"Does that mean I can touch you in the future?"

"I don't know. I just don't know. You treated me like an option. And I didn't even realize I was one."

"I wish I could undo that night. There is no other choice but you."

"How can I ever trust you again? Do you even know what you did to me that night? And the days since?"

"Walking away from you was the hardest thing I've ever had to do."

I threw him a vile look. "You acted as if it was nothing."

His eyes plead for understanding. "I had to, or I wouldn't have been able to do it. I didn't think I had a choice. I was being pulled in so many directions. I still am."

"That makes me feel so much better. So, what happens the next time you feel like you have to? The next time you're promoted or your dad tells you I have to go?"

"I would tell them all to go to hell, because that's what these last couple of months without you have been for me. I love you. I want to spend the rest of my life with you. And whether you want me to or not, I'm not willing to give up on us."

I felt the blood rushing through my head as my aching feet pounded the Nashville pavement on the way to my car. I needed to think, but I was having a hard time at the moment. My ninety-day plan was imploding before my eyes, before Jackson. In an act of self-preservation, I removed my boots when we arrived at my car. My feet said, "ahhh" when they hit the cool pavement.

Jackson chuckled at me. "I guess I better be the one to drive us home."

I arched my eyebrow. "I've got it thanks. You can drive your truck home."

He licked his lips and stepped closer. He ran is finger down my cheek. "Now, what kind of gentleman would I be if I made you drive home so late on your birthday?"

I let out a heavy sigh after I got over the shiver of his touch. "You didn't drive up here."

He wagged his eyebrows. "Coach dropped me off."

"That's a long drive for him."

"He said it was worth it if it got us back together."

I shook my head. "I don't know if I can...or if I should."

He leaned down and pressed his lips to my forehead. "I'm not going anywhere, so take all the time you need."

Time was definitely not on my side. Twenty-nine days. Meow.

Day Sixty-Two

♥

Sunday, September 26

I can't believe he showed up at the concert." Capri stroked my hair on her couch.

I was in a sugar coma with my head in her lap, staring at the remnants of the chocolate fudge layer cake we had devoured. David had some mad baking skills. His disappearing skills were even better. All I had to do was say "coital," and in a flash he was gone. "I'm still trying to process the night."

"He seems pretty determined."

"It appears that way."

"What's holding you back?"

I curled more into myself. "Besides the obvious, the pain he inflicted when he broke up with me and the trust issues, he lives with his dad. When we pulled up to his mini mansion last night, it really hit me that's where he lives. And we all know how his dad feels about me."

"Did you tell Jackson that bothers you?"

"I didn't have to. I think my stiff posture and look of disgust said it all when we pulled up his drive."

"Did he say anything?"

"He said, 'I'm my own man. And am doing what any good man would do.' He wouldn't say anything more. But oddly, his brother's car was there, too. I asked him about it, but he shrugged it off. I hope Daniel and Miranda aren't having marriage troubles. I doubt they were all there. He isn't the warmest of grandfathers, unless you've just won an award or something."

"So what are you going to do?"

"Rehab?"

She laughed.

"I'm serious. You guys could do a Jackson intervention for me."

She kept stroking my hair. "If I thought it would work, I would. Maybe you should give him another chance."

I bolted up and ran my fingers through my messy hair. "You started me on the ninety-day plan. You're supposed to be my voice of reason."

"It's clearly not working. You're in love with him as much as you ever were. And I think he is, too." She reached for her phone near the polished off cake. She pulled up a picture and caption on Jackson's Facebook page and held it up so I could see it.

Tears welled up in my eyes as I stared at a picture he had taken, unbeknownst to me, at the concert. There I was, in all my rocker chick glory, dancing like no one was watching. His caption read, *There are many women in the world, but no one like her. She is as beautiful inside as she is on the outside. Happy birthday, PB. Thanks for sharing yourself with me. I love you.* I leaned back against the couch and curled up like a child. "Why does he have to be so sweet? It's really ticking me off." I wiped my eyes.

She leaned back, too, and smiled. "To love isn't a sign of weakness."

"This isn't the time for you to be smart."

"I'm going to be here for you, no matter what you decide. And if Jackson is your choice, I'll support that. If you want to roll his dad's house, I'm here for that, too."

I grinned. "Thanks for being my girl."

"Forever."

Dear Mr. Bingley,

Jackson has taken a play from your book. You gentleman of fortune are the worst, and kind of the best. I'm still no Jane. I'm not ready to accept his proposal quite yet. No, he hasn't proposed marriage, just being together for the rest of our lives. But, is he his own man? Were you? I mean, Darcy persuaded you on both accounts, first to leave and then to follow your heart. What kind of sway does Jackson's father have? I know he isn't rooting for a reconciliation. If anything, I'm sure he's doing his best to make sure that doesn't happen. Your story ended before we knew if your sisters sabotaged your marriage or if you grew indifferent.

How can I know that what he's saying now is true when I thought what we had before was unbreakable?

What is real?

Presley

Day Sixty-Three

♥

Monday, September 27

THE FINAL WEEK OF FIRST quarter. It felt like the longest nine weeks of my life. At least next week was fall break. I needed a break from life. I was so confused, I didn't know whether to be the lion or the kitten, although the lion in me seemed to be cozying up to the kitten. The kitten was cute.

This was going to be a crazy week, too. It was homecoming and I had to get grades turned in for report cards. Yay me. Administration also encouraged the teachers to dress up for spirit week along with the kids. First up was patriotic day. Easy enough. I threw on my "Born in the USA" t-shirt with some great fitting jeans. What did Jackson say over the summer when he picked me up and I was wearing that shirt? God Bless America? I gave up trying not to think about him. I smiled at the memory of the long kiss. I missed his lips.

I had a surprise visit from Mr. Crandall first thing Monday morning. I had forgotten his promise since I was so preoccupied with my own problem.

"You aren't walking the stage this morning?" I looked up from my online gradebook.

He walked in, ashen faced.

"Are you okay?" I began to stand up.

He motioned for me to sit back down. "I'm fine, dear. I did as promised, but I haven't heard back from Connie." The emotion he felt for her was clear when he said her name.

I sat up, eager to get the skinny. "When did you send the message and what did you say?"

He took a seat in front of my desk and wiped a drop of sweat off his brow. "Late last night. I wrote twenty versions of my letter to her."

I grinned. "That's sweet."

"I'm not sure she will think so after all these years. I don't grovel well."

"I bet it was poetic."

"You give me too much credit, dear. It was basically me rambling on about my insecurities from many decades ago."

"Again, I'm sure it was great. I wouldn't worry that she hasn't contacted you yet. It took her weeks to get back to me and it's a lot for her to take in. I know it would be for me."

A light came on in his eyes. "Ah, yes. I befriended our vice principal on Facebook and saw his birthday tribute to you. You looked stunning, by the way."

I waved him off. "Thank you. Everyone looks good in flashing lights."

He laughed. "Tell me how you're feeling about our new administrator."

I leaned on my hand and sighed. "Tired. I'm not sure what I should do."

He stood up. "I have no doubt you'll figure it out. In the meantime, I asked him to help with the drama department homecoming float for the parade this week."

I shook my head at him. "Of course you did. I'm onto you, you know."

He chuckled his way out of my room.

As soon as he left, the man causing all the angst in my life popped his head in. "Hey."

I smiled up at him. He was dressed normally, in a suit and tie.

"I just wanted to let you know that I have meetings at central office today, so we can't have lunch together."

"I didn't remember that we were."

He grinned and walked toward my desk. "You should probably pencil me in for the rest of the week."

"I never said we were getting back together."

"But you never said we weren't."

"I could fix that."

A sly grin grew on his handsome face. "You could, but I know you still love me."

I rolled my eyes. "Have a good day, Mr. Montgomery."

"You too, Ms. Benson. I'll see you after school. I'll be the hot guy in the tool belt."

I tried and failed at not smiling at him.

"I love your smile. I'll see you later." He strutted out my door.

I felt like menopause had struck by the time he walked out my door. I conceded. Ninety days was not enough. I'm not sure a lifetime was. I was grateful my students started filing in. I took some deep breaths and did my job.

The end of the school day rolled around way too fast. I knew the more I interacted with him, the quicker I would have to make a decision. And I knew the effect he had on me. I had spent the last year of my life loving this man.

I met my students in the parking lot where a parent was kind enough to lend us a flatbed trailer. There were a dozen other groups out there doing the same thing. Mr. Crandall was there with his nephew, Kaine, which shocked the heck out of me.

Mr. Crandall pulled me aside. "I should have warned you. It appears Kaine's fiancée has had third thoughts. And his previous employer wasn't keen on re-hiring him. I felt sorry for the poor louse and let him use my guest bedroom again. I warned him to stay away from you."

By his reddened face and ducking behind some plywood, I didn't think that was going to be an issue. It was weird how unattractive he had become in my eyes. "He doesn't bother me. Thanks to you, I have someone else to worry about."

He gave me a little wink. "I'm just returning the favor."

I gave him an impish grin before walking away to work on the lettering. The students decided to go with a "Hollywood" theme, so I was helping to replicate the famous Hollywood sign above Los Angeles.

My helpers left, though, when Jackson showed up with pizza. He was a show off. I ignored him and kept drawing out the letters to be cut out. But he wasn't going to let me get away with that. He sat right next to me on the tarp, looking sexy in his work clothes. What was it about a man dressed to do manual labor? He came bearing my favorite pizza, barbecue chicken. He opened the box once he was settled in nice and close. His grin said how pleased he was with himself.

"I can't be bribed with pizza."

He took out a slice and teased me with it. Inching it toward my mouth with a come-kiss-me grin.

"There are students watching."

"It's after school and we're in love."

"You know love doesn't solve everything."

The pizza dropped along with his smile. "You're right, but in this case love will prevail." He shoved the pizza in my mouth.

I was caught off guard and I'm sure I looked like an idiot trying to bite off such a large piece. But it was like heaven in my mouth. I brought my hand up and tried to get the bite down without opening my mouth.

Jackson got a good laugh out of it.

I swallowed and swiped the piece of pizza from him.

He kissed the side of my head before getting up. "I'll be right back with a bottle of water for you."

"It's going to take a lot more than food and water to win me over," I called out after him.

"Believe me, I know."

I looked up to see a group of girls giggling and blushing. They all gathered around me once Jackson was nowhere to be seen. "OMG, you guys are so cute," they rang in chorus.

"I want a boyfriend like him."

I wanted to tell her she didn't, but actually, she did. Every girl needed a Jackson in her life. They all needed to see how a girl should be properly treated, again, minus the whole break-up incident.

I smiled at them and devoured my pizza. Sixty-three days and look where I was at.

DAY SIXTY-FOUR

Tuesday, September 28

I WAS WOKEN UP BY A text.

Good morning, beautiful. I hope you haven't blocked me again. I've been patiently waiting to text you. By the way, I saved some of your favorite pizza for lunch today, so you don't have to pack a lunch.

I held the phone to my heart. I missed this. But I was trying so hard to be rational, even though Miss Liliana was calling and leaving me messages every other hour about the saintly attributes her errant grandson possessed. She was begging me to have Sunday dinner with them all. I wasn't going there. His dad was a major cause of concern. Besides, I felt like Jackson was keeping something from me. He'd had to leave abruptly last night. He got a text and he was off with no explanation; he hardly said goodbye. Regardless, I texted back. *I could be having lunch with Kaine, for all you know.*

Kaine? The guy that ignored you and cried all night on the phone when he took you out?

Are you saying you wouldn't cry over me?

Who says I haven't?

Have you?

He took a few minutes to answer. *On a few occasions. I'll see you soon.*

Was he embarrassed by that? He probably was, considering who his father was. It was a shame, because I thought it showed strength.

I got up excited, not to see Jackson—okay maybe—but I got to dress like Marilyn Monroe for the day. Today's theme was dress like your favorite movie star. It was between her and Audrey Hepburn for me. I donned the classic black turtle neck and ankle pants. I had this fantastic Marilyn wig that looked like real hair, paired with some amazing red lipstick. I was just going to say, I was looking hot. And I began to wonder if blondes really did have more fun. Capri thought so.

I scooted my blonde attitude to school.

Jackson was waiting for me in the parking lot dressed like James Dean. Be still, my beating heart. It was tragic Marilyn and Dean never starred in a movie together. Talk about sizzling.

Jackson's slicked back hair with his red jacket, were giving me some serious hot flashes. The fact that I didn't attack him right there was a miracle.

I walked away from him. Lots of self-control.

He grabbed my hand. "Not so fast, Marilyn." He spun me toward him and perused me slowly. His eyes were hungry, but again, they looked worn. "You look too good for school. Let's play hooky."

"Not a chance, buddy."

He pulled me closer.

I pushed back. "We're at school."

He wasn't letting go. "We aren't doing anything against the rules."

"Jackson."

He grinned. "I've missed that name." He pulled me a tad closer. "I still have that blowup pool you got me on my birthday. Remember that?"

I thought about that day back in May. We had planned on going to the beach for the day, but the weather wasn't our friend. So, I bought one of those kiddie pools and set it up in his backyard along with a sandbox, though the sandbox never got any use. I bit my lip. How could I forget?

"As a kid, I never had so much fun in a pool," he whispered in my ear. His breath was warm and I felt feverish thinking about that most magical day. "Let's make use of it tonight."

I stepped back. "Where?"

"Your place."

"In my apartment?"

"Okay. Nana's. She won't mind lending us her backyard."

"Why not your place?"

"Presley." He tried drawing me in.

"I need to get to work." I turned from him.

He followed alongside of me. "It's complicated."

"There's nothing complicated about it. Your dad hates me."

"That doesn't matter to me."

"So he wasn't one of the reasons you broke up with me?"

He took my hand. "Please stop."

I stood firm and held my ground. I stared into his troubled brown eyes. He looked like he was burning the candle at both ends.

"It's not that simple."

"Enlighten me."

He sighed deeply. "I want to . . ."

I raised my eyebrows waiting for his response.

"But I can't right now."

I pulled away. "Then no pool dates, or any dates for that matter. How do you expect us to be together if you can't be honest with me?"

"Could you please trust me?"

"You don't have the right to ask that anymore."

He hung his head and I walked away. It didn't look like Marilyn and Dean would ever get together.

DAY SIXTY-FIVE

♥

Wednesday, September 29

I STRETCHED IN MY BED, PROLONGING getting up. It wasn't like me, but I didn't want to face Jackson. Maybe he was right. It was complicated, at least my feelings for him were. How can you hate and love someone so much at the same time? And it would help if he wasn't a decent guy. I kept running the conversation he had with Leland last night while we worked on the float in my mind. He didn't realize I was privy to their private talk. Leland was asking for advice on how to ask Harper to the homecoming dance Saturday night. Jackson gently reprimanded him for not having asked already. He said, "You shouldn't keep her guessing about how you feel; you're lucky she doesn't have a date yet."

"I know," Leland responded, "But sometimes I'm not sure how she feels about me."

"You have to be man enough to own your own feelings. There is risk involved, but I've learned that a woman isn't going to give you her heart until she knows exactly where yours lay." Jackson paused like it was an epiphany to him as well. "We owe that to them. So, don't keep her waiting. It doesn't matter how you ask, just be sincere about it when you do."

"Are you going to ask Ms. Benson?"

My ears perked up.

Jackson slapped Leland on the back. "I'm afraid I haven't done a good job of showing Ms. Benson how I really feel about her." He sounded spent.

"Maybe you still can." Leland headed toward Harper.

Within minutes, there were squeals of delight.

I took a deep breath and wished for the simplicity of my high school years.

As I lay in bed, Leland's words rang in my head, "Maybe you still can." Were we past the point of no return? Could I ever trust Jackson with my heart again? Why couldn't he just be honest with me? Sixty-five days later and I was as confused as ever.

DAY SIXTY-SEVEN

♥

Friday, October 1

DEAR MR. BINGLEY,

It's October. This was the month I was supposed to be over Jackson. Ninety days, what a joke. Maybe like ninety years. At least I'll be dead by then. Then it won't kill me when I turn him down when he asks me to do things like ride in the convertible with him during the parade and toss candy to the crowd. His tired and disappointed eyes torture me. What does he expect from me? I can't pretend to be something we're not, something I wish we were. Something I thought we used to be.

You know what homecoming weekend meant to me last year. This year, it marks a year since we became an official couple. Last year when he asked me if I wanted to get a drink after the dance, I didn't realize saying yes meant a six pack of Coke on the tailgate of his truck in the middle of a cotton field. I didn't know it would mean staying up all night talking and then watching the sun rise in his arms.

I want all that back.

But how?

Please tell me how,

Presley

Teaching was almost pointless. Everyone's mind was on homecoming and then fall break. The game was tonight and the dance was tomorrow. For most of my classes, I ended up giving hair and makeup tips to the girls. I even showed the girls and boys some dance moves and begged them not to bump and grind. Ever.

Harper was particularly excited. I overheard her talking to her friends. She was hoping Leland would kiss her this weekend so their first kiss wouldn't be on stage. I couldn't blame her. I remembered last year at this time hoping I would get kissed, too, even though our first kiss had been on stage.

I was still wishing to get kissed.

I didn't see the man who I wanted to kiss me until my lunch time. He was looking extra fine in his cowboy boots and hat for cowboy and cowgirl day. Like menopausal hot flash good.

Capri started fanning me with her hand. "You okay, there?" She laughed. "He does look good."

I grabbed her hand amidst my flushness. "Stop. He's coming over here."

He swaggered over, but for as good as he looked, his cowboy hat couldn't hide the fact he was looking more worn down than ever. Was he sick? That thought made me feel ill inside. He wouldn't keep that from me, would he? He sat down at our table. "Hi, ladies."

We both nodded our greetings.

"You guys going to the game tonight?" He did his best to make small talk.

"They better be." Coach bounded up and answered for us. He slapped Jackson on the back, pushing him forward. That worried me. Jackson normally wouldn't have moved an inch.

I eyed him carefully and he caught me. He arched his eyebrow, but smiled. I smiled back, involuntarily, of course. That bolstered his courage. He reached out and placed his hand over mine. "I'm going to try and make it for the second half. Save me a seat."

I wanted to ask him why he wouldn't be there for the whole thing. He lived and breathed football, especially Riverton High and Alabama Football. Come to think of it, I hadn't even heard him mention Alabama's undefeated season so far. I was really beginning to think he was sick. I almost got up to follow him, but Coach took his spot. "What's up with our boy?"

I didn't want to say anything in the teacher's lounge. We were already the hot topic of discussion. According to Capri, the math department was adjusting our odds of reconciliation due to my resistance, which was shocking to most. Even I was shocked. I looked around and lowered my voice. "I don't know. Has he said anything to you?"

"Nope. But he looks like hell."

I nodded my agreement.

"You should talk to him," Capri suggested.

"I've tried to get him to tell me what's going on, but he refuses."

"Have you talked to his grandma?" Coach asked.

"Her lips are sealed tight, too."

"Weird." Capri commented.

That was a word for it.

Especially considering he never showed up for the game. I even gave in and texted him during the third quarter to ask if he was okay. All he texted back was, *Some things came up. I'll see you at the dance tomorrow night. Save one for me.*

What things? Was he seeing someone else? No. That wasn't his style, was it? I wasn't sure what made me feel worse, the thought that he was sick or the thought that he was seeing another woman, or maybe several women. Maybe that's why he was so tired. I remember all the women rejoicing on Facebook when we broke up. Maybe Capri was right. He was a man whore.

Day Sixty–Eight

♥

Saturday, October 2

I DIDN'T SLEEP WELL, BUT WHEN I woke up, it was with a vengeance. I was going to get to the bottom of what was going on with Jackson. I didn't care that I wasn't his girlfriend. I felt like he at least owed me the truth.

Capri and I spent all day prepping for the homecoming dance we were chaperoning, and by prepping, I meant she was pampering me. We did manis and pedis. Followed by some waxing. Tears followed. Ouch. But seriously, you could skate on my legs, they were so slick. She glammed up my hair and squeezed me into a little, but tasteful, black dress.

Capri stepped back and admired her handiwork. She whistled. "Watch out, boys. This girl is a killer."

"Stop it."

"I'm serious. Look at yourself. You're hot and you're going to set Jackson on fire. Forget your Marilyn costume. The gentleman is going to prefer the brunette tonight."

"You know Marilyn, or should I say, Norma Jean, was originally a brunette."

"She's got nothing on you."

"You're a good friend."

"The best." She grinned.

I plopped down on my bed. "You don't think Jackson is seeing someone else, do you?"

She sat down next to me and her eyes had that aha look in them.

"No more online articles," I warned her.

"Fine, but I was just reading something about signs of a cheater, and his actions do match."

"Technically, he wouldn't be cheating since we aren't a couple." I had to hold the tears in. I didn't want to ruin my makeup, but I had hoped Capri would tell me I was crazy. I didn't expect her to agree with my paranoia.

She must have noticed my altered emotional state. She took my hand. "But I'm sure he's not."

"Nice try."

She squeezed my hand. "If he is, he's the biggest idiot I know. In fact, he already is for letting you go in the first place."

I shrugged. "Well, at least this way I will have no choice but to get over him once and for all."

She hugged me fiercely. "I better go so I can get ready. And I think David has played with his online friends enough today."

"Is that what you're calling them now?"

"I just don't get how grown men can stare at a screen all day killing aliens."

"I don't get men at all lately."

"And they say we're the confusing ones. What don't they get? Call us pretty, buy us nice things, call us pretty, and once a month leave us alone."

I laughed at her. "You should write your own online article."

Her eyes lit up. "That's not a bad idea."

I tried not to let my paranoia consume me when she left. I knew he was free to date who he wanted. I had rebuffed his reconciliation attempts, but I had legitimate reasons and concerns for doing so. And he acted as if he was pursuing me, so if he was dating someone else, that made him a pig. Like the big wild ones they have down here. Thank goodness I had never seen one, or I might have already run back home. And honestly, depending on tonight's outcome, I was considering driving home to spend my fall break with my parents. I needed my mommy.

But committing to a twenty hour drive each way was serious.

Chaperones had to be at the school by 6:30. The dance started at 7:00. Jackson was there already, along with Dr. Walters and Ms. Dickson, the other vice principal. They were there to keep law and order. They gave us instructions on the kind of behavior that wouldn't be tolerated, like dirty dancing or foul language. And no leaving the gymnasium and coming back in. You get the picture. Last year we busted some idiot kids who believed we would fall for the whole it's water in our water bottles. Who brings a water bottle to a school dance?

Jackson zeroed in on me after the chaperone meeting and right before they opened the door to let the kids in. The DJ was already blasting music. Capri skedaddled when she saw him coming our way. He was dressed nicely in suit pants and a blue dress shirt. His smile was tired, but sincere. "You look amazing." He looked me over from head to toe.

"Thanks. You look nice, too." I was nervous and barely met his eyes. For whatever reason, I knew this was either the end of the line or the start of a second chance.

"Hey." He tipped my chin up. "I have to greet the kids at the door to check for alcohol, but save me a dance."

I gazed into his eyes. He looked like he had aged ten years. "Jackson, are you okay?"

He smiled close-lipped. "Save me that dance and I will be."

I nodded and he walked off. I needed something cool to drink. I headed to the drinking fountain and drank enough for a camel. I would probably regret that later when I had to pee and there was a huge line in the ladies' restroom.

The dance started hopping and I enjoyed watching my students interact outside of the classroom. I paid close attention to Harper and Leland. They both looked nervous and I saw how their hands played dangerously close to one another. I wondered if one of them would be brave enough to grasp the other one's hand.

But mainly Jackson held my attention, just like he had last year, except last year he was by my side the entire time. Last year that amazing feeling of the hope of something new lingered between us. Those flirty gestures and touches. I could still feel the tingle in my stomach from that night. Looking at Jackson now, I still felt that heat and passion, but it was masked by confusion and pain.

Several of the girls I taught found me and gushed over my outfit. I did the same for them.

Capri and I were shocked to see Mindy and Stella show up, together no less. I heard they were coming back to school after fall break.

Capri pulled our heads together. "I guess that anger management thing is working out."

"I don't know. Do you see how they're staring at Brad? I would run if I were him."

She grinned wickedly. "This could be good."

"I hope they don't make another scene."

"Why? That parking lot fight has had over a half million views on YouTube." Capri was probably five thousand of those. I don't know how many times she had shown it to me and anybody else she could get to watch.

Brad must have noticed he was easy prey and moved toward the entrance and Dr. Walters.

Capri and I watched and giggled.

All in all, the kids were mostly behaving themselves. There was some risqué dancing among a few, but the stern Ms. Dickson put a stop to that. She was nice, but she could be scary.

An hour into the dance, Jackson left his door duty and joined Capri and me near the refreshment tables. If there was food, there you would most likely find Capri. Her metabolism was amazing and quite honestly annoying at times, only because I was jealous and maybe I was still holding on to those chocolate pounds. We all kind of stood there, not knowing what to say. We awkwardly watched over the students.

"You know," Capri interrupted the tense silence, "I need to talk to Lonnie about those odds." She grinned evilly and walked away.

Jackson and I both knew what odds she was talking about. We smiled between each other.

When he looked at me, I still felt that excitement in the pit of my stomach. Even if I wanted to kick him and maybe scream at him. He reached up and ran the back of his hand down my cheek. "You're so beautiful."

"You shouldn't do that here."

"I'm tired of trying to be who I'm not. I love you and I don't care who knows it or what they think about it." He wrapped his arm around my waist and drew me close. And magically, a slow song started. "Dance with me." He wasn't asking. He led us to a dark corner near the edge of the dance floor. There he erased any space between us.

My head landed on his shoulder and I breathed him in. I loved him, too, body and soul. I didn't know which song was playing, but it was becoming my favorite and I hoped it lasted all night. "Are people staring at us?" I was facing the outside.

"There are other people here?"

I looked up and met his eyes. They were full of life. I matched his smile with my own.

"We are the center of attention. I think you're losing in the odds."

"Jackson."

"Presley."

"Are you seeing—"

His phone started vibrating violently in his pants pocket. "Hold that thought." He pulled out his phone and answered it, all while maintaining his hold on me.

I caught a glimpse of the screen. I hoped I read it wrong, but it said Anne. When he answered, I heard a woman's voice. I couldn't make out the exact words, but she sounded frantic.

Jackson's face creased and reddened. "I'll be right there."

I stepped away, more confused and hurt.

He shoved the phone back in his pocket. "I've got to go."

"Are you seeing someone else?"

His tense, lined face shook. "No."

"Jackson, tell me what's going on, or the odds will definitely not be in our favor."

"Presley, I can't do this with you right now. I'll call you later."

"Don't bother. I won't pick up."

"Dammit, Presley, you have no idea." He left. He just left.

I turned around, stunned. To make matters worse, I felt like everyone was looking at me. I had never felt so vulnerable or exposed. And did I mention hurt? But I refused to cry and give everyone more of a show. I managed to walk out into the hall where Capri met me.

"I know this is a dumb question, but are you okay?"

I shook my head no.

She immediately embraced me.

I held back the tears but clung to her. "I think I'm going to go home."

"I'll drive you."

"No. I mean Colorado."

She let go of me. "You can't break your contract."

"I'll just be gone for the week."

"I'll go with you. David has to work anyway."

I shook my head. "No. I need some time alone. But I love that you would."

"That's a long drive for one person."

"I have a lot to think about."

"Is he seeing someone else?" She squinted her eyes bracing for my answer.

"I don't know. I don't know anything anymore. I'm going to go home and pack. Please tell Dr. Walters."

"I don't think anyone expects you to go back in there."

"Maybe I will stay in Colorado. Could I make more of a fool of myself?"

"You could rip my necklace off and I could slap you," she teased. She could always make me smile.

"We'll save that for another time." I hugged her one more time and flew out of there.

Who knew, maybe with this new twist in the plot, I might just complete my ninety-day plan after all. At the moment, I felt no love for the man who left me alone with only more questions.

DAY SIXTY-NINE

♥

Sunday, October 3

I WAS UP PACKING WAY PAST midnight. My parents were excited to have me, although concerned for my mental state. I wasn't sure why. So the man I loved may or may not have been involved with some chick named Anne. It was no big deal, except I couldn't quit crying and I thought I was having heart palpitations. I had this under control. I bent over and sobbed. I lied.

Around two in the morning I fell onto my bed, exhausted emotionally and physically. I promised my parents I would try and sleep before I made my journey home. My dad was booking a hotel for me in Kansas so I could stop midway. I loved my parents. Eventually my shudders quieted and I fell asleep.

I wasn't sure for how long, but it wasn't long enough. I woke up in the very early light to my phone ringing. At first I ignored it. I could barely keep my eyes open, but the ringing persisted. My hand reached out under the covers and grabbed the blasted phone. Whoever was calling this early on a Sunday was getting an earful. Or maybe not. It was Miss Liliana. I could never scold her even if it was only a little past six in the morning.

"Hello." My throat burned from all the crying.

"Are you sick, darling?" She sounded worse than me.

"No. What's wrong?" I sat up.

She began to cry.

I clutched my heart. "Is it Jackson?"

"No. Yes."

I was dying. Which was it?

"Other than tired, he's physically okay, but…my son…"

"Miss Liliana?"

"Darling, I've wanted to tell you for so long, but we all promised we wouldn't. But you need to know. Can you pick me up and take me to the hospital?"

"Are you all right?"

"No, but I'm going to make things better. I'm ready when you are." She hung up.

I was fully alert now. I jumped out of bed and raced to put on a hoodie and some jeans. Whatever I pulled out of my suitcase first. My trip could wait a few hours. My eyes needed spoons badly, but there was no time. They got a few drops of Visine. I pulled my hair up into a ponytail as I waited at a red light in my car. I was shaking. So many questions in my mind.

Miss Liliana must have been watching for me. She walked out of her house before I could put my car in park. She was dressed elegantly, as always, in cream-colored pants and a brown blouse. I raced out of the car to help her. Like mine, her eyes were red.

She took my arm and leaned on me. "I love you, darling."

"I love you, too. Tell me what's going on."

She waited until we were on our way to the hospital in downtown Huntsville. Not the newly built one in Riverton. That wasn't a good sign. The downtown hospital was for more critical patients.

She looked frail, sitting there clutching a handkerchief. "My son…isn't well. He hasn't been for some time. I'm not sure for how long, since he kept it from us until the beginning of this summer."

That was about the time Jackson started spending a lot of time with his dad.

"He probably would have kept it a secret until he died if he could have." She cried into her handkerchief.

I reached over and placed my hand on her leg. "Is he . . . dying?"

She nodded. "The doctors aren't hopeful that he has much longer, the stubborn fool let it go so long before he even saw a doctor that it's spread."

"He has cancer?"

"It started out as prostate, but now it's spread to his bones." She could barely get out the words.

"You don't have to talk about it." She was making me cry and I hated the guy.

"Yes I do. Not talking has caused too many problems. Jackson needs you more than ever and he feels like he's lost you because he kept his mouth shut. He wanted to tell you, but we were under strict orders from my son not to. He has his reasons, I know, but this has gotten out of control. I'll let Jackson tell you the rest."

"Where is Jackson? Does he know you called me?"

"He's still at the hospital with his daddy. Daniel took me home an hour ago."

"You should be resting."

"I will not. Not until I see this mess fixed between you and Jackson. He's beside himself. This has been unfair to both of you. He loves you."

I wiped my tears away and sped down the quiet highway. So many things were starting to make sense, and I dared to hope in a way I hadn't. But there were more questions that needed to be answered.

I held Miss Liliana's hand for the remainder of our silent drive. I ached for her, Jackson, their whole family.

Miss Liliana directed me where to park. The early hour allowed us a spot close to the entrance. Miss Liliana looked done for and I considered asking her if she would like me to get a wheelchair, but I knew what a slight that would be to her. Instead, I helped her and we walked slowly, though every part of me wanted to sprint. We took the elevator to our specified floor. Upon our exit, she held me back. "He doesn't look good, darling. Don't be alarmed." She sniffled into her tissue.

I assumed she meant her son. How heartbroken she must be. All I could do was hug her.

She patted my back. "We're wasting time and it's a precious thing."

We held hands down the hall. The smell of antiseptic tickled my nose. Like the highway, the hospital was quiet, not even the nurses at the station said a word to us as we walked by. The Montgomery's held clout in this town, and they probably knew better than to ask where we were headed. Mr. Montgomery's private room was at the end of the hall. When we arrived at our destination, my nerves flared up. I took a deep breath.

"You go in without me. Jackson needs you all to himself."

"What if he's unhappy I'm here?"

She touched my cheek. "Impossible. I don't want to see you two until you're ready to set a date."

"Miss Liliana."

"I'm serious. Like I said, time is a precious gift and I will not see any more wasted." She stood up as tall as she could and marched away. To where, I have no idea. But that was one lady who could take care of herself.

I turned back toward the large door. I breathed in and out deeply before opening it a crack. I wasn't sure what to expect on the other side. There were two men in there, one who hated me and I hoped one who loved me as much as I loved him. The room was still. The only hint of life was the beeping of machines. I caught a glimpse of both men. Mr. Montgomery was attached to all sorts of medical devices and unconscious; I wasn't sure if he was sedated or sleeping.

Jackson, my Jackson, was sitting by his father's bedside, bent over, holding his dad's hand between his own. He looked as if he was praying.

He didn't stir as I approached. He probably thought I was medical personnel. Or perhaps he was sleeping. Either way, I hated to disturb him. I stealthily took the seat next to him. I took one second to take him in before I reached over and placed my hand on top of his. His head popped up and he turned toward me. A smile and tears erupted. I followed suit. He said nothing. He placed his father's hand gently on his bed before standing up and pulling me out of my chair into an embrace.

I easily fell into him and held him as fiercely as he held me. He bathed my hair in his tears and I wetted his shoulder with mine.

"I'm so sorry," he whispered over and over.

"Please don't apologize. Just tell me what you need from me."

He cupped my face in his hands. "Only you." He pressed his lips against mine.

I sank into it. I had missed this, him.

He released me only to take my hand and lead us to the small couch in the room. He sat down and pulled me onto his lap. I immediately curled into him. His hold was firm and reassuring. He kept rubbing my arms and kissing my head. "Who told you I was here?"

"Who do you think?"

"I'll have to thank her."

"You could have told me." I looked at his father's ailing body. He looked like he had aged fifty years since I last saw him. His skin was sallow and he looked so thin.

"I wanted to, but I promised Daddy I wouldn't. We all did. Hell, he tried to keep it from us. He was afraid it would ruin his career if anyone caught wind of it. The board was already trying to push him out. They wanted fresh blood. I finally convinced him to bow out gracefully and retire early. His body was demanding it."

"How long has he been sick?"

"Only he knows, but I found out in June by accident. I guess he was getting lazy living alone and he hadn't flushed his toilet. It was filled with blood."

"He didn't get treatment?"

"Supposedly he was on a wait and see treatment; they put him on hormone suppressors and watched, but who knows if he was going in regularly reporting his symptoms before I found out. He won't say. He's as stubborn and prideful as he's always been. I've been forcing him to appointments and to take his medication. I moved in with him so I could monitor him, and recently he's started falling. He wasn't happy to have my company, but he's been fading fast. The cancer has spread to his bones. It doesn't look good."

"I'm so sorry."

"I'm the sorry one. I never wanted to break up with you, but when this promotion came up, we had just found out the cancer had spread and the prognosis wasn't good. My promotion seemed to give him some hope and the district's decision hinged on my relationship with you. I agonized over the decision. I talked it over with my brother and even Daddy. Probably not the smartest thing to do, considering. But he promised me if I took the promotion and got my doctorate, he would be there to see me graduate. It's a lousy excuse, I know. It killed me to hurt you, but I thought I didn't have a choice. And you don't know how bad I wanted to tell you what's been going on, but just the thought of anyone outside our family knowing seemed to take him to the edge, and he's already so frail."

I lay still in his arms.

"Presley, I know my words might not mean much to you, but I swear there is no other choice than to have you in my life."

"Who's Anne?"

He laughed. "How do you know about her?"

I sat up to gauge the truth in his eyes. "I saw her name on your phone last night."

He smiled before he pecked me on the lips. "PB, she's the private nurse we hired to help take care of Daddy. It was getting to be too much for me to care for him by myself. Daniel could only come up so much. I was exhausted. She called last night to tell me he fell again and needed stitches. Also, he couldn't urinate."

I rested my hand on his cheek. "I've noticed how tired you look. So, is this Anne a hot fantasy sort of nurse?"

"No one is as hot as you."

"You didn't answer the question."

"Why does it matter? I only have eyes for you."

I arched my eyebrow. "Does she live with you?"

He leaned in closer, his lips parted. "Technically, sometimes."

"Answer the question."

He closed the gap and his lips met mine, but this time my lips parted and I tasted what I had been missing for so long. He was still a gold medal kisser. Soft, tender, but he owned my mouth, my lips, my heart and soul. And he didn't let go until I was breathing hard and wishing we were truly alone.

"Does that answer your question?"

I took a breath in. "Uh-huh."

His wicked grin had me wanting a repeat. "By the way, she's in her fifties and happily married."

"You could have just said that."

"My way was much more fun."

"I'll give you that."

He caressed my cheek. "Can you forgive me for ever making you feel like you weren't the best part of me? That I could live without you?"

I looked behind me. "What's going to happen when he wakes up?"

Jackson turned my face back toward him with the gentle touch of his finger. "He's going to be irate that you're here, but we're a packaged deal. I'm not going to ever let anything come between us again, not even myself."

"Is that a promise, Jackson Montgomery?"

"Yes, ma'am."

"Then I guess you better kiss me like you mean it."

He didn't need to be asked twice. "As you wish." Our lips met and a fire ignited. Rapturous was a good word. Westley and Buttercup had nothing on us.

Day Seventy

♥

Monday, October 4

DEAR MR. BINGLEY,

    You will never guess where I am writing this entry from. Mr. Montgomery's house. Not my Mr. Montgomery, but the Mr. Montgomery. Are you shocked? Of course, you are. I know I am.

    I obviously canceled my trip home. My parents were disappointed, but understood when I told them why. My mom was more understanding than my dad, if we're being honest. Dad is still worried my heart is at risk. But my heart hasn't felt this whole in seventy days. I wonder if this is why Jane so readily agreed to marry you. She felt like herself. Or maybe anything was better than living with her insufferable mother. Did you ever think of that? I'm not here to put you down. I'm too happy.

    Not completely happy, because the man I love and his family that I love, minus the father, are in the depths of sorrow. You see, Mr. Montgomery is ill, an incurable sickness. The doctors are giving him six months to a year to live, at most. Maybe less, since he has been the worst sort of patient, skipping appointments and throwing out medicine. That's why Jackson has to live with him, to make sure he lives. It's been like having an additional fulltime job for him on top of his job. No wonder he was so worn.

I wish he would have told me, but his dad was more worried about what the outside world believed than what his own family was going through. I've kept my mouth shut about the hell he has put his family through, all for selfish reasons. Being sick is not a weakness like he believes. I've never known anyone as self-centered and prideful as him. While he was trying to keep the façade that nothing was amiss, his family has been stressed and catering to his every wish.

How this man raised Jackson, I don't know.

But this I do know. I love Jackson. And together we will get through this.

Very much in love,

Presley

Jackson walked in from the kitchen bearing sandwiches.

I set down my journal and smiled up at him from the couch in his dad's den. "Thank you."

He set a plate in front of me and joined me on the leather couch. He looked at my journal. "How many times did you write that you hate me in that thing?"

I kissed his cheek. "Enough."

He peered into my eyes while running the back of his hand down my cheek. "Thank you for sticking it out and spending your break helping me and my family."

"I would have all along, you know?"

"I do know." He skimmed my lips. "Mmmm, your lips taste good, but I'm sure you're starved, so real food first and then dessert." He reluctantly pulled away.

"I can work with that."

We each took our sub sandwich and leaned back. I rested against him while we ate.

"How's your dad?"

"Daniel says he's awake and demanding to be released. He's still upset we took him to Huntsville Hospital. He's been making us take him to Birmingham in case anyone recognized him.

That's messed up. But I didn't mention it.

"Looks like he may get to come home tomorrow. They're trying to get his pain under control and convince him he needs a walker. And he doesn't know it yet, but they are keeping him catheterized."

Ouch. "Do you think he'll ever use a walker?"

"I doubt it. He'd rather crack his skull."

"Is Daniel staying with him tonight?"

"That's the plan. Then he needs to head back to Birmingham. They're headed to Disney World for fall break."

"Let's do something fun tonight. We could invite Capri and David over for dinner and games. They're dying to get together, or we could do dinner and movie. You name it."

He gave me a sexy grin. "I have the blowup pool all ready to go."

"It's kind of chilly for that."

"I have another use for it, but with the same results."

I arched my eyebrow. "Do you now? And what is that?"

"You'll just have to wait until dark and see."

"And whatever will we do until then?"

He took my sandwich out of my hands and placed the half-eaten sandwiches back on the plate before he pulled me onto his lap. "This will be our warm up." He leaned in and pressed his lips to mine.

"I vote we always have dessert first."

He groaned and parted my lips.

Yep, gold medal, every single time.

DAY SEVENTY–ONE

Tuesday, October 5

THERE IS NOTHING BETTER, I repeat, nothing better than waking up in Jackson's arms in the back of his truck. He threw that blowup kiddie pool in the back of his truck and filled it with blankets and pillows. We spent the night stargazing and talking. Sure, throw in some fantastic kissing, but we both had so much to say. Like for starters, he wanted to marry me, sooner rather than later, so his dad could be there. He didn't ask, he just wanted me to know.

I stared into his handsome face as he slept soundly. I hated to wake him, but I needed to pee. And I refused to go outside. I didn't care that his friend owned the cotton field. I admired his handsome face a moment longer and reflected, not only about his intentions, but the last few months. I laughed inwardly about my ninety-day plan. I'm glad it's something I failed miserably at.

I couldn't take it anymore. I kissed his lips. "Wake up. Your girlfriend needs a bathroom and a latte."

A sleepy grin played on his face. "I love that you're my girlfriend."

I did, too.

I waited nervously for Jackson to return home with his father. I offered to wait at my place, but Jackson insisted that I be there. I appreciated his bold approach to showing his dad I wasn't going anywhere, but angry didn't begin to describe how his dad reacted when he had woken up in the hospital and saw me there on Sunday. I swore he looked like he might have a heart attack. And that man had a vocabulary filled with four-letter words.

Miss Liliana was coming with them, thank goodness. She was as happy as she was sad. But like she said, time was a precious thing and none of us wanted to waste any, so I stayed and fixed his dad's favorite meal of beef braised in red wine. Even though Jackson said the medication he was on messed with his sense of taste, I was hoping the gesture counted. I wasn't holding my breath.

Even with Jackson living there, the house was so sterile. Beautiful, but cold. There wasn't a picture in the house, or any sign that a human lived there other than the furniture. Take the magnificent kitchen, for example. Nothing was on the stainless-steel countertops and everything gleamed. I worried about cooking in it. I wasn't sure I could ever get it back to its pristine condition. I bet Jackson hated living here. His place, though masculine, was always warm and inviting. I wished some of his things were here, but his dad insisted his things not clutter up his home. I was keeping my mouth shut about the unfairness of that, at least for now.

I unloaded all the groceries I had purchased. Jackson had been living off mainly frozen foods. He needed real food, and I needed to wean myself off my chocolate-heavy diet. I found a suitable recipe for braised beef online and began to tackle it. I chopped all the vegetables and fresh herbs I needed. I eyed the red wine and thought we might need extra, depending on how this all went. I wasn't one for alcohol and hadn't had any, per my ninety-day plan, but that could all change once Jackson's dad arrived home.

Within an hour, the house was smelling great. I placed the pot with the meat and sauce in the oven and now I waited, not only for the beef to braise, but for Jackson to return.

I reminded myself I was a lion. I roared. I found I roared louder with Jackson by my side. Together, we could do this.

I heard the garage door open and I wasn't sure what to do. Should I stay in the kitchen? Did I dare try and greet them? I stood up and looked down at my cut-offs and t-shirt. I probably should have dressed nicer. No. I was who I was. And it was a lovely warm fall day and I had spent some serious time preparing a meal for the rotten old man.

I didn't need to worry about what do with myself. "Honey, we're home," Jackson called out into the spacious house.

I stifled a laugh. He had never been one to use pet names. I wondered if he did it for show. I took a deep breath, walked out into the grand great room complete with spiral staircase, and greeted the threesome.

Jackson was supporting his father's full weight and helping him walk toward the master suite. Miss Liliana stood by, looking apprehensive. I couldn't blame her. Her son didn't look well at all. His clothes were hanging off him, his hair was unkempt, and it looked like every step he took might be his last. It was a far cry from the man of steel just a few months ago. But even still, his look was intimidating. Though he and Jackson shared the same brown eyes, they were worlds apart. Jackson's were warm and inviting, they drew you in. Mr. Montgomery's were cold and calculating, they penetrated you and gave you the chills. And not the good kind.

I did my best to stand my ground, all while being gracious. It was a tough line. I stepped toward them. "Welcome home."

Mr. Montgomery turned his head from me.

I had tried. I approached Jackson and kissed his cheek. "Dinner should be ready in the next hour or so."

"You're the best. Let me get Daddy settled."

"Agh," Mr. Montgomery spat.

I paid no attention to him. I drifted toward Miss Liliana and took her hand. She looked like she needed a drink and some rest. "Let's head to the den and I'll get you some sweet tea."

She patted my hand and off we went, slowly, but surely.

Jackson and his father went the opposite direction, at an even slower pace.

When you're younger, you never think of the day when it will be your turn to care for the people who cared for you. And it must be much worse to witness your child prepare to leave this life before you. It goes against nature. I ached for my lovely friend. I got her settled on the couch with her feet propped up on a pillow that rested on the coffee table. "Sit tight. I'll be right back."

"Don't mind my son."

"Don't worry, I won't."

"I think he has finally met his match in you."

That was to be determined. Not that I wanted to battle him, especially in his condition, but there was no way I was letting him come between Jackson and me again. I gave her a smile and headed toward the kitchen.

I was pouring glasses of sweet tea when Jackson approached from behind and kissed my neck. I sighed. "I think you missed a spot."

"This one here?" He kissed the nape of my neck.

"Uh-huh."

"Anywhere else?" he whispered into my ear.

I had to catch my breath. I turned around and caught his lips. He picked me up and I wrapped my legs and arms around him before he set me on the counter and kissed me like he meant it. His hands wove through my hair as he drew me as close as he could. He tasted of cinnamon and I savored every moment. The taste of salt hit our lips as tears streamed down my face. My emotions had overcome me.

Jackson released my lips to peer into my eyes and wipe my cheeks with his thumb. "Did I do something wrong?"

I shook my head. "I just didn't ever think we would be us again."

He kissed my forehead. "I'm not going anywhere."

"I know."

He hugged me tight. "I need to get Daddy to take his medicine and then check his catheter bag."

I cringed. "Have fun with that."

"Thanks." He stepped back. "But later tonight you and I are going to pick up right here."

"Promise?"

"I guarantee it." He walked off whistling to himself with a glass of sweet tea.

It was definitely hot in the kitchen.

Day Seventy-Four

♥

Friday, October 8

DEAR MR. BINGLEY,

It has been one of the best, but most emotionally exhausting weeks of my life. They say you have to know the bitter to enjoy the sweet. I understand that now more than ever. I never knew being with Jackson could be so good, and that's saying something. I treasure it now. Even if it means putting up with his cranky and downright rude father.

For as sick as he is, he made sure to speak loud enough so I could hear him complain about the food I made, my clothes, my attitude, and upbringing. If you didn't know me, you would think I was part of the Beverly Hillbilly clan. Just call me Ellie May.

Poor Jackson feels the need to defend me, which only seems to do more harm than good. His dad usually ends up in a coughing spell and yesterday he threw enough of a fit his catheter came out. Not only was it a mess, but Jackson had to take him back to the doctor. It's taking a toll on him, physically and emotionally.

I've offered to stay away, but Jackson insists he needs me by his side. There is no other place I would rather be. Though I say that lying in my own bed *away from him. Jackson has meetings today. I didn't realize administrators didn't get the full time off. I think there are a lot of things I didn't or don't realize.*

Maybe I judged your Jane too harshly. Who am I to say what she should have done? Not to say you weren't a lucky man.

I am lucky too,

Presley

I set down my journal, stretched, yawned, and decided I should get up. I couldn't believe fall break was almost over. What a wild week it had been. I was planning on a lazy day of going over my Marilyn project and lunch with Capri. I hadn't seen her all week. But my plans changed with a phone call.

"Hi, handsome."

"Hey, beautiful."

"That was unenthusiastic, what's wrong?"

He let out a huge amount of air. "Anne's sick and I need to leave here in a half an hour. But I can't leave him alone."

I tried to think of anyone but me who could help. It's not that I wouldn't do anything for Jackson, but I wondered if my help would be more of a hindrance considering his dad's aversion to me. But who else could he ask, especially on such short notice? I took a deep breath. "I'll be right over."

"Are you sure?" I could hear the relief in his voice.

"No, but I'm coming anyway."

"I love you."

"And I must really love you." I hung up and tried to pull myself together in five minutes. I threw a bag together with my makeup and other essentials before heading out the door. What was I thinking?

It took all of ten minutes before I found myself in front of Mr. Montgomery's house. I couldn't call it Jackson's, because no part of that house reflected him. And I knew he couldn't wait to have a place of his own again. A place with me in mind.

I mustered up my insane side and headed in.

Jackson met me at the door with a grateful smile and a kiss. "Thank you."

"You're welcome. Tell me what to do." I kind of already knew, but I had never entered his dad's lair before.

"He knows you're here, so hopefully he'll behave. I warned him that he better, but you know how he is."

Yes, I did.

"He has a recliner in his room he likes to sit in and watch TV or read. But he needs help getting up from the bed and making his way over. You need to check on him frequently, because he thinks he can do whatever he wants. I left a list of the medications and their dosage amounts and when he should take them. He's eaten breakfast, but you'll have to feed him lunch." He grimaced.

I reached for his hand. "It will be okay. Maybe." I teased.

He squeezed it tight. "Call me if you need anything. I've told central office and Dr. Walters of Daddy's condition, so if I have to leave, they'll understand."

I pulled him close. "You go do your thing. And try not to worry."

He leaned his forehead against mine. "Have I told you lately how amazing you are?"

"I'm freaking amazing for doing this."

He chuckled and kissed my lips. "Agreed." He took a deep breath and let it out. "I'll be back around four and then I'm going to show you how appreciative I am."

"I can't wait."

"Me either." He headed for the door. "I love you."

"I love you, too. Have a good day." That sounded so domestic. I was channeling my mom. I could live with that. My mom was the best.

Now what was I supposed to do? I looked around the museum styled house that glistened unnaturally. I headed for the patient's room and peeked inside his open door. It looked like he was sleeping. Or maybe he was faking it since he knew I was there. Either way was fine by me. I took a second longer to take in his surroundings. It looked like a stately manner kind of a room. Dark wood furniture filled the space, except for his charcoal colored recliner. The only pop of color came from some paisley patterned curtains that were shut tight. I turned to walk away, but—

"Coming to survey what you think will be yours when I'm gone?"

I spun back around with a smile on my face. So maybe it was an evil grin. I entered his room, if just barely. "You couldn't pay me enough to live here."

"How much would it take for you to leave my son alone?"

I took a few steps forward. Enough to see the cold calculation in his barely open eyes. "There isn't enough money in the world."

"You're not good for him."

"Don't you mean good enough?"

"Don't tell me what I mean, young lady."

So, it was on. Was I terrible for arguing with a dying man? He did start it, as my students would say. I boldly took the chair by his bedside and moved it to where we could see each other clearly. I sat down, but before I could respond to him, I noticed a picture of Jackson's mother on his nightstand. She was beautiful. Jackson and Miss Liliana had shown me pictures of her before. She had chestnut hair, like Jackson, but I never noticed before that she had green eyes like me. She was in a summer dress, sitting on a tree swing. It could have been a magazine cover. I picked up the photo, which didn't make the dear old dad happy.

"I didn't give you permission to touch that."

I smiled up at him. "I didn't ask."

His eyes opened all the way. I felt the heat of his stare.

I ran my fingers over the glass of the frame. "She's beautiful. I see a lot of her in Jackson and Daniel."

He looked up at the tray ceiling. "No one was her equal." It was the first nice thing I ever heard come out of his mouth.

"You must miss her."

"That is none of your concern."

"You see, it is, because someday, whether you like it or not, we're going to be related."

His head turned painfully back toward me. "You're not good for my son."

"You've already said that. The question is why?"

His face reddened. He didn't like to be questioned. "Love is an Achilles heel."

"It makes you weak. Is that right?"

"It has that tendency."

"You believe Jackson is weak? And Daniel, too?"

"Daniel knows where he's going in this world. And Miranda knows her place."

I clenched my fists. His chauvinistic attitude and ideas had no place now or ever. "So, that's your problem with me? That I have a career?"

"Among other things."

"Such as?"

"You're holding Jackson back from his potential. And your brazen attitude is unwelcome."

I set the picture of Georgia Montgomery back where it belonged. "My attitude only reflects the way you've treated me. I have done my best to be polite to you, but this is the twenty-first century and I refuse to be regarded as unequal because of my gender. And whether you believe it or not, Jackson is a success. There is more to life than titles and money. Your son has a gift for teaching and helping people." I peered into his eyes.

He lifted his head, but it expended too much energy and it fell against his pillow. "You don't know the world."

"Maybe not, but this I do know, it would be a whole lot better place with more Jacksons in it than your kind."

"Young lady, I built a company that launched rockets and satellites that have protected and secured your way of life."

"For that I thank you, but your greatest accomplishment was raising a son that cares more about you than he does for his own welfare. He was willing to give up his own happiness to please the unpleasable. So what does that really say about you?"

I never fully appreciated the phrase "if looks could kill" until that moment. I should have been dead on arrival with the hatred that ran through his eyes. But I didn't back down. Our eyes stayed locked for what seemed like minutes. And by some miracle, the heat in his eyes dissipated little by little.

"I only want what's best for my son."

"Then we can agree on something. But you need to come to terms with the fact that you don't know what that is."

"You are pertinacious, aren't you?"

"Something else we can agree on." I smiled.

"My wife was, too."

"You know, I think she would have liked me."

He narrowed his eyes before turning his head away. "She probably would have," he muttered.

It made me grin. "Can we at least call a truce for Jackson's sake?"

He turned back toward me. "I still don't like you."

"Good, because I'm not very fond of you." I smiled. And if I wasn't mistaken his lip twitched like he might smile, too. "But that being said, I love your son and this is hard on him, you are hard on him. Use what precious time you have left to show your son how much you love him." I stood up. "Can I get you anything?"

He shook his head as best he could.

"I'll be back to check on you. Don't try to escape." I winked.

He closed his eyes in dismissal.

I took the hint, and a large breath.

The rest of the day was not so eventful. Jackson must have texted me a dozen times to check on us. He was like the worried father of a new-born. But Mr. Montgomery took his medicine and ate the best he could.

He even used his walker to get to his recliner, but I think that had more to do with the fact he didn't want me to touch him. I didn't mind at all.

By the time four rolled around, I had dinner in the crockpot, Mr. Montgomery was watching some World War II documentary in his room, and I was going over my Marilyn outline in the den.

I heard Jackson come in through the garage entrance. He headed to his dad's room first. I heard a muffled conversation before Jackson came and found me. He stood near the French doors and grinned at me. "Daddy was almost agreeable, what did you do to him today?"

I grinned slyly. "Nothing. I just told him he wasn't the center of the universe."

Jackson shook his head. "I do love you."

I set down my laptop. "I'm ready for you to show me how much."

He was to me in a second flat. It was a gold medal moment all the way.

DAY SEVENTY–SEVEN

♥

Monday, October 11

THANKS TO SOCIAL MEDIA AND Riverton's small town nature, everyone knew Jackson and I were back together by the time school started up again on Monday. Yep, another holiday—Columbus Day. Nothing was sacred to this school district. I braced myself for the onslaught of stares, and maybe dirty looks from the likes of Mindy and Stella. Though if I were them, I would play nice with everyone after their hiatus for anger related issues.

As predicted, smiles and turned heads followed me into the school. I even got a thumbs up from Dr. Walters. I was glad, because I was worried about the little show we had put on at the homecoming dance.

I headed toward the auditorium first to see how Mr. Crandall's break was. He and his nephew Kaine had planned to work on the set, so I wanted to get a peek at that as well. I walked in to find Mr. Crandall where he always was, but there was something different about him. Instead of pacing, it was like he was waltzing to a silent tune in his head. I approached the stage to investigate. He looked like he was walking on cloud nine. Gone was his bowtie; it had been replaced by a handsome red tie. I had never seen him at school without a bowtie.

He opened his eyes and grinned when he noticed me. "Ah, my dear."

"You sound chipper this morning. I take it you had a good break."

Always the gentleman, he reached down for my hand to help me up the stairs. "It was marvelous."

"Do tell."

"Sit, sit." He waved.

I did as he asked and he joined me. I was anxious to see where all his liveliness was coming from.

He had a childlike glow to him. "I had a most interesting message from my dear Connie."

"Your dear Connie?" I grinned.

"Yes, yes, dear, keep up. After a little animosity, she said she was open to more contact from me." He was all lit up. "I seized the moment and asked for her number."

"I'm proud of you."

He beamed. "We have spoken several times and we're meeting in Atlanta this weekend. She lives in South Carolina now. It's a halfway point."

"Look at you. I'm so happy for you."

"As I am for you."

My cheeks pinked. "I don't know that I've ever been happier."

"It shows. I'm glad our new VP finally got his proverbial head out of his buttocks."

I held my heart and laughed. "You and me both."

I headed to class and met Coach, who threw decorum out the window and picked me up and swung me around. "My boy is back. PB and J are back."

"Don't cry on me now." I held onto the wall. My head was spinning from his greeting.

"Tears of joy, baby! Now maybe we can get back to planning that engagement of yours on the field."

Huh? I wondered when and how Jackson was going to propose to me. I had a feeling it would be soon. I kind of hoped under the circumstances it wouldn't be anything flashy like some halftime proposal on the field. I would take the back of his truck or the prop room. But however he did it, I knew what my answer was going to be.

DAY NINETY

Sunday, October 24

DEAR MR. BINGLEY,
 I fear I may have misjudged you. Either that or staring at the engagement ring on my finger has made me delirious. Deliriously happy, that is. You're the first to know. It seems fitting. You have seen me through my awkward teenage years and into adulthood. I haven't even told my parents, Capri, or Miss Liliana yet, though he did ask my dad for my hand in marriage like a gentleman should.

I know you're dying to know how it happened, so I will keep you in suspense no longer. Earlier this evening after we got his dad settled for the night, he took me to the den for what I thought was going to be an evening of him reading to me while I lay in his lap. It was becoming a nightly ritual. But instead of reading, he just stroked my hair and kind of chuckled to himself. I sat up, wondering what was so funny to him. You know what he said?

"Isn't this a special day for you?"

I couldn't figure out what he meant. He laughed some more.

"Isn't this the day you had planned to be over me?"

Can you believe he said that to me? Me either. But as you know, I knew he knew. So I grinned and informed him he should probably make sure the *next time that I really was sleeping. But, honestly, we both had a good laugh over my foolish plan. It had been doomed from the start.*

That's okay, because he said he wanted to offer me another plan. The forever one. He reached behind the throw pillow on the couch and handed me a white box. He got down on one knee, and you know the rest. It didn't come with any fanfare or flowery words. Just a simple I love you and please be my wife.

It was beautiful.

Men definitely do not suck,

Presley

I set my journal down and stared one more time at the gorgeous round solitaire diamond my finger wore so well. Then I stared at the man who lay asleep in my lap. I stroked his hair and smiled. Maybe I should write my own online article. *How Not to Get over Your Ex*. I'm expert at it, after all.

Day One-Hundred-Forty-Three

♥

Wedding Day

MAYBE IT WASN'T A GOOD idea to have all my sisters, my mom, Capri, and Miss Liliana help me get ready. I was being poked and prodded in places I didn't know existed on my body. Not to mention the serious teasing that was going on with my hair. "If I look like a hooker, you're all fired."

Loud laughter rang in my ears. "You're going to look gorgeous, baby girl." My mom pinched my cheeks. "And I bet Jackson wouldn't mind one bit if you looked a little sleazy."

"Mom."

More laughter.

"We don't need to have any wedding night talks now do we?" my sister Jen asked.

I rolled my eyes. "Thanks. I think we've got it covered."

"Wait, wait," Capri shouted over the loudness that was my family. "I just read an article online about wedding night jitters."

"Please, no more articles. Remember the last one?"

"Yes, and your welcome. Trying to get over him totally worked to your advantage. The fact you were trying, and succeeding I may add, and he was failing miserably, only made him come to his senses sooner."

I wouldn't agree I was exactly succeeding, but I did give it a go. "Well, regardless, I'm not at all nervous about tonight."

Capri didn't listen and pulled up the article on her phone anyway. "How to Get Over Wedding Night Jitters."

Everyone stopped what they were doing and listened intently to Capri. "Number one, relax."

"Really, I'm fine."

She ignored me. "Number two, you don't need to make a big production out of it."

"Okay. Thank you."

Still being ignored. "Number three, have a drink. Finally, a list that makes some sense. I'll pack you a bottle of wine."

Everyone but me laughed.

"And last but not least, don't put pressure on yourself."

"Okay, enough. I get it. Can we please finish my hair? I'd like to get married today."

"You've always been so bossy," my sister Michelle, who was the closest to me in age said. She gave me a little squeeze.

I wasn't bossy, I was excited. Jackson was downstairs waiting in his nana's parlor for me. We were having a small wedding at her house since it wasn't good for his dad to be around large groups of people. And if he needed to, he could use a room here to rest. My parents were gracious enough to come here. My mom and I had always dreamed about my wedding in Colorado, but Jackson, and maybe even I, wanted his dad to be able to witness our marriage. Mr. Montgomery and I weren't the best of friends —yet—but I was working on him. He even smiled at me once. So maybe it's when I stubbed my toe on his bed and used some of those four letter words he's so fond of, but it was a smile nonetheless.

But honestly, I didn't care how he treated me as long as he treated his son with the respect and love he deserved. He didn't flip out when Jackson told him he was putting off getting his doctorate for the time being so he could focus more on family, so that was a start. He even sort of gave us his blessing. Not that we needed it, but it made Jackson happy.

I hoped, though, that he didn't blow his top when we told him we purchased that fixer upper around the corner from Miss Liliana. My dream home with the trellis and ivy. It didn't look like much now, but we had a lifetime to make it ours. We probably wouldn't move in until... well until... I hated thinking about it, especially on my wedding day, but Mr. Montgomery was fading fast. It was one of the reasons we were getting married now. That and the fact we were crazy in love.

Before I knew it, I was stripped down and stuffed into my ivory ball gown dress. It was very Princess Bride. Just call me Buttercup—but don't really.

Miss Liliana touched my cheek. "I always knew this day would come. You're lovely, darling."

I held her hand against my cheek. "I love you."

Her eyes misted up. "Don't keep my grandson waiting."

She didn't have to tell me twice.

Capri and my sisters all hugged me and left me there with only my mom.

"I knew he was the one. Make sure to take good care of each other. And remember this day in those moments you hate him."

I arched my eyebrow.

"I know you can't imagine that, but those days will come. And on those days, you have to remember that love is a choice, so always choose love."

I nodded with tears in my eyes. I hoped I grew up to be like the woman in front of me.

My dad knocked on the door. "Are you decent?"

My mom yelled out, "She's ready."

My dad walked in and stood there, stunned for a moment at the door. "You're beautiful." He reached out his hand to me and I took it, suddenly filled with overwhelming emotion. It was a good thing I had on waterproof mascara.

My mom kissed my cheeks. "I'll meet you down there."

I nodded. Words escaped me.

My dad looped my arm through his and off we went to the tune of "Sunrise Sunset."

"Are you sure about this guy?"

I knew he was teasing. "Pretty sure, but I thought what the heck, since he's pretty and all."

My dad belly laughed. "Keep that sense of humor, kiddo. You'll need it."

My parents had warned me for years that marriage wasn't a cake walk and it would be the hardest thing I'd ever love, so I wasn't surprised by their advice. But no matter what the future held, at that moment I was blissfully happy and in love.

And by Jackson's look of adoration as we neared him and his preacher, I would say he felt the same way. His warm brown eyes glistened with tears, making me wonder why I bothered with makeup at all. It wasn't going to survive the onslaught of happy tears.

I took one moment to look at all our friends and family gathered there. My eyes landed on Mr. Crandall and his date, the lovely Connie. They both seemed to twinkle. Who said love was for the young?

Jackson held my hands tight as we faced each other. I kept waiting for the preacher to say, "Marriage is what brings us together today" just like in *Princess Bride*, but he never did. But he did say "man and wife" and "you may kiss your bride." And my absolute favorite, "I now present to you Mr. and Mrs. Montgomery." I always knew that had a nice ring to it.

Now on to my honeymoon, where I was hoping to work on a nine-month plan. I'll let you know how it goes.

PREVIEW

His Personal Relationship Manager:
Dating by Design Book One

So, let me get this straight. You've created a program that chooses the perfect mate for someone?"

I smiled, and refrained from sighing at the young male business reporter from *Atlanta INtown*. How many times had I been asked that question? I knew what I did for a living was, let's say, a tad out of the ordinary. Okay … it was a lot out of the ordinary, but there was no denying its success. "The program is only part of the service we offer. That's where we begin. Once we input each client's personal data, it gives us an array of options, and from there we do more homework. For example, each one of our clients is required to go on one test date with a member of my staff before we ever set them up with another client. Purely platonic, of course." I smiled slyly.

Bradly, the skeptical reporter, smirked. "Yes, of course. So how is the program you designed different from something like an online dating service?"

I stiffened in my very comfortable, yet highly stylish, leather office chair. "Besides the tailored and personal involvement we pride ourselves on, it's all in the algorithms."

"Care to share what those are, Ms. Marshall?"

I smiled as if to say, *what do you think?* "That is strictly proprietary and well-guarded."

He almost sneered. "And how much do you charge for your services again?"

"I would encourage people to call us, or better yet, come in for a free consultation." I hated talking price. And the punk in front of me, who was barely out of junior college, would probably exaggerate it anyway. Or perhaps he would call it extortion money, like the last reporter I'd had in here. And really, did price matter? I had hundreds of happy clients, and not once had anyone ever asked for a refund.

"One last question." His faux smile seemed more like a sneer. "Don't you feel like what you do takes the romance out of it, maybe even cheapens the experience?"

I loved this question. I was well-versed in my answer. "Not at all. Most people's problems center around relationships. What we are doing, through our tried and proven method, is giving them the best chance to find success in a romantic relationship and, dare I say, even love and marriage. In this day and age, we do research on everything from the best school to attend to the car we buy. Why not do the same for the most important decision of your life?"

He looked at me thoughtfully for a moment, like perhaps he believed me. At least for a moment. "Does that mean you do the same for your relationships?"

"Time's up." I stood up and held out my hand to shake his.

He eyed me carefully before standing up and holding out his hand. "Thank you for your time, Ms. Marshall."

"The pleasure was mine. Our receptionist, Meg, will validate your parking." Without another word, I went back to work. I had more important things to do than talk to skeptical journalists. I'd had some new compatibility research come in and I wanted to include the data in my code before running the next batch of clients against it.

My partner in crime, Zander, popped his head in. Or should I say, Alexzander? He was so proud of his Greek name that meant "defender of mankind," though he was neither Greek nor anywhere close to being foreign. He had grown up in the suburbs of Atlanta, like me, and looked like the all-American male. He even had a little bit of a Southern drawl.

"Hey, darlin', how was the interview?"

I rolled my sable-colored eyes at him.

"Same as always, huh?"

"Well, at least this time he didn't insult my intelligence by being surprised a woman developed the software we use, or call me a matchmaker." I despised that word.

"Yes, I noticed he had all of his limbs attached, and he wasn't wailing."

I shook my head. "I'm not that bad."

He looked around our posh surroundings. "No, you're that good."

"I knew we were best friends for a reason. Now if only we could share clothes."

"I've always wanted to see what you would like in one of my button-down dress shirts."

"If I didn't know you were kidding, I'd fire you."

He laughed. "Oh, you can't fire me, honey. No one else would put up with you. That, and I'm good at what I do. And you know you love me."

He was right, I did love him in that brotherly sort of way. We had been friends for fifteen years—half our lives. Alexzander Grainger and I were lab partners in high school chemistry, but thankfully there hadn't been any between us—chemistry that is. We did try kissing once when we were seniors, just to try it out. You know, to make sure we weren't missing out on anything before we parted for higher education. And we weren't. It was the most awkward kiss of all time. I mean, he was a good kisser, but it felt incestuous. We both decided to never mention it, until death do us part.

I opened up the folder I needed on my computer. "So who are you 'dating' tonight?" He was the best of the best. He did a lot of the "platonic" dating of clients. He knew how to read women and weed through all the embellishments everyone puts in the surveys we ask them to fill out on their initial visit.

"No one. I'm taking the night off, remember? My old college roommate, Jason, recently moved to town and we're having dinner to catch up. You should join us. I think the only two people I've ever considered real friends should meet. Besides, you look good on my arm."

"I'm too tired to pretend I'm your girlfriend tonight. You'll have to fight off all the ladies on your own." And I knew there would be some. He wasn't drop dead gorgeous, but he had a presence that drew people to him, women in particular. His amazing algae-colored eyes that invited people in, paired with his wavy chestnut hair always done in this messy-yet-stylish look, not to mention his buff bod, made him desirable. Again, it was why he was good at his job. That and he never planned to settle down, at least that's what he always said. He had always claimed we would marry each other when we were too old to care about having a physical relationship, but he knew I was never walking down the aisle again.

He brushed off his tailored suit coat like he was put off by my refusal to be his pseudo-date. "Fine, the next time a man asks if you're available, I'm going to say yes and give him your personal cell number."

I narrowed my eyes at him. He stood there smugly and dared me to call his bluff.

I didn't say anything to him.

"You're the best, Kenz. I'll pick you up at seven. Dress casual." He walked out the double glass doors of my personal office into the loft-style suite.

I chucked my squeaky softball stress reliever at the door after him. I kept it on my desk especially for situations like this. He laughed when he heard the squeal of the ball when it made contact with the glass.

"I love you, Kenz," he called out.

I needed to find some girlfriends, or maybe any friends besides him and my older brothers, Rick and Dylan. I let that thought quickly leave my head. I knew it wouldn't end well.

I gathered my things and walked through the office toward the exit. The only sound to be heard was the click-clack of my stiletto heels on the wood floor. I was always the first one in and the last to leave. My momma encouraged me to get a life, a real one outside of work, but work was easy. And I had a life, just not the one she hoped I'd have. Sure, she was proud of me and my accomplishments, but she wanted me to have what she had. You know, a man who adored the ground I walked on and children who considered me the center of their worlds. But for me, that was never going to happen. My life was about making sure other people got the life they wanted, whatever it was.

For each client it was different. Some were looking for temporary companionship, or even a rebound—someone they could nurse a broken heart with, with no strings attached. Then there were the white-picket-fence people, and of course those who were looking for their perfect soulmate. And guess what? We could find someone for each scenario. We hadn't failed yet. I turned to the wall of bliss for confirmation, and to revel in our success. Staring back at me were pictures of happy, smiling couples on their wedding day. The wall was becoming crowded. It gave me a sense of pride.

I looked around one last time, set the alarm, turned off the lights, and locked the door. *Until tomorrow*, I thought as I admired the sign on our entrance door that read, "Binary Search" with our tagline "Dating by Design" right under it. I gave myself such props for the company name. I thought it was quite clever to use a computer term to describe the kind of services we offered. It fit so perfectly. Some people didn't get it, but it was so unique, as was what we did, that no one ever forgot it once they heard it.

I waved goodbye to Ellen, the owner of the building and event planning company that occupied the lower half of the building. We leased the top half from her. It was a perfect setup. We had struck a deal that anyone who got engaged using our services would get ten percent off if they used Ellen's wedding planning services. In return for the referrals, we got cheaper rent.

She paused to talk to me on the way to her car. "I'm off to meet with Wayne and Julie."

They were our most recent success story. I was pretty sure they were planning a fall wedding.

"Please tell them hello for me."

"I do hope you'll come to the wedding this time."

I smiled without answering, as I always did when asked that question. I didn't do weddings. I was happy to send a gift, wish them well, add them to my wall, but I never, ever accepted invitations to the actual ceremony. I could barely attend church with my momma without breaking out in hives. Too often weddings and churches go together. Don't get me wrong, I was no heathen, I've always been a properly bred Southern woman. I just have a severe allergy to anything remotely related to wedding ceremonies. "Have a nice evening." I waved at her.

She gave me a knowing grin and wished me the same.

Maybe if I were more social, Ellen and I could have been friends. Again, I let that thought slip right out of my head. I was settled with my life. I didn't need or crave any more than I already had.

ABOUT THE AUTHOR

JENNIFER PEEL IS THE AWARD-WINNING, bestselling author of the Dating by Design and Women of Merryton series, as well as several other contemporary romances. Though she lives and breathes writing, her first love is her family. She is the mother of three amazing kiddos and has recently added the title of mother-in-law, with the addition of two terrific sons-in-law. She's been married to her best friend and partner in crime for a lot longer than seems possible. Some of her favorite things are late-night talks, beach vacations, the mountains, pink bubble gum ice cream, tours of model homes, and Southern living. She can frequently be found with her laptop on, fingers typing away, indulging in chocolate milk, and writing out the stories that are constantly swirling through her head.

♥

If you enjoyed this book, please rate and review it on
Amazon & Goodreads

You can also connect with Jennifer on
Facebook & Twitter (@jpeel_author)

Other books by Jennifer Peel:
Other Side of the Wall
The Girl in Seat 24B
Professional Boundaries
House Divided
Trouble in Loveland
More Trouble in Loveland
How to Get Over Your Ex in Ninety Days
Paige's Turn
Hit and Run Love: A Magnolia and Moonshine Novella
Sweet Regrets
Honeymoon for One in Christmas Falls

The Women of Merryton Series:
Jessie Belle — Book One
Taylor Lynne — Book Two
Rachel Laine — Book Three
Cheyenne — Book Four

The Dating by Design Series:
His Personal Relationship Manager — Book One
Statistically Improbable — Book Two
Narcissistic Tendencies —Book Three

The Piano and Promises Series:
Christopher and Jaime—Book One
Beck and Call—Book Two
Cole and Jillian—Book Three

More Than a Wife Series
The Sidelined Wife — Book One
The Secretive Wife — Book Two
The Dear Wife — Book Three (Coming Soon)

A Clairborne Family Novel Series
Second Chance in Paradise
New Beginnings in Paradise — Coming Soon
First Love in Paradise — Coming Soon
Return to Paradise — coming Soon

To learn more about Jennifer and her books, visit her website at www.jenniferpeel.com.

CPSIA information can be obtained
at www.ICGtesting.com
Printed in the USA
LVHW030916010420
651870LV00004B/742

9 781795 342674